UPON A BRIGHT RED BENCH

A STORY OF STORIES

Pallavi Rebbapragada

Om Books International

First published in 2017 by

Om Books International

Corporate & Editorial Office
A-12, Sector 64, Noida 201 301
Uttar Pradesh, India
Phone: +91 120 477 4100
Email: editorial@ombooks.com
Website: www.ombooksinternational.com

Sales Office
107, Ansari Road, Darya Ganj,
New Delhi 110 002, India
Phone: +91 11 4000 9000
Fax: +91 11 2327 8091
Email: sales@ombooks.com
Website: www.ombooks.com

ISBN: 978-93-83202-10-2

Printed in India

10 9 8 7 6 5 4 3 2 1

Pallavi Rebbapragada is a print journalist in the Indian media. In 2010, she started her career as a correspondent with The India Today Group. In 2013, the falcon of her dreams landed in Dubai. Here, she worked as features editor with *Forbes*. Her next stint was with *The New Indian Express*. She has recently started writing for *Firstpost*. She has reported from India, Europe, the Middle East and the Far East.

From the vibrant worlds of fashion, food and luxury to the dark alleys of death, drugs and homelessness, her pen has journeyed across human realities.

She earned her Master's degree in Sociology from the Delhi School of Economics, where she was also awarded a National Scholarship. Her love for prose grew in 2014 at the Yale Writers' Conference.

Home, she feels, is where the printing press is.

To my parents

Contents

Contents

Once the pen is picked up, the id turns against the ego turns against the superego. At some indefinite moment between the dipping of the nib into the inkwell and the pressing of the nib onto paper, the three make peace to resolve one ceaseless conundrum: The clash is mostly, if not always, within.

The writer is deaf and mute; the writer is withdrawn from the misery and pleasure of existence. Only then is the writer able to see necessity in misery; only then is the writer able to find deception in pleasure. The writer is alone in a room, dark and distanced from other rooms. A mere window opens out into the world, from where the writer watches with sleepless eyes. In the confines of this room, the writer discovers conflict and develops its cure. This room is the mind, and the writer is both a master and a slave in it.

Upon a Bright Red Bench

I am a bench, a bright red bench. Stillness is my journey, solitude is my companion. I have held the same four feet of ground, for years, for a decade perhaps. I stand on empty sand. Some of it infects onto my wrought iron legs until the rain frightens it aside. I am tulip red, as if a field of bloom was squashed into a warm tin of lacquer and then slithered along my length, my breadth. It has hardened over me, autumn after autumn. Every year, bursts of salty brown erupt over my skin. I am their ageing muse, my ruin is inevitable. Yet, they leave a coat of young paint over my flaws, in denial and in revolt. Once the imperfection is hidden, they believe, it ceases to exist.

I am equidistant from two avenue trees that were cosmetically grown to beautify the garden we're all in. These trees, they look less man-made than I. At the distance of a thrown stone lies a winding track of mud. I stand and watch the passage of life. Every morning, a reluctant believer shows up to purge his sins. Sins made of chocolate and butter. He looks both overfed and hungry. His spirit is defeated by the sight of that singular sprinter in glossy spandex who paces ahead, her bouncy ponytail pendulating in the breeze. The spikes in her sole leave their mark in the mud, which the mud soon forgets. She feels she is in control until a happy couple cycles into the scene. Then, she feels lonely. The tender peddles are trying to keep pace with one another, even at the risk of losing balance. The couple watches an old man and his grandchild crawling out into the distance; it is difficult to tell who's walking whom. The husband chooses to see the old man and resents retiring broke. He thinks of the cars he hasn't driven, the champagnes he hasn't corked open, and the deep seas he hasn't dived in. The wife's gaze is fixed on the child. Sooner or later, she wants her own.

I am a bench, a bright red bench. I stand away from the road. I stand where nature is in its details. The glossy dew on my cold surface is swept off by a soft palm and a leather boot creates the crackle of a golden leaf just below me. That ladybird looks chic in red and black, she crawls up my right leg like an ant. If I could talk, I would remind her that she can fly. There's a pigeon, its plumage grey as steel, perching on my right arm. He brings along friends, and they never care to clean up after. If I could talk, I would explain to the chirpy folk how they'll repent coming back to their own mess. But I cannot talk, for I am a thing. In a world where people are considered ordinary and available for a price, I am only a thing. In a world where things are extraordinary and priceless, I am just a thing. In principle, I am eleven cast-metal slabs hammered together in a dark, greasy warehouse; a pair of legs and arms welded on later. In practice, possibly, I am a little more.

They come and sit on me, some old and some new. They appear to disappear. I feel their furry hoods resting on my back. I sense their straw hats and silk scarves left unattended on me. The cold canopies of their umbrellas spring open on my foot, I enjoy their shade. The stretchy polyester in their pants is mucky with sweat, I don't know if I like it.

Some come alone, with books. They flip seven pages and leave. Others come with others, to talk. They talk of broken relationships; they talk of not having talked earlier. Those who married to better their social standing have drawn status and wealth from their decisions. They now criticise patriarchy and feel burdened by bondage, and complain they never fell in love. Some married for beauty, in complete enchantment. Beauty aged, the way it was meant to. Why are they surprised? Are they sitting here and taking offence at the course of time?

Some say they are moving on, casually, from their "break-ups". They have terms for everything, because terms make sorrow social and simple. Can a calculated removal of a partner's presence from their lives be defined as a loss? Will these break-ups somehow prepare them for death, the least romantic of losses? Some reveal they've been cheating in greying marriages. They croon over monotony and seek surprise. In such cases, an honest admission to a trusting friend acts like an antidote, it shields the mind from sin and restores the body for further sin. Upon a bright red bench, they come as sinners and confess and leave. Conversations lift them from their undoing.

They talk of spending more time with parents, of how they keep forgetting to call up parents, of how they're happy to be away from parents, and if they'll ever turn to their parents. The strongest bonds seem to form around economic and emotional dependence. With age, that dependence lessens. No, they don't stop calling them up, they just don't do it every day, or every week. Are they just orphans of the earth, like me? The parents, now older and weaker, once hoped their children become independent and free. Have they succeeded or failed?

If I could talk, I would explain to urgent minds how vastly underrated nothingness is. Only on empty benches can new stories and more stories be written. They talk of deadlines, some enriching and some unhealthy, and they invent ways to live between these deadlines. They share with each other, images of traffic jams, coffee mugs and messy work desks. With much more enthusiasm, they share images from their holidays. They talk of interesting new ways to earn wealth, shrewdly pointing out what they've identified as "market gaps". Suddenly, they claim to have struck million-dollar epiphanies. Should they be successful, will they never have time to come back and idle on a little bench like me or will they come back in search of another great idea? I wonder.

Sometimes, they open compact mirrors and stare into them seriously; the dab of a lipstick here, the wipe of a tissue there. With such concentration, are they seeing something they've never seen before? The precision with which they tweeze those soft arches bending over tear ducts and fill in chapped lips with a shade of scarlet, do they instantly forget their own imperfections? How hard is it to live with imperfections? Aren't imperfections as much their own? I will never know.

They talk of dead uncles and fathers and how simple life was when those few good men were walking around. Also gone are their hobbies. That dusty guitar in the storeroom, they say, has broken insects and rusted nails in it.

They talk of friends in front of whom the secret workings of their hormones became visible: the first sprout of facial hair and the first stains of dark red on funny underwear. Those friends, without whose sanction crushes were crushed quietly and in whose company mistakes were made willingly, why are they not on the bench with them? The rolling of strong smokes and the mixing of drinks in the madness of their evenings, only to feel their chests choked up and their throats burnt in vomit—the madness was theirs and its price too was theirs. Is the price of that madness too high or does no one have the willingness to spend on it?

Only in the cool distance of retrospect does the intensity of embarrassment turn into sweet stupidity. Together with these friends, they identified capitals on atlases, highlighted footnotes on classics, solved algebraic riddles till hangnails bled ink. Once the knowledge is attained, do they like to erase the memory of its attainment? Do they feel comfortable believing they've always possessed that knowledge? Today, those friends have collapsed into memories bittersweet, and with time it has become difficult to tell the bitter from the sweet. Those friendships are now just a handful of anecdotes that vary a little with each narration. I enjoy listening to stories of lost friendships. The existence of those friends has shrunk into the tiny templates of social media profiles. They scroll over them and open new windows with perfect strangers in the hope of finding newer best friends.

Sometimes, they come with sketchpads. They say this reminds them of a time when they created landscapes with graphite. This was where the stride and slide of a pencil took the shape of mountains and a river that indefinitely originated between them while a boat floated along the river and a hut, just one hut. A complete universe, all ready to be hidden in the heavy depths of a spiral notebook. They might have signed these off. Back then, their signatures were unformed. They now draw childishly than before, but the signatures seem certain. Is growing up an ongoing victory of one sense of self over another? I would like to know.

I am a bench, a bright red bench. It is not my job to change the world, to raise consciousness, to mend differences, to bring people to read and dream, to get the grieving to smile, to get the warring to love and to keep the child alive inside every adult. I am just the audience to the theatre upon and around me. In poor theatre, like in real life, it is easy to point out the difference between the actor and the character. They feed off fiction, off music, off opium and God, to fill the void between what is and what could be. Then, there are those who have forgotten how this is done. It is the latter kind that I worry about the most.

Some scoff at the necessity of God and spend a life looking for rational alternatives. Their decisions are their own. They believe in theories and questions, and outgrow those theories, and then search for new ones. Others leave things to God. They listen to God and God speaks to them, and a mute dialogue happens someplace hidden from the naked eye. They expect miracles and blame fate. Everyone is searching for something powerful to endorse their morality. Everyone suffers, everyone survives.

When little girls come and play on me, they bring along dolls. I hear nasal giggles as they braid and clothe them. They even mate them, four Barbie dolls and one Ken. Ken enjoys the benefits of being born a "pretty" man. They probably imagine a bench as a fortress from a fable where these toys are respectable citizens. I almost chuckle at life's sanctioned hallucinations. Some girls bring miniature houses with little beds and chairs, and pans and pots. The miniature is imagined in magnitude. Poor children come up here with empty cardboard boxes and used glass bottles, half-filled with pebbles, and possibly imagine more. Little boys load soapy water in their bubble-guns. They try to harm each other, playfully. Does harm begin in harmless ways? The awareness of one's ability to cause harm to another and the pride and thrill one derives from it—how is the playground readying them for the future?

I am beginning to understand how things keep humans entertained and engaged, and distant from other humans. Things, rattly little things, pacify crying infants. Things turn partners into fiancés, and things sit on mantelpieces as memories. Things remain, even after life doesn't. They endow things with reverence and call them brands, and God. They live their life acquiring and building things they affectionately call assets. If they have the will, they hand them down. In the presence of things, for the sake of things, humans are compelled to think, to imagine, and to believe. What is then human and what is not a thing?

I am a bench, a bright red bench. I was planted in honour of a dead soldier. That was a strange time. I was coming to life in furnace sparks and he was losing his life to gunshots. I was a thing and I was coming to life, he was a young man and he was dying. The world thinks my presence can substitute the sacrifice of his unlived youth; how little the world knows. His name is scribbled on a copper plaque on the side. Already bleached out, it will be burnt dry by next summer. And then, all that will remain buoyant in a drowning world would be a bench, a bright red bench. Is that why they've smothered me bright red? To distract collective conscience, however briefly, from destruction?

On weekends, more people show up at the park. Sometimes, a synthetic shuttlecock falls flat on me. Soon after, a shuttler comes searching for it. He sits on me, ties up muddy shoelaces and syncs into one tone the varying rhythms of his breath. I am his respite; he makes me feel powerful. Some evenings, when the weather is mild and delightful, a middle-aged couple drops in. Their problems seem real and insurmountable. They speak of dying parents, of jobless children, of unpaid home loans. I am stupefied at their calmness. Where are they deriving such strength from? They hold hands in hope. I marvel at the strength of human belief. They forget their worries and laugh from within. Even at the risk of exposing their crooked teeth and cavitied gums, these people laugh.

A young couple, four or five years into their marriage, has stopped having conversations. They don't mind if I listen in on dull chatter that starts with a 'Yes' and ends with a 'No', another 'No', another 'Yes'. At an earlier time, they've kissed here in the clear vision of maids pushing prams and dog-walkers in track pants. Scandalous! Now, they come here out of habit. They were always opposites. He now fancies nothing more than slices of home-baked vanilla cake on chequered oven mitts and she stares lustily at window displays in malls, at the buyable spectre of leather, velvet and linen. She now calls him an 'underachiever'. Opposites attract because man carries a void within him, once the void is filled up, what is left for man to do? They sit further away from each other. But as long as they come to the bench, they still face the same way.

Maybe, conversations aren't dead after all. A girl in college is romancing her beau, who lives beyond the seas. She blows kisses into a small window in her phone where he sits, one tenth of him, shirtless and unshaven. Distance makes hearts grow fonder. Will hearts remain fond when distances are bridged? What if she presses the call cut and slides her phone into her pocket, and topples over into the warmth of a real guy's arms, one she can touch and smell? Will she soon park herself on me with that other, real man? The call from the distant boyfriend will tremor silently, deep inside her pocket. I will feel it and she will feel it too, but neither will do anything. Will she love the tremor as much as she loves the touch, as much as she loves the absence, as much as she loves the feeling of the touch removing loneliness, returning again and again?

I am a bench, a bright red bench. My life is about other lives. I see ordinary people living mysterious, almost miraculous lives. I have tales to tell, their tales; tales of how the normal suppresses the pathological within it and pretends to be normal all along; tales of how mad and wild the average human mind really is.

Numbered in municipal records, I am only a bench like other benches in the world that stand in the bloom of lawns, in the brown of woods, on stone-tiled pavements along big streets. And these are just people, doctors, engineers, artists, bankers, journalists, dreamers and doers, who roam the world in need of love and attention. They seek something, they seek it in ideas, and they seek it in things. If they are unable to find it, they seek it in change. Why do they strive to define the present, knowing that it mostly never escapes the past, knowing that it almost always fears the future? Can the present ever be unconditionally realised?

What they understand as the present, is it just an attempt to extract an actual and finite moment from the vast lostness that is as romantically scattered in the nostalgia of their past, as it is scientifically pinned in the projection of their future? Through adage and ideology, they repeatedly remember that the present is to be seized. They try. They try every day, to wring out of this distant and eternal continuum, a small, personal sense of now.

The past is passion. With its tragedies, comedies and farce, it survives. The future is fantasy with its thrill of the unseen, it will live on. What dies every instant is the present.

They sit upon me, they think and speak, and they wish that the present was made of silver and gold. Why do they seem unqualified to look beneath and find to their immeasurable delight that it might be a bright red, a hopeful if not beautiful bright red?

And that is when I think to myself, are they present in the present at all?

Nun on a Train

In Palakkad, the rain fell upon the innocent like a curse. Cloaked in a gunmetal cape, a bitter monarch pointed a finger to the sky and ordered the shatter of a mirror that dared to lie. A million water droplets were its shards, withdrawing from it in sudden reluctance and crashing to the ground; in seconds a deafening shudder, in minutes a wet blur. Down below, civilisation readied its defence plan: jet-black umbrellas. A war, a benign and bloodless war, had broken out between nature and culture. The streets decided to play dead till ceasefire.

Braden George stood, facing a window on the second-and-highest floor of his red-brick home. His bony legs took his body a little over six feet into the sky. In a pair of deep blue denims and a buttoned white shirt, his vanity was disciplined. He softly released one hand from the tight clasp behind him and reached out to a cup sitting on a brass stool. He trapped one thumb betwixt its ceramic hook, as his left palm greedily soaked in the heat escaping the roundness of the cup. He felt the cup on his lips and noisily drew in sprays of his dark-roasted Monsooned Malabar coffee. All this while, he was vacantly staring at how the mesh grills that trapped the rain, freed the rain and slashed the arrogance of its waters, drop by drop.

'George, come play with us,' yelled out his friends, when they all were seven, when they all were friends.

'No. I won't,' said George. 'No. I won't,' he said again, and ran back in.

The showers were a game that George never wanted to play. So, even at 29, he just watched the rain. He watched push-karts being hurriedly polythened by men. In their attempt to get home, women were swift, as swift as someone wrapped in nine yards of silk could be. They crumpled delicate drapes in sick ways, turning a lady's presumed civil experience into the handiwork of a four-year-old boy. Those jasmine buds that were once bobby-pinned into greasy ponytails, broke off and floated along in puddles.

Just then, a long gong chime pulled George's sight toward the cathedral-like façade of St Thomas School that stood across the road. Here, the last hour had been the longest; each minute was a restive yearning for the school bell to go off. Muddy footprints bridged the outside with the inside and wet raincoats rose in heaps along corridors. Though uniformed and under singular charge, schoolers were never a collective lot. They were different times thrown into one space. Those fresh from the bed-wetting stage were unhappy, the rain had stalled their daily play on the swings and shoelaces were now too grimy to be tied, or touched. The adolescents wished they could only excuse themselves from the moist indoors and run amuck on soccer grounds, like puppies free from the leash. The children began to huddle out, three under one plasticky umbrella. They moved in a cautious phalanx till the buses at the gate were only a splashy jump away. George had been a student here and his only childhood memory of the rain was his running away from it.

'George, come play, we are having so much fun,' his classmates would say.

'No. This is not my kind of fun. This is not fun. This is not fun,' George would say.

George took another sip of his coffee and noticed how the flickering tube lights hung above thick shop shutters were competing with the lightning, only to be defeated by it. Canines weren't notorious in a chase for bread because in the time of rain, refuge was the greater reward. Cats dug into municipal garbage bins and, without admitting the incoherence on their part, unassumingly pawed their way under parked cars.

He took yet another sip and rolled his eyes in the direction of Ramanujan's dosa stall next to the school. This served as a trench. Upon entering its thatched confines, foot soldiers wrung out the remains of rain from their garments and seated themselves on soggy wooden stools that threatened to crumble any minute. The foldable tables were rickety over a floor made of wet mud. George hated that this decades-old food joint didn't believe in repair work. He hated when places gave up on themselves. There were young servers running about in sleeveless vests and white wrap-around mundu skirts. The podgy counter clerk was covered in a steam-cleaned version of the same outfit. He was just a face, flanked by crunchy piles of banana and tapioca chips and stale prawn crackers.

Sometimes, George came here for breakfast. The nutty smell of curry leaves and cumin seeds, fluttered around and settled on different spots like a swallowtail butterfly. Gift-wrapped in banana leaves and fresh from a steam bath, fish was food. Milky coffee inspired a bittersweet froth. It was streamed from a height and poured—in millimetric-measure—into paper cups. The pulse of pulses was beaten to death to form a thick creamy batter, rich in protein. In pancake fashion, this was spread out to form dosa sheets on a flat black stove that was the size of a foosball table. Folded and served alongside neutrally-flavoured coconut paste and red-chilli pickle of nefarious intent in sparkly stainless steel equipment, the food made people sweat in the rain. Somewhere within, a crackle of deep-frying mimicked the racket of rain only to amuse itself.

In Palakkad, monsoon was a welcome beast. Situated at the foot of India's Western Ghats, this was otherwise a land of small rock-ribbed outcrops and diminishing streams. In drying times, the palms could barely breathe alongside its muddy streets; there was thirst. As if sketched out by a bored child's charcoal pencil, it was a town of silhouettes, sharpened against sun dust.

At some point, during standing and staring at the spectacle of wet sliver, he remembered the happy drizzles from the day he brought home his girlfriend of 10 years to begin a life of holy matrimony. It was on that day that she clutched the trims of her pearl-white gown as he whisked her off the ground. That was still his happiest memory.

She saw his loving eyes through her white sheer veil until they both dizzyingly dipped into the depths of their canopied bed. A bed they were going to share for life.

As undergraduate students, they spent rainy days on the leathery insides of locked cars, feeling the same vulnerability felt by children giggling under little tents made out of bed sheets. They never wiped the mist off the windows. On occasion, they got dirty in hostel dorms, and flirted over Maggi noodles and watery tomato soup served in government cafeterias. On houseboat excursions along Kerala's criss-cross backwater canals, when their classmates broke into huddles around lending strings to Dylan's blues, George and his girl visibly separated themselves. Even the breeze rising out of southern India's blissful inland lakes couldn't cool their fiery embrace. On bright red benches, being with her was an extension of his solitude.

'Will you always hold me like this,' asked his girlfriend.

'I will never be able to forget you,' said George.

But marriage is more than its weight in cake sponge. Marriage is more than the ring that looks twice its size as it settles on the bottom of a bubbling goblet. Marriage is what lies beyond the brass-on-wood borders of a photo-frame. Marriage is an evolution, a parallel evolution of two minds. In the years that followed 'I Do', George was growing into a community shaper, a mentor to many, a kind of all-encompassing force that oversees the fulfilment of his society's needs. He was somebody with big, broad goals. She, in innocence and in idleness, wished to remain the same girl he had met on the first day of engineering college, outside the library at half-past noon.

'Why do you wait for me for dinner? Don't you feel hungry?' he would ask her while removing his shoes after a long day.

'We always eat together and go to bed at the same time, George. It's nothing new?' she'd say, asking him if she's doing anything wrong.

'Nothing new. But do your own thing, na? Don't tire yourself and waste your time like this,' he would tell her.

He was outgrowing her, a little more disrespectfully each day. The founder of a public-private sector organisation that incubated business ideas, George was regularly invited to speak at universities. He looked tireless on stage, raising his fist in roman salutes. Until the mic was soaked in spit, he kept harping on the benefits of thinking beyond classrooms and curricula. He wanted to lead an entrepreneurship revolution and had started appearing on TV debates. He dealt with government officials, who were not too enthused about cooperating with inventors-slash-investors. He approached hard-to-impress corporate investors, urging them to put their money into young ideas. While all this was happening, his wife remained the same person who wanted to come home early to dust table tops and bake walnut cookies after her 9-to-5 job at a small marketing firm.

Back in his world, George was busy giving talks.

'Work cultures are being rethought. Ours is a co-working space where people can take power naps and run on treadmills to get ideas. Your skills will no longer be embedded in hierarchy, and no emotional energy is to be lost in massaging egos. In this ecosystem, a techie will meet a financer, a financer will find a lawyer, a lawyer will hire a publicist, a publicist will use the services of a designer and a designer will go back to the techie to build his or her website.'

The method was good-old mutual dependence, the same method that marriage is believed to be based on. The other thing he believed in were ideas. His theory was that ideas begin in the black liquorice oozing out from board markers, then move back and forth and round and round in alphabet and numeric doodles along a clean white board. And no matter how small or silly an idea seems at first, it needs to be given a chance in the world.

Even his wife wanted a chance, a continuous chance.

George was a change-maker. Change comes as shock; change comes as surprise. Change poses challenge and brings relief. Sometimes, change calls itself revolution. Change is seldom one-dimensional; change is mostly overwhelming. Life experiences are either an acceptance or a resentment of change. If he saw possibility at work, he wanted possibility at home. New ideas, new people, new faces, new journeys and new books, there was much to experience out there and a marriage of two people was just between those two people. In George's case, his work-self was now his only self. As he saw it, the Just Married placard, with ribbons and balloons on it, had served its purpose on the rear of his car and he was left driving for the sake of driving and toward a dead end.

They say nobody realises restraint till it is institutionally imposed. When the world rubbed George's sexual unavailability to his clean-shaven-almost-juvenile face, he began questioning the structure of marriage and why he was functioning within it.

"A happy ending is an ending after all. An ending of choice and of the freewill to exercise that choice," George started to think.

His newfound rationality was negating the need to commit, or fake commitment. Is reason a lot like sweeping a ball of dust under a hand-tufted wool carpet, and then leaving a vacuum-cleaned shine on it? Does reason sanitise vision? Like religion, reason directs morality. The church postures life through sacred imposition, it checks sin and balances suffering. Is reason a dynamic of personal faith? George's rationality was like secular religion, where the chasm between thinking and doing was his own instinct. He was his own convict, he was his own judge.

What is reason, really? What they have defined as reason could be just a misty reflection of what they have watched, possibly half-asleep and at most times half-interestedly in what went on in the world known to them. Some of it was formed at night, when they left that favourite song playing and sank layers and layers into it. A radical professor, a stern parent, a cynical best friend, they all painted portions of the reason they now called theirs. They just sat there, heard them out and drew whatever they could from each one. When their freedoms were threatened, they declared they cared far more than they did. Is their reason a product of their laziness, of their boredom, and of the fears they still don't want to fight? Then why is it so hard to replace that reason?

They think they need to marry a certain kind of person, with whom they have already imagined a life full of mutual affection and sympathy. They know where they want to be two decades from now, with more certainty and interest than where they might want to be tomorrow afternoon. Out of habit, they worry about the loss they haven't had and repent repeatedly over what they have established as a pathetic mistake. What kind of reason compels them to take family for granted? What kind of reason makes them turn down people who offer them love? Reason isn't the opposite of passion, it is as fluid as passion, as human as passion. There is as much reason in erring, in feeling weak and even in wishing to run away. Sometimes, when no one is looking, they might remove that mask of reason off their face and feel the passions they've been hiding.

Like everyone else, George too was in love with his own reason. His first affair was clandestine, with a friend's willing sister. The second one was more deliberate, with what he perceived as a "provocatively-dressed" co-worker, who showed up in a leather bustier and hot pants at a corporate off-site held at the Kumarakom lake resort. The third was just a kiss, or three, which might have been the desired consequence of an intoxicant. His actions were in question, only because his wife didn't have an answer to them. She wanted to stop denying her husband's waywardness. She wanted to draw him back into a warm hug or beat him with a nightstick and drag him into their cave. Had a guy done this to her best friend, she would have picked up the phone and abused him. If a boy had been this unfair to her little sister, she would have killed him. Few in the world are strong-willed when they battle the people they love. Everything ever said about self-respect on women's rights forum, or on a feminist's blog, or even in a late-night-girl-talk session, seemed hasty and harsh to her.

When reality chewed into her fantasy completely, she threw the remains of her married life into three black suitcases and dragged herself out while he pulled another all-nighter at work. Her weeping shadow disappeared behind the black shrubs in his backyard, forever. Two years of a quaint and bizarre marriage, where she was learning and he was unlearning, came to a halt—a red-stamped, black-inked, paper-worked halt. He felt cheated at how easily she accepted his misdoing, without questioning the inconsistency on his part.

Even in his guilt, George was never wrong. He had loved and lost, everything from then on was physical pleasure.

It had been two years since his divorce and it was hard to tell if George felt a void, sometimes, or at all? He couldn't understand why his family and friends mourned his divorce like, in his own words, 'The death of a young biker hit by a landslide in a steep valley'. He was no longer capable of sensing personal losses. What he could do well, however, was look for larger solutions like creating a colossal collective future. But those little things, reasoning out patiently, keeping the partner tempted toward oneself and more, all of that, he just couldn't do.

Every other week he travelled for work, carrying a distressed-leather shoulder bag that held together a sleek laptop, a pair of headphones, a moleskin notebook and a ballpoint pen. When he rolled back the sleeves of his either black or white shirt, the digital matrix of his Casio G Shock appeared on his hairless wrist. Wearable computing excited George.

Today was another day of travel. The rain receded into a noiseless drizzle. It left the sky with the shine of a bald head, as though an electric shaver had been run through grimy dreadlocks that choked and fell dead to the floor. George had to board the train to Cochin, the commercial capital of his state. He had reduced his hot beverage to one tiny cold sip. He took it. Turning off light switches and locking the windows of his minimally furnished, almost empty house, seemed futile. Still, he did all that and left.

The wiper blades of his company's mini-van wagged exactly a hundred times and the station arrived. George had been listening to the soundtrack of A. R. Rahman's *Bombay* on Internet radio, through the ride. The percussion of thunder clashing into waves under gloomy skies was condensing the melancholia of the rain, if it could be condensed at all. He never created a playlist on a music device, because he stopped enjoying songs once he owned them.

The platforms looked unimportant, it was hard to believe that the tracks could lead to far and beyond. And on that rainy day, it looked empty like busy trains wouldn't bother stopping there even if the station master were to wave his brightest red flag. There were some old men sleeping on concrete benches, and they looked dead. George walked past them, disinterested in their life or the lack of it. There were three families with children who pestered to sit atop suitcases. The parents, too exhausted to argue, obliged.

George saw one young couple move out of town, with six big bags and three small ones. Paintings, gigantic Ganesha idols and dismantled wooden screens were sticking out. He smiled. For no reason, a stranger like him could picture what their next house would be like. To George, most people on the station looked like they were forgetting something. There was also an army man going back to his military base, possibly after a short holiday. He was in casual clothes but a crew cut and a steel trunk were clear hints. At the sound of a sharp long whistle, everybody fused together in the singular purpose of passage.

George plucked out a business magazine hung on a clothes line in a small stall. He also picked up strips of paper soap from the stall adjacent to it and got into compartment C3. There were a handful of people entering the train, but they quickly disappeared into its length. He threw his bag on the side upper berth dangerously close to a black railway fan, whose unstoppable little blades had plans of chopping at least three fingers in their lifetime.

George flung himself at the mercy of the window. An empty train, a short ride, time to make notes, he thought. He was on his way to deliver an annual lecture on decision-making at a management college. The train started to jiggle forward, or was that the train on the parallel track offering a false sense of relief? George couldn't care less.

'Seat No. 13?' said an anaemic voice. He lifted his head from the scribbling he'd made and noticed a young girl who had skin akin to an almond soaked in mineral water overnight, even the texture and the flavour could have been the same. She wore an onion-pink saree that was painfully pinned back, drizzles were fading on it. Her hair too was pulled back into a low bun. For George, the height of a woman's bun was directly proportional to the sex appeal she exuded. Dangling over the flat front drape of her mathematical-looking saree was a chrome-plated metal cross. Entangled between her fingers were black-wood rosary beads dramatised by an ornamental crucifix. The train moved. It left an electric current running through the beads, they too moved. The crucifix stayed firm on her chest.

'Yes, that's my seat,' he addressed her question after a north-to-south glare.

'May I sit down here with you? It's a short ride and I don't feel like climbing up to my berth', she said, and she wasn't seeking approval. She noticed how his bag had encroached upon her seat. The train had been moving for a couple of minutes and George was still staring at her high cheekbones, her wet eyelashes. She was white. Not Caucasian white, just a luminescent Indian white. He could go close and spot blue veins under that sheet of bloodless skin. She had the worldly evangelism of an unsure nun.

She knew he was emitting an unblinking stare. Men always did that to her. 'It's your complexion', her family always assured her, but she felt it was symptomatic of something potentially life-altering. She didn't trust men too much. "Nothing is skin deep, nothing whatsoever. If he is lured by my skin, he will do anything, from wooing me to raping me. The choice will be his and the price will be mine to pay," she used to think. At 26, the wrath of youth had set in.

Back in the train, she twisted her backbone to face the window and gave the moving paddy fields a long stare. The showers had flushed the dust off them, they were now emerald green. Hers was a fake stare, a mere deflection of his stare. She then began distracting herself, click-clack of a hair-clip here, tick-tack of a safety pin there. He kept staring at the irresistible virgin in front of him.

The wide four-berth booth adjacent to them was empty, but they still sat across each other's stare.

'Does God smile at you?' said George, as he made a strange attempt at conversation, possibly to end the awkwardness.

'God smiles at everybody, from the distance he's at,' she answered the kind of answer that begets another question. Even she sensed relief in conversation.

'Are you implying he's smiling away, and no one's looking?' he said. He was only too happy to take the conversation forward.

'Man is never looking at God. Man is looking at other men and imagining God,' she continued.

He didn't expect this answer. He looked below and smiled.

'So then, God is something we imagine?' he said, and the conversation was getting real.

'There is something we don't imagine?' she replied, this was a conversation she could handle.

'Yes. All reality outside the binding walls of the convent is against imagination. Because it is lived. Sin is lived, penance is lived too,' said George; this wasn't the first time he was deriving pleasure from shaming the church.

'Perhaps, you are conscious of what sin is and what penance is. Aren't you then using imagination as a tool to outline and separate the two?' she asked. She could smell the blood of a non-believer, it was as thick as water.

'Is celibacy a part of God's plan?' George questioned. He always knew what he wanted from the women he found worthy of conversation.

'Everybody isn't living the same plan. Some of us can choose to stay out of God's plan, which is made of miracles,' she raised her arched eyebrows, her eyes were still quite wet.

'Lady, I wasn't referring to progeny…' George stopped short of his words at the growing sight of the ticket collector who walked in, staring head down into a printout, pressing the pusher of a cheap ball pen up and down. He had the general effect of the principal of a convent school who had spotted George hopping over barbed walls to stare at girls during exercise, or an invigilator who had caught George cheating during an exam. He felt a recognisable guilt warming his earlobes. The girl was unaffected by this clerical intervention. The intruder, the messenger sent by the railway lords, left after a casual checking of tickets. George felt notorious again.

'I was talking about sex,' he continued in a tone so direct, almost mean.

'Sex is the living of a sentiment,' she stated; the clergy kept sermons handy.

'In the name of the father, the son, and everybody else in the family, sex is just a physical act,' George exclaimed. He never called himself a non-believer, he just had different beliefs.

'Really? When you look at a woman as an object of desire, isn't your judgement based on your taste? And isn't that taste based on what you are socialised into considering desirable in the first place? From the curves on her waist to the colour of her skin to how naturally she gives herself to you, to how attractive or bold her thoughts seem to you? Is that all just physical?' she interrogated. She was breathless from the length of her sentence. George felt thrown off his game. A clean and clear answer to that one could have won him a prize at this stage (a fridge magnet with Da Vinci's *The Last Supper* or a glow-in-the-dark baby Jesus—anything biblical that could be bought and sold).

George pulled back till his spine straightened against the seat fully. It was his turn to throw a stare or two out the window. Shake-shudder-shiver, shake-shudder-shiver, the train brushed along bridges and flew past fields. Outside, a family of power towers had distanced itself from each other to share their energy with the world. The current running between them was alive. Their arms were stretched out like giant scarecrows, and their insecurities and fears were hidden under the bold front they were putting up. This bold front could survive the strike of lightning. This bold front always expected the strike of lightning. Tearing through the storm by trusting the balance of its wheels, the train too was brave.

George thought about how the church could fight back. For once, religion didn't seem kind and forgiving, especially in the hands of a divine-looking crusader. He gave her another long stare. She didn't have the vibe of the first minister of a state church; she certainly couldn't make the blind see. She looked more like someone in charge of the confessional box. She wouldn't throw up vintage Celtic terms like "the holy one", or would she? This was someone profanely low in the hierarchy of a sacred order; someone open to the idea of cheating. George had once overheard a pastor saying that, 'In Kerala, nuns were away from the constraining eyes of the church only when they were in trains.' And, didn't the church once declare forbiddance a tasty fruit? As usual, George made and sanctioned another one of his plans.

'No offence to catechism, but I think chastity is trapped in its own findings. Pre-marital sex with my girlfriend was celebrated as romantic but extra-marital sex once she became my wife was condemned as adultery. On both occasions, I was just outsourcing physical pleasure in exchange for emotional bliss. I must also add that the emotion is muted in an affair. It is more of a naked pleasure, of escapism, of release,' articulated George, hoping his rationality could untie many a prodigal robe.

'Sin isn't in the act. It is in the consequence of the act. You promised somebody loyalty and then denied it. Adultery is a broken promise,' she first addressed the second half of his question. She then lent the church her voice: 'Chastity and the cinctures one chooses to wear in its name are an independent decision. Just like being childless or being in a live-in relationship. It is not the carnal opposite of sexual adventure. Those who dedicate their hormones to reverence know exactly what they want to do with them, just like you claim to know what you are doing,' she explained.

George was too self-important to be spoken to in this manner. Except a whiny mother he never listened to and an older sister he couldn't ignore, no one dared to speak sense to his face about anything even mildly personal. But, she went on, and on… 'Weddings also happen in churches you see, chastity is never imposed…'

George had nothing to say, he had dropped all but one weapon to the ground. He was aroused by the intellectual foreplay that had been staged between him and his newfound nun. He used the sword of his intentions to shred her saintly cloak. He had undressed in layers, her surprisingly aggressive mind. He had expected benign reluctance, the sort of grandmotherly ignorance each atheist expects the church to possess about the ways of the world. Surprise heightened the excitement of this man, who had once broken a heart to heal his boredom.

A couple of minutes later, when she stopped to hydrate her tired throat, he moved forward and kissed her on her cheek. He waited for her to resist him. She didn't, so he moved down and rolled his tongue on her neck. It was how he had imagined it to be, like sweet almond if not better. Why wasn't she resisting him? Was his flesh the temptation of her blood? A little more temptation, a little less resistance; a lot more temptation, a lot less resistance. George began sinking into a sin. He may have been conscious of committing a sin.

Soon, he was biting her lips and pushing them apart with his tongue. Trapped inside his mouth, her tongue was slippery. He lifted her roughly and laid her flat on the sleeper berth next to theirs. His cold hands unpinned her saree, nobody was pricked. He then purged another layer of clothing till he reached a woman's visible secret, her breasts. They were beautifully big and partially white.

By then, his tongue had a will of its own. She breathed in his Old Spice cologne and circled her palms all over his bare back. She captured the firmness of his hairless chest on her fingertips. Her psalms were unhooked, his heresies were unbuttoned; every bit of clothing was strewn to the floor. Only her metal crucifix and his rubber watch interfered with their nudity. His watch was on his side, it turned seconds into minutes and quickly, it was too absorbed in mechanical mapping to even notice how people lived within time. That day, George wasn't feeling as mechanical as his machine. He kept looking at her metal crucifix every now and then. Was it making him mindful of the sin he was in? He had always been an atheist, and weren't atheists free of sin, free of bondage and belonging? Or, was rationality just a conscious subversion of dogma? Isn't a construing of collective faith a more streamlined, but equally radical, kind of faith?

His thoughts weren't stopping him from what he was doing. George was inside her, almost touching her soul, rubbing and shaking her soul. They vibrated within the train, they vibrated along the train. He left her with a long, loud moan. Their breaths were shorter, sweatier. They gradually straightened up. All of a sudden, worried about a possible unwelcome glare.

The train decided to slow down, as though somebody pulled the red chain of conscience on them. Thrissur station was almost here. Her hair was breaking out of the bun, untidily. The pins were pulling at her scalp, painfully. She agitatedly removed them and left her hair open. It was thick and black. He wished she had let it open earlier. All dressed up and tired in the thighs, she pulled at the handle of her small suitcase and rolled the magazine he had been reading.

'If you ever call me, you'll burn in hell,' she grinned and winked as if nothing meant anything. She took out the magazine, knocked it on his head and left the compartment. George was a little confused. He was ridden with guilt and she was leaving the train scot-free.

He spotted her at the station, thrust his upper body an inch-and-a-half outside the window's five horizontal bars, and announced, 'Lady, I think I forgot to ask. What's your name?'

She wasn't startled at the question. As if prepared to answer this one, she calmly wheeled her suitcase forward and left a warm whisper across his face.

'Madhuri Swaminathan. That is my name,' she declared.

'I…I don't understand…I mean, are you not a…I mean…your belonging to the church and all that?' he said, fumbling in astonishment.

'When did I ever say that? I am playing a nun in a college play and I practised some of my dialogues with you. In fact, I made up new lines thanks to you,' she stitched on a grin of a Cheshire cat, a patch on the pale fabric of her face. He could see cherry-coloured gums defining her huge sinister smile. Had it been there all along? She left him with a fright, turned her back toward him, walked up to a bright red bench on the platform and sat on it with poise. The train budged forward. George, still holding onto those window bars in reluctance, tilted his glance backward till the bright red of the bench faded into a dot in the corner of his eye and then disappeared.

Guilt had taken sides. She was free to walk away and he felt charged with a crime he did not commit. It wasn't just in Palakkad that the rain fell upon the innocent like a curse.

Mr & Mrs Singh

A lukewarm sun hid behind a thicket of smoky grey on the fifth afternoon of December. An erstwhile refugee colony in the narrow depths of West Delhi was struggling to absorb its fading warmth.

Meanwhile, outside a government colony in Central Delhi…

'Refugee colony chaloge?' Sarita Singh yelled out to an auto rickshaw driver. His vehicle, like marbles rolling on oiled roads, stopped slowly against its will, at a distance. She dragged herself up to him, arms caught in a cross inside the warmth of a factory-spun woollen shawl worn over a raw silk salwar kameez, and feet covered under skin-coloured nylon socks that were jutting out of stained leather sandals. The 50-something with henna-dyed orange hair had a conflicted frown cracking her forehead. She looked needy for the ride and equally willing to bear the winter wind a little longer for a cheaper ride. She was on her way to her brother's house for a funeral. Exhaling white fumes outside the vehicle that was underdressed for the weather, she tried to rehearse her behaviour and recollect her thoughts about death.

To her surprise, he agreed to turn down the meter and saved them an unpleasant negotiation. She didn't wait a second to hop in. She pulled the shawl over her head, now somewhat guarded. She lifted the rubbery side-curtain and stared at the colonial languor of a Delhi that had gracefully tiptoed out of Edward Lutyens' red carpet imagination. She felt the open frame of the auto rickshaw like an AC vent that had been pointed at her face. The breeze had numbed her against the thought of death. And the thought of death had returned the favour by numbing her against the breeze; the saddest kind of win-win.

She watched Delhi's roads that stood firm with pride. This was a Delhi of chalky-white bungalows that were square and straight, guard towers on edges and important nameplates polished in gold. This was a Delhi that held onto British legacy like a little boy locking tiny fingers around his father's brawny thumb. This wasn't the first time she was seeing a Delhi unmoved by the moods of sun and shade, a Delhi whose roads held hands and leapt far and wide and detached from each other gracefully at roundabouts.

And at those roundabouts, she clasped harder the stubborn drape of the curtain. She thought of the possible life inside those bungalows. The high-brow pain of declining a serving of canapés at a lawn party may be happening inside and here she was, painfully pounding her way in the direction of grief.

Inside those bungalows, were there men in Nehru jackets, ears studded with solitaires, getting chattier while passing around glasses of scotch? Were there some women inside too? Women wrapped in Pakistani kaftans embroidered with threads of gold, ash-pink Japanese pearls touching fair necks, and Turkish emeralds on fingers manicured and spoilt? And were they all drinking hard drinks with a vengeance, coughing and excusing each other in the most delicate of ways?

In there, they might be sitting on buttoned leather sofas, she thought. Here, her own buttocks bounced up and down at speed breakers.

She was inhaling the smoke of burning leaves outside their homes, when they might be nosing perfume; top notes: 25 ml tuberose, 10 ml iris, 5 ml gardenia. Inside, there might be frail old ladies, much older than her, who would have buried their freckled cheeks under pinky-white foundation creams and tucked their loose stretch-marked tummies inside stockings, with flabby arms stuffed into velvety jacket-blouses. And these gentle ladies might be hanging off the suited arms of their sons and husbands. And these gentle ladies might be praising each other in accents that were acquired on foreign trips like magnetic souvenirs. However, when they switched languages to communicate with their drivers, would these accents remain intact?

She wasn't interacting with the driver of the amply well-ventilated vehicle. She looked at a Delhi that knew how to remain genuine in pretension. The *trrr-trrr* of the auto rickshaw was keeping her seconds away from a depressing silence. She kept looking, sometimes at the meter, sometimes at a Delhi that stood there issueless and spoilt. If there had to be privilege in this world, why was it born in front of those who didn't have it? Why was it shining, laughing and enjoying around those who couldn't afford it? Did some people have a right over all the good times?

She stared at a Delhi that wasn't aping the occident, a Delhi that wasn't escaping the orient; in nonchalance, in hypocrisy, this was a Delhi that was only binding the two.

In 20 strange minutes, she arrived at the gate of Block C and instructed the driver to take two left turns and stop. Away from a Delhi of power was a Delhi of power cuts, where it was either too hot or too cold for comfort. This was a Delhi of fewer trees trapped inside strict municipal barricades, and outgrowing them unaesthetically. Unlike in Central Delhi where nature was trimmed, tamed and trained to fall in line with architectural order, nature was defiant in its ways over here. Tree barks broke out of small boundary walls, lime-green branches descended disturbingly low into the walker's path.

Under a wind-bashed tree, the three-wheeled rickshaw halted. Her cold hands trembled with fear as she searched for those two banknotes rolled into an unclothed pocket.

Ahead lay the disturbing energy of a hearse and a police van, their sirens muted. It sent a shiver down her spine. She paid off the driver and began tearing through the crowd that stood facing house No.19. A nameplate, slanted at the loss of one hook, read "Mr & Mrs Singh". The house stood at the first sharp turn of what was informally called the Refugee colony, but didn't have anything to do with the "politically distressed" tag the municipal records assigned to it.

Some widowed grandmothers in the neighbourhood, who sat on wooden cots drinking chai out of steel glasses, still had some Partition stories to share. They repeated them again and again till people lost interest. Lahore, Islamabad and Multan, how far had the future travelled from its past. The grandchildren of a bloody era in history were living their happily-ever-afters in small single-unit bungalows that had grown up with them over the years. There was the addition of a couple of floors and the appearance of a spiral staircase. The large balcony where a tiny wall once united women in an exchange of small-talk, pickle and pride was now completely covered and windowed.

The lady walked out into a crowd of women, who were sobbing into their chiffon dupattas and lint-laden, inadequately sunned and smelly scarves. They stood slightly away from the men who were mostly in wintry grey fleece jackets with damaged zips. The jackets looked more industrial and naphthalened. They had huddled into groups of four and five, reasoning out causes and consequences like small-time detectives.

'This shouldn't have happened,' said one. 'What did these good people do to deserve this?' said another. 'It's all destiny. It was all meant to happen this way,' somebody remarked.

She walked faster. She wanted to spot a familiar face. Her brother sat on a corner of his own chip-floored driveway, as if he had fallen there and couldn't help himself up. He stared into stillness, in deep thought, or no thought at all. He was stiff as if rigor mortis had set in. She ran toward him, hugged him and let out a dry howl. The bridge of her nose was deep pink, it wept along with her eyes. He wasn't answering her plea to cry along. She rose up and ran inwards, in search of more mourners. Her sister-in-law was beating her chest to the tune of small, tired shrieks. A band of women held her from all sides, they too were crying. Mourners were seated on mattresses spread out on the ground. The wind, like the sharp edge of a new kitchen knife, made cracks on cheeks dry and flaky. In the rapt stillness of the afternoon, the wind made its presence felt with an occasional slap of the door. A makeshift kitchen, set up just outside the house, boiled batches of cardamom tea every hour. Mere seconds of warmth were being exchanged for acidity.

Sofas, beds, a study table and chairs were dragged out into the little front lawn. In the absolute centre of a blank white drawing room was the photograph of a young man within a gilt frame. It was smiling Mona Lisa's carefree, almost wicked smile. As if sadistically witnessing another's loss, it smiled and smiled ceaselessly, behind the pure fragrant fumes of incense sticks and under the soft burden of a garland of marigold.

This was the portrait of Abhimanyu Singh, who had lost his life of 29 years in an accident. His physical remains were absent from his last rites. A group of five young men, believably the dead boy's closest friends, came forward and took charge of the arrangements. In white pathani salwars and biker jackets that had serious-looking metal studs poking out of sleeves and cuffs, they ran around frantically. With heads tilting into headphones and arms waving like windmills, they supervised a workforce that was burying cold and hard poles into playground mud to stretch out a bright blue tent. Here, a prayer meeting was to be held.

Brash boys didn't know how to express grief. They grew up overnight, possibly at the age of nine, when they stumbled upon porn lying next to video game DVDs at poorly-supervised stores. They grew up with the desperation to ride a bike, to drive a car, to kiss a girl, to build muscle, to taste alcohol, to inhale hookah fumes, to travel to Thailand, to dodge the police, to dodge death.

Abhimanyu was one of their own and they were going to miss him. That clutter of beer pints from their last gathering was still lying on his terrace. Ticket stubs from last Friday's movie were still stashed away on dashboards. Their drunken bromance had sobered down, for good. But they couldn't cry. It was believed that crying was for the weak, for the women, for the old. Was the lack of weakness a weakness in itself?

Is crying a sign of mental weakness? Isn't there as much point in crying, as there is in laughing? Isn't it just a release? A normal, natural release. Nobody likes an ending. Isn't crying the breaking away from delusions, isn't crying the death of denial? It looks like a fiercely private dialogue with one's inner self done in a manner universally identifiable. Is it the bastard child of drama, longing to be accepted? The eyes warm, the lashes sticky, it is the fever that has fallen upon a face at its wrinkled-most. Then why are they told not to cry?

'Where's Anwesha?' the aunt spoke, between a series of short sniffs. No one uttered a word, waiting for someone else to make the first move.

Abhimanyu's mother, whose loss seemed the greatest, expanded her sobbing eyes angrily and screamed. 'That witch, she jinxed my son's life and brought bad fortune on him. She must have done black magic…she stole my son away from me,' cried the mother of a dead son. Her sisters held her by the shoulders, as if to stop her from running away. 'I want to see his body. I want to touch his face. Please show me his body. I want to hold him once more,' the mother said what nobody wanted to hear.

'Where's Anwesha?' This time the aunt whispered more persuasively. 'Come with me,' said an unknown face, a neighbour's maybe. She was taken deep into the sad, cold house till she reached the backyard.

She crossed the tulsi plant that looked drier than usual, and ashamed at its inability to protect the life of the child of its garden. Here was Anwesha, in the company of her sister, her mother and two school friends, all of whom were softly crying in a huddle. Even after the death of the groom, they were still the bride's side, inhibited and scared. Anwesha was Abhimanyu's wife of four years. At 25, the tsunamic tide of widowhood had sunk her hopes. She looked like flotsam, afloat and alone.

One week ago, the couple had driven off into hilly wilderness that lay many miles north. Abhimanyu drove and drove madly. Steering a wheel forward meant driving a life forward and in that sense, the one who controls the wheel also controls the lives of all those who share the ride. A control fetishist, Abhimanyu switched between lanes to the blare of a loud horn, confusing rowdy trucks and making them feel powerless. His black SUV had the tempo and mode of a Jamaican sprinter on stimulants, it gathered splatters of yellow dust, lap after lap. Anwesha had become used to living like a passenger. She sat next to him, pulling her sweater sleeve over her palm to wipe the dust off tinted window films. She stared at the traffic, at large trucks she could fit her life's belongings into, at bulls and goats that won't put up a fight if something fast and sharp left them injured. She stared at everything that was being left behind, urgently. Why was everything being left behind, urgently? What was it that lay ahead that won't be left behind, urgently?

'I get scared when you drive fast, Abhi,' she said.

'Have we ever had an accident?' he shot back.

Behind the wheel, Abhimanyu swore at all of humanity, and at the slightest provocation, and was ready to beat up people on the street. But, every single day, he went and bowed down at a Hanuman temple on the way back from his father's garment factory, where he worked. Anwesha sensed emptiness in his faith. Was religion in its acts or in the deeper feeling those acts evoked? Her strength came from ensuring her family's safety and satisfaction. She was silent about her beliefs, silent about her disbeliefs. Abhimanyu held a Bachelor's degree in Commerce, but wasn't educated in emotions. Actually, he wasn't even properly educated in Commerce, he bunked classes all year and memorised borrowed notes the night before each exam. He knew his family business would fall straight into his lap, and that immediately negated the need to do anything else except show up at his factory on a day of his choice.

In the bright of dawn, they reached Akhnoor, a small town by the banks of River Chenab. It had a small fort of minor historic repute, a confined military cantonment, some colleges and shops. Mr & Mrs Singh had booked Suite No. 07 of the Apple Wood Resort. It stood all by itself upon a little hill at the farthest end of this town. With its back toward this sleepy township's buildings and streets, the luxury property held its chin up and faced the mighty currents of the river. There were muddy paths snaking in and out of villas, clusters of evenly spaced-out cottages and one all-suite building. The latter was where they were.

There was a fluffy white bed with a deliberate mess of rose petals and a peachy welcome drink with three strands of sweet saffron. Abhimanyu drew open the thick curtains with one hand. The river could now be seen, heard and felt. There was an angry charge of mutiny in its waters, it was struggling to get somewhere, threatening and defeating its own waves. It liked to be lonely, even the rays of the sun couldn't befriend it. The wild isn't that wild from a distance. In the sealed warmth of their glass room, they only felt the freshness of the river's cool mist and its happy gurgles.

That night, the resort had planned an anniversary dinner for them. They had until evening and Abhimanyu wanted to make good use of the time. They had three rounds of sex. The first soft, the second wild and the third evermore ghastly. He made her go down on him against her will. For her, these were trying times. She sucked in her tongue, kept its tip dry and moved it up and down his rubbery penis. She pretended it was actual rubber and not a penis. She didn't like it when he went down on her either. In such a situation, she stared at the ceiling fan in envy. She was envious of how inanimate objects were free from the pain of force and the pressure of compulsion. Physical objects lacked the consciousness of misery.

'Abhimanyu, I don't enjoy this. I don't feel sure about it when you make me...' she tried to talk to him about it.

'Are you mad? Don't say all this. You'll learn to enjoy it,' he cut her off.

Rape, like any other crime, was a victim of its own description. Because he was her husband, no one had an interest in hearing her plea. Because he was the husband, he had bought a share in her soul and her will. Because he was her husband, he held a stake in her identity and voice. Because he was her husband, was she all and only his wife?

The couple was inebriated on one of the three Indian wines in the mini-bar. Abhimanyu was lazily surfing the television, still naked in bed. Anwesha, enthused out of habit, began ironing her saree for the evening.

'Anu, why do you have to dress up? It's only us,' he commented, as he surfed the television disinterestedly.

'Abhi, I want the occasion to be a memorable one,' she yelled from the powder room where she stood in a bathing gown.

'Okay, whatever. Iron my blue shirt, I'll wear that,' he ordered.

As the sky turned dark blue, a silver-haired manager with cheeks and jawline sagging like that of a purebred bulldog, showed up at their door. He looked at least two decades older than he possibly was. At the sound of two brief knocks, she grabbed her phone and slipped into pointy heels. He pulled out the key card and dabbed his spiked hair in front of the mirror. They were all set. The couple walked behind the footsteps of this dog-faced man, right through a stuffy corridor.

Hotel corridors had a strange insight into the lifestyles of guests. A hotel corridor knew who was hungry for French fries, who needed a soap bar or a dental kit and at what odd hour, and who didn't take in the new-born newspaper into the room. Still, that carpeted stretch didn't show any interest in knowing what went on behind the doors that opened and closed on its face.

Soon, the couple found themselves out of the resort's back gate and onto a narrow path defined in gravel. On either side of this lay the dense stripe of rock and grass that was energetic with short, shy chirps. Things weren't eerie till the manager pointed to a hole in the bushes and urged the couple to shoot a long glare into it. He wanted them to spot a pair of owl eyes that were widely awake inside two circular facial discs. Abhimanyu didn't show any interest in this strange proposal of gawking at the creepy nocturnal bird. As usual, Anwesha followed her husband, now gripping his arm tighter.

The tiny gravel under their shoes made crushing sounds but looked unhurt. There were tea-lights in lanterns. About 10 or 15, maybe 15 minutes later, they reached the riverside. The trail ended at the foot of a broad wooden staircase that was leading up to a machan. The manager, doing his bit to extract a leafy tip, wished them a happy anniversary with a broad smile a second time. Abhimanyu asked Anwesha to pull out a 20-rupee tip from her purse.

Below a kind moon and above a cruel river, this middle-earth was theirs for the evening.

'This has to be one of the most gorgeous places I have seen,' she remarked.

'I know. I wish I could own such a place,' he said.

The river mist had defined the invisible winds. The endless sound of water left them with a constant sense of where they were. The wide deck was airy. Some lanterns from the pathway replicated their shine on it. The bulbs of blue hyacinth tied together in bunches on the floor looked dark, as dark as their shadows. The hotel authorities had seen a lot of the same kind of movies, where the distance between two smiles is lessened by a table of steel domes, candle holders and napkin rings. And where chairs made of wicker are swathed in white and suited elbows crumple over pure white table runners. Years may go by, the young may give up on their youth, but romantic tear and cheer will live up to the grandiloquence expected of it; the truisms of a tender love forevermore. And, such tender love is expensive and difficult to draw together. Yet, such tender love is outlined, and those who fail to feel it aren't in tender love. To honour what lay tender between them, the hotel had left a chilled Cabernet Sauvignon, its spicy grapefruit body leaning on a metal bucket. On one corner was a barbecue, where succulent slabs of meat waited to be seared over briquettes of charcoal. Abhimanyu fired up the grill and Anwesha took up the skewers. She marinated the meat till it turned sweet. He chewed softly. Abhimanyu loved the toxic energy of the Chenab and liked the sense of being close to something that was routinely fierce.

'You are so lucky, you came here as a child. Was it as pretty even then?' she asked.

'Oh god. Just look at the view. I wanted to come back so bad,' he said.

Abhimanyu came to Akhnoor with his parents long ago and stayed in the army cantonment with his uncle, Colonel Randhawa, who then commanded a regiment. Years before the hotel acquired the land from the government, it belonged to the Army. His uncle had arranged a dinner get-together on the deck. Abhimanyu remembered those decorated army generals with moustaches, each word they mouthed was loud and clear. Cheerfully drowsed on the champagne and the breeze, he melted into his memories. He relived the sight of his young father joking about his marriage, with other men, while swirling a glass of scotch killed with soda. Those men stood on the edge together. That night, his mother wore a rose from the valley on the slant of her crimped bouffant and a cushion-cut sapphire pendant. The memory of kids asked to stay put on a large couch with plates of greasy finger food and bowls of ketchup placed before them, also came back to him. Little Abhimanyu wanted to run toward those wooden rails and grasp them. Instead, he felt denied. He didn't like being a child that night. The seeds that denial sows into young minds rarely fail to germinate within them. And denial is a tamed beast, at some point it frees itself terrifyingly.

Abhimanyu felt he wasn't a child anymore.

'Just come here right now and look at the view,' he invited her to the edge.

'I am scared Abhi. I can't, I won't, and I don't want to,' she said.

Anwesha knew all along that she was the mother to this man-child. Being a child is hard. Children are stubborn because the promises of childhood are immediately inconsistent with themselves. A man-child needs to be calmed and entertained by people who hide the painful coercion with which they do what they do, mostly to keep their own peace intact. In childish arrogance, he then walked up to the barbeque and devoured cottage cheese that slowly acquired a golden crunch, and bell peppers that still felt raw. He kept shoving piping-hot chunks into Anwesha's mouth. She was vegetarian, but was in the habit of staining her hands with the smell of slaughterhouses for him. Later that night, he held her hand and whisked her away to the edge. She felt dizzy. The railing was fragile and thin.

'Abhimanyu, let's take a step back,' she begged him. He held her tight and stood firm. 'Don't worry, you're here with me,' he said. There's a thin line between ignorance and arrogance, and it's mostly hand-drawn with a blunt pencil.

Every four minutes, a white flash from a lighthouse shone the pale blue of her cushion-cut sapphire pendant, the same one his mother had worn on that deck. Damaged in places, that stone looked empty until a throw of light illuminated specks of green, pink and purple along its cuts.

She looked desirable. He kissed her violently, till her lipstick smudged all around her mouth. He kept his cold palm on her waist and wanted to capture her in a photograph. He grabbed her phone, which was playing an old Bollywood song. He zoomed in on her.

'Abhi, you are too close to the edge,' she warned him. 'Shhh,' he hushed and touched his finger to her lips. He stepped backwards, centimetre by centimetre, to catch her in the frame. 'Anwesha, smile, Anweshaaaaa,' were his last words. He was out of sight in seconds. The railing broke into two. One portion of it accompanied him. The mouth of the river swallowed him up. He drowned in its salivation. His last cry echoed in the plains… 'Anwesha...'

'Anwesha, Anwesha, Anwesha,' his aunt called out to her with her hectic throat, in which beads of tears had jammed the traffic of breath. She heard her name and felt the warmth of affection from this one and only member of her deceased husband's family. She picked herself up and limped forward. They met in a powerful hug.

'Anwesha, I feel your pain. I know how much you loved and cared for my boy. Be strong, Anwesha, you are now the son of this family,' she stopped to swallow the tear that sneaked down her throat. 'You have one more responsibility.

Be strong.' She uttered some words. The hug had all the warmth Anwesha had been searching for.

Grief is a strange little thing. There is no one kind of grief, there is no one way of healing grief. Is it a failure on the part of society to expect all kinds of people to grieve in one manner? Death is devastating, but the realisation of one's loss in the company of others can be embarrassing or insulting. It curates a situation in which destiny seems to have singled one out for greater misery, as the others are allowed to go home and sleep blissfully. Do those others secretly feel relieved that it didn't happen to them? The wife of a dead man is expected to announce her renouncement of indulgences, the sons are meant to shoulder their fathers' bodies, the sisters and mothers aren't allowed to be present at the funeral. What if the sisters are more evolved to deal with death? What if the mothers are ready for the loss, and what if they are the ones who will shoulder the responsibilities those dead men left behind? Does social norm override the diversity of human sentiment? Some death rituals seem horrifyingly rigid. Maybe, just maybe, the pouring of sacred water into the deceased's mouth and the rubbing of sandalwood paste on its forehead might make the loved ones uncomfortable. Won't these death rites ultimately pile onto the disturbing memory of the incident of death? Symbolism, however scientific and sociological its merits, can be burdening. The grave is hidden, the epitaph is abstract, the dead are gone, and the burning pyre only blinds those alive around it.

Anwesha wasn't a stranger to death. She had lost her father on her 18th birthday. He was on his way back from the bakery on a rickety two-wheeler when a black SUV crushed him and drove past casually. She had lived through the sight of her father's cracked body on a busy Delhi road, when the blood leaking off his limbs mixed up naïvely with a damaged black forest cake. The blood was dead but the coffee frosting would have still tasted sweet and fresh, his affection was still on it. The tip of his dead tongue peeped from the edge of his lip, covered in cake. It resembled that of a child passed out on chocolate.

Anwesha ran forward to guard her broken father from the glares of the passers-by, especially those bus passengers who flocked toward one side to gape at his wounds. His blood lay on municipal property, no different from a spillage of petrol or dog urine. Shivery from shock, she pulled out a floral handkerchief and tried to soak whatever she could into its softness. This was the only way to fight the state to stake claim over her father's mortal remains. How much of one's sense of security is lost with a father? And, if he dies in the public square, will that resemble a crucifixion being telecast worldwide? With every wild strand of pubic hair, with each unsightly deposit of fat being spread out and pinned on a board for public viewing? Watching another's pain from a distance, is there a faultless pleasure in it for others?

After the incident, Anwesha became her mother's support, worked part-time, and put her sister through high-school and college. She bought a second-hand car and drove them around. She was rebuilding something for her family with all her strength and spirit.

'If you marry this boy, I will feel relieved,' said Anwesha's mother, when her sister conveyed the news of the proposal.

'But I don't know if he's a nice boy,' she replied.

'Why will he not be nice? Marriage with anybody is a gamble,' said her mother, settling it once and for all. Anwesha could never disagree with her mother.

Abhimanyu married her because he found her pretty, pretty like a showpiece designed on order. Besides, she also resembled his ex-girlfriend of five years from his school and college days. Her pink cheeks had a dry dimple in them. At each slow blink, one could see a brush of candy-pink on her wide-apart eyes. Her hair, like a rope curtain tieback, was elegantly tasselled. It fell from shoulder to shoulder. At Abhimanyu's funeral, the lampblack lining her eyes had broken up like hardened nail paint that was falling off in scratches. It had settled under her eyes. She hugged the aunt and let out a hoarse cry.

The poor little girl would be denied the respect of her community. Respect is the desirable sentiment that is more than the sum of its gestures. When it's active, it's fear; when it's passive, it's pity. For now, she might just be pitied. With age, some respect could come her way, depending on how well she performs at picking up the pieces of her life.

'Don't worry, Anwesha. You are now the son of this family,' repeated the aunt.

Patriarchy dictates that sons are sons of the soil. The fact of having a healthy male successor led to the myth of his assumed greatness. Mothers and aunts and sisters and wives, they all rotated on an axis around the son. Was the weight of this social honour taking away his ability to co-exist, his ability to set aside his ego and feel what others feel, feel how he makes others feel? These sons were burning in their own brightness. Anwesha might have felt son-burnt too, but she had hidden the tan marks under a cloak of pretence.

Anwesha's marriage to Abhimanyu made her conscious of how she spoke, what she wore, and whom she kept in touch with. He doubted her character; his doubt was independent of her character. She was always under watch, he called her on her phone often and her phone-bills were cross-checked for "unusual activity".

'Whose number is this with a 007 in the end, and why have you dialled it 10 times in the last 10 days' he once enquired, flashing her phone-bill in her face.

'That's my friend Mahima's number, she got married last year. Remember, she sent a card?' she replied, nervously.

'Okay. I will find out,' he said, and dialled the number.

Ten minutes later, he returned fuming from the bedroom because Mahima's husband had answered his call and maybe it was him Anwesha had really been speaking to. For weeks, he blamed her and cursed her, even though she did her best to clarify.

Anwesha knew that cheating on him would have been such a nuisance, and loyalty was peaceful. Strangely, when they went out, it was de rigueur that she be in tight jeans and a skin-hugging top. By the watch-dog logic, he was lugging around his juicy bone, waiting to bark and bite the predators away.

'I don't want to dress up in these clothes. I don't like to,' she expressed her discomfort at his demands.

'You can wear anything when you're with me. I am an open-minded person.' he declared his bold stance.

As a result, she became socially awkward. Anwesha, who once had an infectious smile, now waited for others to declare something funny before she started to laugh along.

Anwesha was damaged. And widowhood was going to make matters worse. The aunt bemoaned as she thought about Anwesha's fate.

'Anwesha, why was Abhimanyu being this adventurous? Why did this happen? Why?' she couldn't avoid discussing the issue, she too had solace to seek. Anwesha stopped crying. She sat with the aunt on the bright red bench in their backyard, holding a cup of tea, looking like a spent storm.

'It happened, Aunty, it just happened,' Anwesha's voice was prickly, as though she had swallowed rusted nails. She leaned on the aunt's shoulder and shut her warm eyes. Mourners came and went. Some wept along harmoniously, others expressed distant concern with intermittent *tch-tch*s. Anwesha was still leaning on the aunt in the darkness of her closed eyes. The aunt thought about the poor girl's relationship with her in-laws. Oh, her poor life, without children of her own, without cheer and colour of her own, what was she to do now?

'How did this happen?', 'Why did this happen?', 'What will happen now?'... Anwesha couldn't soak it in any longer. She felt nauseous and sprinted to her room. She latched herself in and fainted on the bed. She hit her head on its raised wooden edge, it started to spin, and spin faster. She shut her eyes and took her mind to the scene of the accident. In what resembled the negative of a camera roll, she relived the sequence cinematically and came face-to-face with memory.

Once dinner was done, Mrs Singh asked her husband to a dance. Like always, he drank at least thrice as much as she did. The wine from the day had blended with the champagne from the night. The yellow beeswax of tea-lights evanesced. She took out her cell phone from her purse and placed it on the table. She scrolled to her father's favourite song and clicked on it, "Mere mehboob qayamat hogi, aaj ruswah teri galiyon mein mohabbat hogi" (My darling, it is doomsday today, love will leave your streets in dismay today). She buried her face in his chest as they teetered to the tune. He held her waist, pushed her hair to one side and began kissing the other. They swayed, slowly.

The episodic beams of the lighthouse spotted them every four minutes, but they didn't seem to care. He was dangerously close to the edge and kept dancing closer and closer toward it. At the third minute of darkness, even the tea-lights went off into the wind. The song was still in the air and Mr Singh's eyes were locked in ignorance and the bliss it brought along. At the edge of the cliff, she pierced his foot with her sharp heel. He flushed crimson, and bent down in a weakness triggered by a shooting pain.

The red lava of pain spread across his face and his neck in a visible, violent undercurrent that turned him warm. He bit her shoulder to silence his scream and grabbed the other one; an instinctive attempt to thwart the pain. Recollecting whatever was diminishing inside of him, he took her off his chest and made eye contact. He wanted to see an affectionate apology in her eyes. He brushed aside the strands the wind had coldly thrown over her eyes. Her eyes weren't closed like that of a sleeping baby, lying without a worry over her mother's chest. They were open. Under all that hair, why were they wide open? In one go, she enlarged them to twice their size, imitating the hunger of a tiger in the middle of a wild roar. He fell inwards into the cesspool of his own confusions, which weakened him in the knees. As he reeled back and forth from the centre of his balance, she used all her force to push him into the waters below.

The song was still disseminating into the desolation, the lyric and tune of the melody shielded her senses from the intensity of his holler. The lighthouse was back on the scene. All it saw was Anwesha standing by the side of a broken wooden rail, with her palms piled up in shock over her face, about to let out a cry. The next 10 minutes were both strong and weak. Some locals paraded up to her and held her, another group motor-sailed to rescue whatever was left of him. They only found one shirted arm, nibbled on by fish. Anwesha looked at it and remembered her father's dead arm, sullied in the same manner. He was killed by a rowdy boy's black SUV just like Abhimanyu's, was it Abhimanyu's?

"Aaj ruswah teri galiyon mein mohabbat hogi."

She woke up from her bed. Remorseless, she walked back to the bright red bench in the backyard and thought to herself, "The firmness of your muscle was ceasing my soft arm, the sharpness of your nails was searing into it, leaving marks red, blue, deep purple...there was a stream of blood beneath it, which too had a colour, which too had a life, a life you were killing each day.

And, if there is hell somewhere, I will meet you there someday."

The Government Wife

'Sarojini, go up to your room,' said her mother.

'Sarojini, do as your mother says,' said her father.

'But Maa, I only want to know what a condom is... It's not a good thing? Why does the government say it's a good thing?' the 13-year-old defended the innocence in her curiosity.

'I said go up to your room, right now,' her mother warned, more forcefully this time, repressing a lot more than the curiosity of her young mind.

Sarojini was her name and she was a small-town girl in greasy plaits and a home-stitched dress. She was wary of alien men, distant from world wars, and shielded from familial feuds. One would picture a Sarojini to be like that, wouldn't one? Are the syllables of one's name an endless chain of signification? That's how convention usually works, doesn't it? By that logic, it is correct to believe that someone named Monica would blossom into a halter-top-wearing-vodka-drinker at the age of 17. Or a Ramola would make a sexy 30-year-old, who spends her Friday nights holding champagne flutes, in low-cut blouses and oxidised silver amulets that bite into her porcelain skin.

Maybe, a Nandini would walk into a party on time, unsurprisingly with a bouquet of fresh red roses. She'd never leave her pearl-white smile at home. A certain Chandralekha would be waiting at a bus-stop in a cotton saree and a black bindi, holding her broken leather sandal.

The nomenclature stretched over to the boys too. The one named Ankit couldn't, at any point, be older than five. The Pulkits were studying to be mechanical engineers, always approaching a board exam, or its critical result, either of which wouldn't matter once they cleared the JEE anyway. The Akshays were neighbourhood playboys in mirrored aviators and acid-washed pants; even streaks of rebellion stuck to dogma laid down by VH1. The Adityas of the world had managed to find summer placements with marketing firms, the previous winter. They wore formals and looked dutiful in them. Then, there were the problem-of-plenty Nehas & Shwetas, considered too cosmetic to be intelligent; anybody with neat coats of blue nail polish doesn't have a plan larger than dinner with friends at 8. On a weekday, even on a Monday, one could see them dawdling down shopping malls wearing tangerine Zara jackets. On a sunny day, they slipped into floral dresses from flea markets in Goa that were picked up with the express purpose of sticking out in a New Year group-selfie. They were comfortable in their world of flip-flops from Bangkok, and Guess watches encrusted with synthetic diamonds. What a life!

The creation of such convention was necessary. Even adults, with their developed identities, hadn't the ability to confront it. A Poonam Aunty held a double B.Ed from a recently renamed state university and she only made use of the degree to outdo her sisters in finding a good match. Of course, the degree meant an upper hand in her marriage of 23 years to Mr Poonam. She made humble efforts to keep up with the times, quoting gyan from Shobhaa De's columns in the passing and wearing short kurtas from Fabindia with jeans and sports shoes on morning walks. She could learn authenticity from a Gayatri Aunty, who ran a school for poor children on her terrace and wrote poetry. Hers was a pretty garden where plants grew out of wine bottles and painted old kettles. She knew some botanical names. She could identify the species of exotic birds that perched on the muddy rims of her ferns and conifers.

A Srivastava Uncle could summarise into six clever points, any of Bipin Chandra's Indian history textbooks. The D'Souza folk knew how to bake a rum cake and mull a red wine, and their oldies could dance arm-in-arm, and they could even raise a toast. The Rustams were stealthily rich. Even though they still dragged around their sky-blue Ambassador 1965, there was some secret wealth stashed away somewhere that would ultimately be bestowed upon a nephew or a niece. They never had children of their own. The Chatterjees had, for some mysterious reason, named their daughters after Nivea creams: Olina and Oindrila. Both were PhDs in Women's Studies from JNU.

The Akhtars were not poor Muslims; they had nothing to do with a pet goat. They were territorial about Urdu. They might have invented it. The drawing room of their ancestral home had real paintings made by famous painters and signed copies of coffee table books. Their evenings were spent discussing intelligent things. They made poetic references to civil rights movements alongside kebab cutlets and chutney sandwiches. They were the sort of family that always had guests over for dinner. They served soups, and croutons (not breadcrumbs) on off-white silk napkins.

The Aroras couldn't handle their whisky. The Jains sent their son to Warwick to study management so he could later join the family's hardware business, of course. Junior Jain was using that one year away to kiss at least 20 white necks. Then he came back for good with an Arsenal jersey for his younger brother and not half a mind to go slog in a stinky warehouse. The Nairs had a fridge full of magnets from their time in Sharjah. Their children were both medical doctors, and they now lived in Indiana. The Menons weren't the sort of Mallus who migrated to the Gulf in search of forex. They taught at state universities.

Is convention a creation of convenience and breaking down the world into familiar images, an inexplicable civil practice?

It seems that the mind is made on a potter's barn. There's a spinning wheel of existence upon which the moist clay of beliefs to be accepted, errors to be avoided and ideals to be chased are clamped and thrown in. All right and wrong is the work of two small thumbs that decide what to press in and what to trim out. With time, a thin but defined wall takes shape. This is perception. If a mere crack causes a crumble, it's time to re-evaluate. If a first shot begets a perfect pot, it's a clear case of good judgement. On being exposed to the heat of a kiln, patience is tested. If it hardens, it dies the death of an experience. If it doesn't, it lives on as a lesson. The mind is made on a potter's barn, where expression is only an impression.

However, Sarojini Shukla's mind was more like an imitation of a Ming Dynasty vase. The outside was artistically glazed, in deep cobalt blue, to appease her immediate surroundings. The inside was left dark, deep and hollow with doubts unresolved and questions unanswered. The inside didn't matter because society snipped and stuffed ash-pink roses down its throat. The world was only able to see petal curls on top, drippy with dew, cool and soft to touch. She looked ordinarily effervescent on the outside. It was somewhere in the underbelly of her roots that a decay was developing. The waters that held her together were turning yellow, green and black. But nobody wanted to look at the impending devastation that lay beneath. The beauty of flowers, and life, was best left a fleeting delight.

The only child of a bureaucrat father, Sarojini was born and raised in small towns in the heartland, or the Hindi-speaking belt, of India. Her childhood featured hair oil, in unhealthy measure. Her mother would heat it and pour it into a cup of smelly herb powders. Flipping through comics (Super Commando Dhruva, Archie and Tintin), she spent sunny afternoons with her stomach flat out on a teak plank tied to four formidable iron chains of an ancient-looking garden swing above a brick-floored verandah. A steel cooler made breeze. Its jaws were eternally widened and trapped onto a window grill, drool dripping down its rusty legs.

Sarojini was common looking. One would eventually run into the other six faces that resembled hers.

Afternoon upon afternoon, she lay on that swing, palms folded inward like that of a baby's, and eyes rolling to the graphic advance of a comic. A half-eaten chocolate bar with a bite mark on it, sat next to her.

Her father, Kishore Shukla was an Indian Police Service officer; 1979 batch. He was allotted a large government mansion to serve the country better. It had a straight driveway, the size of two stretched limousines. It was furnished with one military green jeep and two white ambassadors with cherry-like lights on top. The cars were fitted with little net curtains and tiny fans that ensured the comfort of the occupants and made that comfort visible.

A retired clerk with tobacco-stained teeth, Ram Singh had been assigned gardening duties at the Shukla residence. Every morning, around the time Shukla Sahab got into his signature blue track suit, flexed his moustache and brisk-walked out of a large wrought iron gate with his Alsatians, Captain and Shaitaan, Ram Singh would be on duty. He hosed down magenta bougainvillea vines, pitch-forked crisp golden leaves off the garden's brick-worked borders. Occasionally, and especially, when he had a favour to ask of his master, he fetched newspapers and wheeled the tea tray into the wet morning lawns.

Meanwhile, Ram Singh's young brother-in-law Bhim Singh spent his life checking if the soil was right for the birth and growth of green beans, eggplant and pumpkin in the kitchen gardens. But this wasn't his full-time job. Bhim Singh was also a runner, quite literally, running around with files, flasks, unstitched blouse pieces, train tickets and umbrellas. They were both at Shukla Sahab's beck, call and all.

There was another level of domestic bureaucracy operating inside. Here, head cook Babu took all the important decisions. His face was always sweaty with spicy steam and he kept a cloth spare on his shoulder to hold handles of hot pans and occasionally blow his nose into. Of course, Mrs Sangeeta Shukla had veto power over him. She could rule in anytime, condemn recipes, amend garnishing tricks and repeal evening menus. The lowest in the rung was Raju, who did the chopping and the serving.

During garden parties, for hours, he held heavy trays loaded with plates of snacks. Bureaucrats loved making waiters hover around till they finished making their point. Those who were government servants in theory were masters of those destinies that hierarchy had placed below them. Typically, an aggressive take on public policy would be delivered between the plucking of a paper napkin and tonging out of a fried snack onto it. Raju, red rings imprinted on his palms from that 18-inch silver-plated brass tray, always looked painlessly servile.

The seating arrangement at social gatherings was gendered. Young girls sat by their mothers sipping orange-and-white soft drinks. The higher the husband's rank, the heartier was the reception of his wife's views. Womenfolk found creative ways to fill the emptiness of a small-town existence. They rated each other's gardens, at the end of which the giving away of cheap china tea-sets or bright pink-and-green mink blankets absorbed into the shape of their PVC bags, took place. Sarojini always sat next to her mother. She was just shy, or scared. If she picked up Sprite instead of water from a serving tray, she'd pretend to sip along as if it was exactly what she'd wanted. 'Sarojini, don't have more than one glass of soft drink. It's not good for your teeth,' advised her mother. In cursive writing, her parents drew her fate across her textbook mind, and they sharpened and erased as they liked.

Though mere blocks away, Sarojini was driven to her all-girls school. In the evenings, she was chaperoned to her horse-riding lessons. Just as she was getting better at it, her parents pulled her away from those young trainers in gumboots, who fell like thunder upon dusty tufts. Some years passed. A piano teacher and the harmonious coupling of a kathak guru and a tabla vaadak appeared in interludes at the Shukla household. She rode, she danced, and she did all that her age expected of her.

At the bend of Sarojini's street stood the nearly 100-year-old Jain bakery. With her arm attached to her mother's, she would enter the bakery's vanilla-smelling insides, wondering if cakes and patties existed so far back in time. Around its refrigerated convex counters, her mother invariably bumped into one of Sarojini's school teachers, most of whom were also wives of officers. Her parents even invited her classmates and close friends over to their place.

In small-town familiarity, social interaction was monitored. This was the living of a life inside a warm, fortified cocoon. But children were not moths. Then why were they attempting the spinning of silk cocoons around them? The boundaries they were weaving were made of silk, a fabric one could see through but not tear through. Within these silk cocoons, caterpillars were expected to blossom into butterflies, in hiding, in complete silence, on their own. Why was culture replicating nature? And, if mankind was doing what was normal, then would the human butterfly be allowed to flaunt its colours, flitting from flower to flower? Culture seemed to be a mere miscalculation of nature, a chivalrous bastardisation of nature. Some small towns, like cocoons, were trapped in their own soft muck.

When Sarojini was growing up, she was warned not to wander beyond the gated confines of her government colony. 'The world is full of the bad and the ugly,' said her mother. 'They can do anything to you,' she added. At night, scary thoughts would keep her awake. She would imagine strangers, male strangers, throwers of glares carrying daggers or smaller folded knives sharpened with the satanic intent of tearing up a little girl's clothes, or mortifying her naked body or selling it for a strange price. Such thoughts would make her nervous and more desperate for parental shelter.

It was a given that any Hindi-speaking man below her class was a bhaiya, which eliminated the possibility of a sexual liaison and rendered her secure and superior. Her mother censored what Sarojini watched and read. The memory of her mother casually tear up the sex survey edition of a national news magazine, was something Sarojini couldn't make sense of. How gory and other-worldly was the sight of a cleavage scant inside two unfastened buttons? Why didn't her mother want the servants to chance upon a magazine cover dripping with innuendo? What harm could it have done?

Puzzled at the delphic message conveyed in a condom ad on television, she asked her mother what the point of condoms was. What was this informed choice that lay wrapped inside that box? 'It's none of your business,' was her mother's one-and-only reply as she switched off the television.

Sarojini began menstruating at the age of 12. It happened during a sultry summer that was approaching a slow end at her mother's childhood home in the company of cousins, who were around her age, and aunts who were clarifying butter and her grandmother who was pickling mangoes and lemons in quantities that could animate the taste buds of an entire village. Sarojini, along with her little cousins, was then attempting a brave ascent on the banyan tree in a large backyard. She sensed an unfamiliar wetness in her underwear. She sank her finger in, it returned red. Oblivious, she ran to her mother and held out her stained finger.

Her mother, who was then in the company of aunts, maids and male cooks, was left red-faced. 'Sarojini, keep quiet,' she took her by the hand and rushed her to an inner room, as if she was going to be detained for a crime. In an allegedly friendly initiation into womanhood, her mother spoke, 'We are women, we are born to bear pain, don't be scared, Sarojini, just be careful. Watch how you sit. You will not be wearing short skirts anymore and don't go touching my temple when you are bleeding.'

'You are now the honour of your father's family,' she declared. Sarojini, still 12, still a little girl, suddenly shouldered the weight of something heavier than her bones. Once the initiation was done, the mother didn't let her step out. Sarojini wanted to ask why this was happening to her, and if this was happening only to her? 'Does my friend Radhika also bleed from there,' she asked her mother. 'You should never discuss these things. Have you ever seen me talking about my periods with anybody and have you ever noticed me buying sanitary napkins?' replied her mother, as she lined Sarojini's underwear with a sticky white sanitary pad. 'When you want to change your pad, first hide it with a dupatta and then take it into the bathroom. I will be very upset if you come running to me in public to tell me that you are in pain. And there will be pain but you need to bear it because medicines are not good in the long run…' she droned on and on.

Outside, her little cousins were playing hide-and-seek. Lying alone on a four-poster bed with carved mahogany pillars on all four corners in the darkness of her widowed grandmother's bedroom, she turned sides toward the green-tinted windows that were shut tight, and bordered by thin lines of light that managed to break in. The sight made her sleepy. It was still bright outside. Like sporadic founts, their laughter shrilled up and down. They were still playing hide-and-seek. Sarojini was hiding too. But, hiding is fun with the knowledge that a friend will come seeking and a foe shall not find. Slowly, the noise and the light coming in from the outside faded.

Back at her school, another rough game of hide-and-seek was on. Girls who didn't have the strength to seek, hid themselves under social norm that prescribed no interaction with the opposite sex, except under the supervision of adults. Those who did find the strength were seeking pleasures, mostly unchecked. On sleepy afternoons, girls were leaping over the backyard fencing of their homes to unite with their beaus, who stretched their brawny pelvises over second-hand bikes and clink-clinked the edges of their cheap Chinese cell phones into metal gas tanks in happy anxiety. Together, they *vroomed* past back-lanes to hit the restaurants along the highway. Their kisses tasted of jalebi and samosa.

'Do you know, Reena has a boyfriend and she meets him every evening after school? Yesterday, they went to watch a movie, and last week they were about to…,' gossiped Sarojini's classmate.

'Let's not talk about her. She's not a nice girl,' interjected Sarojini.

Occasionally, these girls would go to better restaurants, the ones with laminated menu cards and stands full of shiny steel spoons. They could only afford a plate of veg manchurian and two fresh lime sodas (sweet-salt mix). The girls would return in the evening and unassumingly blend in with their gang of girlfriends at the park. Hickeys were hidden under scarves and mouths were repeatedly rinsed. If anybody found out what the girl was up to, she was the subject of colony gossip. Even if she became an ISRO scientist one day, people would first draw a reference to her shady growing up days. Sarojini was growing up in this censored world, where habits were either clean or dirty.

When she was 14, she ended up attracting a stalker. He was a college dropout who cycled behind her car and hid in bushes surrounding the badminton court to catch a glimpse of her newly-formed breasts that bounced up and down. He befriended Sarojini's servants and drivers. He once pretended to be her older brother and broke into her classroom to take her home. A petrified Sarojini told her teacher she didn't know him. The matter reached the Principal and the Shuklas were summoned to the school. On reaching home, Sarojini was slapped hard by her mother.

'What did you do with him? Why did you attract him? What did you do to attract him? Did you lift your skirt or remove your shirt for him? Has he touched you there?' her mother lashed out a set of accusations that were embarrassing for the family.

Her father, arms crossed behind his back, hung his head in shame. Between each slap, she raised her head a little, in the hope that her father would say something or do something to stop this. 'Pa' she muttered affectionately, like an infant hoping to land into her father's cushioned arms after he tossed her high up in the air. It was too frail a plea, it was only a syllable and her father had decided not to hear it. He had succeeded in providing a safe and sanitised life for his family, which meant he could neatly excuse himself from any emotional responsibility. After making his favourite dismissive declaration, 'You women resolve the matter amongst yourselves,' he shrugged his shoulders and walked out of the room. Her mother cursed her a little longer and left her crying in the dark. Sarojini observed her father's back, walking away from her, leaving her alone. That night, for the first time, she felt her father was dead.

Young Sarojini wept into her brocaded pillow, trying to consume her tears. Maybe, she wasn't even allowed to cry? 'Krishna, the world you have made to protect me, why does it only hurt me? Answer me, answer me,' she whimpered softly, so her mother wouldn't hear. The tears corroded her throat, but she kept drinking them up. She tired herself to sleep.

The rest of Sarojini's growing up was scandal-free.

During her 23rd year, her father was completing his second tenure in the city where holy ghats descend into the sacred froth of the Ganga. It was then that the Chaturvedis, who were locals, expressed an interest in securing Sarojini's hand in marriage for their eldest son Gopal. The Chaturvedis were saree merchants and had recently diversified into jewellery. Gopal had joined the State Civil Services after completing his Master's in History from Delhi University whereas Sarojini had studied English Literature from

Benaras Hindu University and was now translating Hindi history books for her department archives.

Initially, second generation civil servants, the Shuklas were hesitant about marrying their daughter into a business family. Sarojini's father had a theory that if a family's wealth is visible to its members in the form of overflowing cash-counters, and if sales and profits are discussed by brothers and sisters in front of aunts and uncles over dinner, one day or the other, they will all start fighting over it and turn against each other in greed. Shukla Sahab's father was an honest civil servant who sold his medals and government rewards to get his sisters and daughters married. In his view, all stature was sacred and any money was profane.

After reassuring phone calls from relatives and common friends, Shukla Sahab invited the boy's family over for tea. He decided not to tally horoscopes just as yet. He felt astrology could be the most issueless excuse if they decided to turn down the proposal after the first meeting. Sarojini knew what was going on. She felt a new kind of excitement. It wasn't alien. She had wanted this since a really long time. She had visualised the sequence of meeting a boy and his family in her drawing room thanks to at least 1,000 movies and 500 television shows. She imagined a stiff family demanding dowry, sometimes a decisive mother-in-law handcuffed her with an ancestral gold bangle, and sometimes there were skittish sisters-in-law who elbowed their brother to point out how lucky he was. In the cosy confines of her drawing room, with the approval of her parents, an innocent romance was about to be born. When convention is the only choice, do people learn to romanticise within it?

Without letting her imagination down, a Mahindra Bolero full of Chaturvedis poured out at their gate. There were aunts, hair messy, sarees crumpled, clearly exhausted from a bumpy ride. The uncles came in suits. There was a newly married brother-in-law and sister who had a mountain of vermilion parting her scalp into two silky halves. There was also a little girl, who was a restless source of potentially awkward questions. At any point, she could pick up a showpiece and pretend there was life in it. Then, there was the suitable boy, Gopal, in raven-black trousers and a parrot-green shirt.

Shukla Sahab, who was then Assistant Commissioner of Police in his state, looked casual in a white kurta-pyjama and welcomed them with folded hands into his mansion, which he humbly described as Gareeb Niwas. It was like declaring truce, and pre-empting a greater war of patriarchal egos between both sides. Interestingly, Shukla Sahab stood amidst sprawling lawns that circled his 10-room mansion where three armed guards and two old Alsatians patrolled. But, because it was government property and belonged to him only till the last day of his service, they had reason to believe in his humility. The Shuklas laid out a feast of biryani and refreshing mint-muddled curd. Also present at the venue were the pious middlemen who sanctified the meeting of the two sides, dragging planets and stars into the making of this match.

Once both sides put forth their ritualistic take on caste, sects and ceremonies, they announced they were modern and that the decision of the girl and boy was supreme. Sarojini appeared in a translucent crepe-chiffon saree that was slipping off her thin shoulders, it was turmeric yellow.

Sarojini's face had pleasingly bordered itself along her pear-shaped nose. By virtue of being the object of attention, she looked prettier than she was. Everyone in the room stood up, as though she was a Supreme Court judge and this was the final hearing before a lifelong sentence. Gopal, the criminal in her custody, raised himself, to surrender to the glow of her radiance. He noticed a slim silver chain lining her sleek waist. She lifted her downcast eyes, for some seconds, memorising the sharp cuts of his face. Members of his family murmured at length about how tall she was, worrying if she was taller than the boy. The women dabbed three fingers along her cheeks, as if to check texture quality. Soon, Sarojini and Gopal were sent off to another room to talk. Seated on the same side of the couch, they threw side glares at the person they were expected to sleep naked with.

'So…who is your favourite cricketer?' he asked.

'Rahul Dravid,' she reacted.

'Do you like Rabindra Sangeet,' he asked.

'No. I like Sufi songs and Norah Jones?' she answered.

Soon, it was time to make up their mind.

For the next two months, they met thrice, and always in the interfering company of his sister and her cousin. Among the topics discussed were Bareilly's jewellery, Jaipur's leather market, Switzerland's glacial glory and Chinese food joints in Benaras. Sometimes, he called her up on the landline and asked what she was wearing and how she was looking. Her mother flailed about in the same room, dusting clean cushions and lending to the awkwardness. He told her he keeps thinking about the chain on her waist and those tiny pearl earrings that appeared and reappeared from behind her long brown hair.

'Hmmm...okay...,' was the only reply Sarojini could muster the courage to give, especially with the mother around.

Exactly two months on, the Shukla lawns were dressed up in glitter-sprayed canopies. There were bouquets of peach-pink and ivory roses, wild foxtail orchids and timid frangipanis, their stems caught inside napkin rings and tied together by soft blue yarn. There were pillars crafted out of pots, glittery with cut mirrors. On that windy December night, the lawns were planted with propane heaters that looked like standing ashtrays around which guests huddled with paneer tikkas and ceramic cups of sweet corn soup.

The music was a mix of folk and remixed Indian songs. The men showed up in sherwanis, feathers and large crystals broached on chests. The women were dressed up in jewel-toned ruby reds, peacock blues and rani pinks. Gemstone necklaces and gold-threaded saree borders sparkled in the glow of hundreds of twinkling lights and the holy flame that consecrated the marriage of Sarojini and Gopal.

Within hours, she found herself in his bed, hidden under a cake of make-up, with jewels tying up her nose to her ears to her head like ornamental shackles. He chose to surpass the excesses and firmed his sight on her tight blouse and her untouched breasts breaking out of it in a crack. He unscrewed her jewels, with a little help from her, then held her face and began kissing her lips. With graceful poise, she closed her eyes, giving herself to him completely.

The black of shut eyes joined up to form one big vacant screen where her mind projected scenes from movies songs that ticklishly elaborated the night they were going to be awake through. His invisible touch was lending character to her thoughts. The touch that bound them was neutral. It belonged neither to him nor to her, but to those songwriters and filmmakers whose work she was imagining.

The songs were about to reach her lips and turn into words. She opened her eyes. She saw his paunch. It was naked and dewy with sweat. In her mental absence from the scene, he had gotten out of his wedding outfit. Its pieces fell, some on the bed, some on the floor. The sight of his nakedness horrified her. This wasn't what she had seen in any movie, or read about in any story, or even heard of from friends. She was excepting clean, hairless abs like Salman Khan's.

Are women allowed to be lookists? Can they disapprove of a man, however suitable he is, if they don't find him attractive?

In this animalistic avatar, he wasn't the same Gopal she had first seen. There was a strange odour of undigested peas or was it the stench of mildew on a wet towel? In her sheltered world, the one her parents brought her up in, this act would be deemed dirty. Sarojini began to panic. She felt her mother was watching what she was up to. Could she be beaten up for committing this crime? Was Gopal that stalker from her childhood, now seeking carnal revenge? This wasn't the same legitimate romance she was allowed to watch and observe everything about. This was the sex her mother had warned her against. This was sex; the sex that puts one's character in doubt, the sex that was banned, the sex that was designed for servants and deviant girls. Sex was like entering someone else's dirty bathroom. Sarojini had nothing to do with this sex.

Ecstasy was pregnant with agony. She pushed him aside. The songs in her head stopped, on their own.

'Is there anything wrong?' yelled Gopal.

She didn't know what to say. 'I am a little...I am a little tired...from the ceremonies... I don't know... Can I please...can we please sleep?' she tried to defend herself.

He looked at the floor to cool down for a few minutes. 'Please, relax Sarojini. I understand. It's a new place. I understand,' he said to the best of his congeniality.

Gopal's masculinity was trying to revive itself from what had just happened. He felt unable to attract and arouse his spouse, but self-doubt soon subsided. All this was new for them and he knew Sarojini was the only child of her parents, and more guarded in her ways.

The women were usually in fitted clothes, a lot more skin was on show and the cuts and curves on their bodies were far more defined. What about men? Under full-sleeved shirts and tapered trousers, there could be patches of discoloured skin, big brown moles: two entangled strands of hair creeping out of their centres, there could also be man breasts and a wide forest of hair. Because societies poeticise a woman's appearance and obscure a man's behind his stature, his intellect and his humility, does it not matter at all? Sarojini buttoned up and turned her back toward him. She slept through the pain, which returned minutes after she woke up. And, she woke up alone. She felt a strange guilt inside her, partially toward Gopal, majorly toward her mother.

When she dressed up and came out the next morning, the Chaturvedi women were seated in the living room amidst ceremonial fruit baskets that were exchanged during the wedding. In one corner, a maid had squatted to broom out the frippery of confetti, straw and wrapping paper.

Gopal's sisters and aunts lit up with joy when they saw her walking in. They ignored how she looked homeless and aimless, and harangued her with pointed questions like, 'How was it?', 'Are you tired?' Sarojini felt deeply offended. What was going on? How could they be forthcoming about something as filthy as sex? She smiled and said nothing. In any case, wouldn't a positive and descriptive answer to that question gross them out? Then why would they show interest in what shouldn't concern them to begin with?

She thought about her mother again, about how livid she would be if she found out what could have happened the night before. Sarojini sat next to Gopal's grandmother and left the rest of them busy unwrapping and rewrapping presents. His grandmother observed the unsettled look on the face of this new bride. She turned her wheelchair in Sarojini's direction, took her soft palm between her own rumpled ones and left some caressing pats on it. She then asked her to give her a little Krishna. Sarojini stared into the recesses of the lady's old eyes, vexed at the ridiculousness of the request.

Sarojini too wanted children of her own and had picked out their names. But not this way. She gently took her hand back and put it on her head, which was heating up. Her bejewelled bare feet, tinkled their way into Gopal's huge kitchen, which was the size of a small badminton court. She pulled out a freezing bottle of cola that was hiding behind boxes of sweets sealed in red-and-yellow cellophane. At this point, she could soak her hair in cold cola, for that relaxing feeling of the weaning away of a heavy headache.

Gopal returned at night. Sarojini, anticipating his return, pretended to be in deep sleep since long before. She was almost desperately waiting for him, waiting to deny him his due. Night after night, she used sleep to shield her soul. She wasn't going to give him what he wanted because she was an honourable woman. He showed no signs of irritation, or worry.

Within a month, they moved into Gopal's brand new government house in Vrindavan, her own government house, where Sarojini was the government wife. It had the smell of freshly-cut wood and varnish. She decked it up with large paintings that were drunk on colour and furniture made of dyed bamboo. She painted the window panes yellow-and-green and dropped block-printed curtains below them.

When a boy and girl set out to start a family of their own, they become man and woman in exactly one night. Isn't this an existential change that expects them to depend suddenly and only on each other? Arranged marriages, although cushioned by custom and familiarity, jerkily impose the abrupt expectation of complete intimacy on that night.

One wrong move between Sarojini and Gopal and the friction from that night would reprise, tunelessly. So, they started enacting their platonic childhoods. They chatted about the television shows they grew up watching, and discovered their shared love for cricket and comics. Sarojini placed a bright red bench in their lawn, upon which they became friends. Gopal gave her space and time. Virgins within their new marriage, they spoke of dance and music. They spent hours listening to music on their lawn. On that bright red bench, they first held hands. His palm reached out to hers and she enjoyed his warmth on her, each finger in it was innocent. They bought new gadgets and also a puppy. Soon, the smell of young wood and varnish faded away and the warmth of muslin table covers, cushion cosies, grass mats and jute carpets turned this government house into their own home. Sarojini was happy living the safe, sanitised life with him. The same life her father had provided her with. She politely deflected his come-ons, but they didn't make her that uncomfortable anymore.

During the first summer of their unconsummated marriage, Mr & Mrs Chaturvedi were invited by the state government as special guests for a dance-drama fest on the rain-drenched lawns of Vrindavan. Gopal and Sarojini found their VIP name tags in the front row. They sat down to experience the first night of the annual Vrindavan Sangeet and Nritya Mahotsava.

The lights went off. The first few strains of moonlight descended upon parched groves that acquired an ashen glow. The world outside was sinking into deep, meditative slumber. Vrindavan was waking up to the sprinkle of young drizzles. A group of milkmaids in flirtatiously flared skirts arrived on the scene. The biting of a lower lip, the throw of a cold palm on a blushed cheek, ever adorable were the efforts that failed to hide the unease in smiles.

A gentle wind shook the shrubs. They fluttered for minutes till the wind left them alone. Hidden in the shrubs were the furled feathers of a peacock. The wind passed through the holes of a reed pipe and turned into sound. The musical current threw open its feathers far and wide. The bird then opened its black eyes.

The peacock is a pure lover, it mates with loyalty. The women sighted a man's silhouette, in the dark blue yonder. They were already in pure and loyal love. In operatic grandeur, a thousand spotlights cut through theatrical smoke and brightened the blue-and-yellow silk that wrapped his muscular body. The copper beads on his feet jingled to his thumps. The women owned him in sight, and in song and dance. They pleaded for more. They danced around him, in disbelief. They fell at his feet to submit their egos before him. They wrapped their bangled arms around him, inviting him into an embrace.

In the backdrop, powdered fingers were slipping over sitar strings, and turning merry in the company of the tabla and the pakhawaj. Like a herd of Chital deer with glints of want in their doe eyes, they danced about restlessly. The percussion that strained through the moist air was blessing their union with the hunter of their choice. He multiplied himself to entertain their individual imaginations. They left every material reality outside the peripheries of this garden and united their souls with his. Is he man, is he God? Bluish-black like a drifting night cloud, he engulfed them in the moment.

Shrouded in mystery he will remain, yet they will wish to decipher him again and again.

Sarojini wasn't a stranger to Krishna's tale, but in the context of her relationship with Gopal, she understood the raas leela in a new light. The union of man and woman wasn't being prescribed, but celebrated by tradition. The mist of Krishna's myth was still in the air. It was departing from convention only to return magically to it.

The next day, they visited some temples they both had seen, but not together. Sarojini held on to Gopal, in public. His arms felt reliable. Nidhi Van, where they toddled in together, was a dry garden with thorny shrubs. The aged guide, in his own kind of English, described this as the place where Krishna reappears every night to unite with the milkmaids and his mistress Radha. Unexpectedly, there was a room fitted with a double bed. Legend has it, here the lovers united in sacred love, away from the regularities of the world. This made mythology less ancient than it was.

Sarojini was staring into the modernity of this mythical room, till the guide clapped and said, 'Time is money, madam. Time is money,' urging her to keep walking. Gopal, who decided to refrain from yielding his bureaucratic authority on their first holiday, didn't like the thought of a man being disrespectful to Sarojini. 'Come, let's go,' he took her by the hand, till they walked away from the precincts of that garden.

On her way back to the hotel, for the first time, Sarojini thought about Krishna as a force greater than her mother. Strangely, this was also a force she viewed as human, as if he was consecrating the making of love. Will the making of love then be that wrong?

The next day, on the ride back to Benaras, Sarojini found herself listening to Krishna bhajans. The next couple of days, she dwelled over Krishna's love tales. She made rounds to the same public library she frequented for history books during her college days. On dusty racks, she found yellowing papers that chronicled Hinduism's pragmatic acknowledgement of sex as a powerful act of creation.

Residing in the city of Lord Shiva for years, she perceived the phallic symbol of 'ling' as chaste masculinity that was breaking out of 'yoni', refusing to be contained by it. This constitution of fertility was worshipped by her parents. She came to realise that only Shakti can bring Shiva to the peak of his potential. How holy is that union which harmonises nature and brings it to a cosmic balance, and unites energies to give birth to life. Sarojini was theory-minded. Theory was beginningless. It stood above the word of her mother and her father. In the light of what she read, she re-imagined her physical relationship with Gopal as something that had the potential of being sacred.

She began facing him while sleeping, without feeling threatened by his accidental touch. In the weeks that followed, she introduced her thought-thirsty mind to the concept of Ardhanarishvara, the lord who is half-woman. To Sarojini, the form that carries male and female biological dispositions wasn't about the lord who had chosen to embrace a woman's calmness within him, but rather about a man and a woman finding their place within each other's bodies, homes and lives. Androgyny maybe biological in manifestation, but is social in essence.

She came across a book on the Khajuraho temples of Madhya Pradesh, where her parents had once gone on a holiday without her. The Chandellas of Bundelkhand, as modern as 1150 AD, engraved on their temples scenes that depicted the natural thrill of watching other people involved in sex, the possibility of homosexual instincts in some minds, and the state's disapproval of animal sex. Inscribed in sandstone were threesomes and women wilfully performing oral sex; experimental lovemaking was left in the public eye till eternity. In thin friezes of relief carvings, maidens lustily wringing out water from their hair or plucking thorns out of their feet were displayed outside the sanctum sanctorum in which Krishna idols resided. She ran her palms over the glossy sheets of the book that displayed these figures in pure peanut, dark coffee and caramel yellow; more than 50 shades of brown. The literature she was reading, disassociated the temples from the *Kamasutra*; the two were in fact six centuries apart. But the book told her that some guides tried to forge that link to hot sell India's erotica to foreign tourists. The Duladeo Temple was notoriously referred to as the Suhag Raat Mandir; this was a manufactured linkage to potency during a nuptial night.

Khajuraho taught her that even in an earlier time, societies have dared to accept sex as it was, as ordinary, as spectacular, as a secular reality like any other.

She began holding onto Gopal's arms, with a new kind of passion. He felt proud of it, as if he had earned her consent. She thought of having a child, but now, that wasn't the only reason she wanted to put herself in an intimate relationship. As soon as a woman conceives, she goes from being a seductress to a nurturer, the carrier of an heir. The growth of the unborn child is measured in medical care and ritual norm, and all talk of sperm and egg is termed genetics. Science and religion are man's favourite tools to code and colour the world. They justify whatever can be imposed, nullify what shouldn't be imposed and vilify whatever comes in the way of the previous two. Tradition has elements of both religion and science. Sarojini made her up mind.

The lust in watching nature's miracles on herself drew her toward Gopal. She had felt like a child with him before. She now wanted innocence within the adult act, so there wouldn't be a need to regain it at all. With open eyes, she made love to him. It was love free of malice. When she felt she was up to something dirty, she dismissed it as a fetish, just the kind of treatment the thought deserved. And, like her mother, she did have a child of her own. Her son Krishna was her victory over mystery.

Upon the same bright red bench in the same government house, where his hand had once mistakenly fallen on hers, they kissed in love, and in front of their child.

In a post-God society, morality is checked and controlled in unjust and unreasonable ways. Traditions pose difficult questions. Some turn to modernity for answers, others search for answers within tradition. Maybe, social mores are just like those five-metal alloy bells that weigh a few tons and are hung at the entrances of temples. Tradition prescribes that a devotee must beat their tongues hard till they squeal out a gong. Not everyone has the intent and, certainly, fewer have the strength to do that. Some feel startled at their sound that others find soothing. Like the five-metal alloy bells in ancient temples, traditions will live on and people will keep offering their lives to them, in appeasement, in resistance, in submission.

The Artist is in Love

Paris. A dinner date. Two strangers in mutual fascination. Wine. The holding of hands. More wine. The locking of legs. Candles. Victoria's Secret fishnet tights. Romance. Paris.

A cobbled street was slippery from a bashful drizzle. It had the dusty shine of an old mirror. She saw in it the delicious reflection of her black Mary Jane platform pumps.

There was breeze, not so much breeze to ruffle up her pleated skirt in awkward measure, enough perhaps to blow open her soft Grecian curls. The juice of wild strawberries had been squeezed onto her lips through a lipstick. She was high on breeze, as though lifeless, she drifted about in it.

In Paris, imagination was never too far from reality. Tenderness lived on the exactness of arch-bridges, of renaissance brushwork, of chequered berets. In Paris, melancholy was melody. It could spill out as naturally from the strumming of a rosewood violin inside a velvet-embroidered opera house, as from the guitar of a street star.

She tiptoed along, as if to the drawl of Sinatra's "Strangers In The Night", clasping slippery railings that lent a sense of direction to Montmartre. Like the carefree slithers of a broad brush dipped in a warm tin of oil pastels, the distant canvas of Montmartre melted into the sunlight.

Whoever painted Paris, knew how to conceal in colour and reveal in grey.

Halfway up the northern hill stood a rundown warehouse. It was stuck to an electric blue door. This was a Franco-Italian restaurant indulging in the bourgeois habit of gourmet. Dangling above its rustic frontage was a board and it crooned in calligraphic French: Cirque D'Amour. The breeze hadn't ceased. Plastic awnings all around were dancing to it and lavender-scented candles planted on the tables outdoor were dodging it.

She was Sharanya Sharma and was here to meet her Clark Kent, a happy neighbourhood boy who would turn into superman on her command. Superman could fly and save lives and soft land on her terrace, and make sweet love to her. He could take many forms, each as spectacular as the other. A man like the one she was going to meet tonight.

Sharanya was in Paris for her Master's in Fine Arts. She shared scholastic space with a dorm full of bizarre and bold minds. They spent full evenings, purging the varnishy scent off gin with more and more tonic fizz. It was easy to believe that only at a watering hole of Irish roots must their art school pretence be drowned in. After some drinks, they poked fun at their gay classmates, spilling out how they didn't really want to wear the badge of gay pride and painted their faces pink-and-purple to rally down city squares only to be welcomed within the liberal arts space.

Others hoped to cash in on a traumatic past to market their work. Suppression and assault were hot favourites. In a world easily amused by tragedy, they used their fingers to tickle tragedy in the tummy. In sweeps of palette knives, big bold sweeps, they compressed death and other suffering that survives.

Then, there were those like Sharanya who found it entertaining to draw and read and just experience literature and art as one turf, their turf. Their 20-something minds resembled the stained-glass blocks they were learning to create in art-deco class. The paint, heavy and sticky like honey, crossed the black geometric demarcations. It turned a little black and spilled over into other counters. Art had mixed up their beliefs had mixed up their art! Or were they just chunks of mosaic with a pattern running through them, trapped in the wider aesthetic and too powerless to alter it? As free as it claimed to be, art too had boundaries. It promised a world full of possibilities and then imposed restrictions of genres and eras. Was art incongruous with itself?

Sharanya didn't mind any of that. She only lost composure at the stereotypes they caricatured about her people. Yes, there were cattle straying on the roads in her home town, but not on every road and definitely not on the roads of her native Central Delhi whose stone-tiled pavements were larger than the roads of many other towns in her country. These pavements were shaded with neem leaves and bougainvillea vines in pink, purple and white. Together, they broke out onto them in autumnal grace, whichever be the season.

There were manicured greens between important state buildings, a crumbly Mughal tomb or two. This was the city's way of reminding itself of its heritage. Cities needed to do that. Their merit wasn't certified by nature. There was no drama of wild seas and the taming of them by shores, there was just barren land that man strived to make as purposeful as he could. And, man was insecure. And, man was looking for approval, for praise, for power. And, man wished to remind himself of his ability to build, destroy and rebuild. Cities were made by man. Cities were made in exodus and revolution. Cities tried.

What architecture did to cities, art did to man, allowing the madness and escapism of parallel possibilities to exist within. Sharanya's life was protected to the extent that it seemed ordinary. Like everyone else, Sharanya was told to live in the moment. What if the moment is ordinary, she asked? What if the moment isn't majestic or musical, what if it lacks inspiration? What if the moment is just the desperate urge to break out of the moment?

As a child, she ran around her house, grasping the armrests of large couches and curling the corners of long Turkish carpets in a close game of chase with her siblings, one brother and one more brother. She would stop to catch her giggly-spitty breath and sense her eyes coming back to the cluster of Monet prints nailed onto one corner of her large drawing room that was always flooded with white light. Her mother could name each of those prints. She was a connoisseur of fabric prints, if there is such a thing. But, she had laminated them poorly, there were air bubbles blowing up on their surfaces. Sharanya ignored her own broken reflection in them. Her little mind was convinced that the longer it stared, the more layers it was likely to see, the more layers it was likely to create.

The painting that consistently fascinated her was *Women in the Garden* (1867). Back then, she didn't know it had a name. The painting displayed a bunch of women in brilliantly white summer dresses. There was one with a parasol, plucking flowers along a path; so pastoral, so pure. Sharanya was drawn to the painter's immediacy to pull an instance out of history. She studied how the creator used gradations of light to indicate the time of day and how important the time of day actually was. The hot sun had poured in and made all that it touched a shade lighter. Sharanya felt the passions that ran beneath those calm frames. She realised that the extraordinary was to be found within the ordinary, and inside the everyday. The human mind could look at the same situation with a range ever so wild. It could imagine deep sorrow, a happy instance, a moment of boredom, everything, in a single frame.

To her international friends, Sharanya was the un-Bollywood, no-spicy-food-please sort of un-Indian. At first, they were confused about why she was drawn to western art and philosophy. Sharanya could have explained to them that an Indian identity, like any other cultural identity, wasn't monolithic. In fact, the term cultural identity is a rough patch of contradiction and Sharanya didn't want to waste her creative energy in stitching it up with an appliqué needle.

"Let contradictions stay. In any case, if they are able to figure me out, then they'll never be compelled by anything I paint. And that's why I let contradictions stay. Let them keep assuming what I'm like," she spoke to herself and walked away. She was too musically self-engaged to think about fighting the wider world, or even interacting with it. She was perfectly at peace when alone.

The business of stereotypes is a lot like firing a machine gun, where recoils of equal momentum almost always fall inward. She too considered the French emotionally superior, the custodians of art, of parallel cinema, of marble busts, of wrought iron statues, and of pigeons on them.

On balmy days, she sat on bright red benches and spent hours in the company of her geometric sketchpad, oblivious of the afternoons wearing on or of the hedges operatic with the trembling arias of crickets. She walked barefoot on grassy stretches in the amber of street lamps. The summer unleashed on the streets those dandies in red pants and ruffled crop tops, and those capitalists who were busy looking busy in Armani. She saw priceless logos embossed on a sea of leather totes, some even had snappy little dogs peeping out of them.

As she felt it, Paris was amazingly unfinished. It was an ongoing swirl of colours and textures under the clear sun. The order was wild. Had it risen out of Renoir's *Moulin de la Galette* (1867), where an air of friendliness surrounded men and women dancing around the flour-grinding windmills of Montmartre, where everybody knew everybody and they all flirted and rejoiced? Nobody feared or envied anybody, everything was fine. The relaxed brushwork of soothing blues, pinks and oranges was carefree. In Paris, like in the painting, pleasure was momentary respite.

Some of her classmates were living in groups of three. There was a term for it: *ménage à trois.* These were consensual unions of three, who shared fear, saliva and wine.

Sharanya secretly condemned such arrangements. She disliked those who said they "swing both ways". How can these people ever be in love if they're undecided about the form in which they want love? "I am sure about what I want," she thought. This woman wanted her one and only man to guide, inspire and console her. Her friends spoke about their parents' divorces, about going fishing with the stepfather and board-gaming with the half-brother, and warming up to the mother's new boyfriend. Sharanya embraced new family ideals intellectually, and often thought about what it would be like to cope emotionally with evolving family structures. Such thoughts disturbed her.

For good or bad, in her life, things remained the way they were and she only evolved on the will of her own decisions. Her parents were still together. Sharanya, who was now miles away from the petty detail of the disagreements her parents' relationship might have accumulated over the years, derived strength from the truth of their togetherness.

In Paris, she could spend hours and hours, just walking, without feeling banal or directionless. She planted her easel under the stretched shadows of the Eiffel Tower, sliding her charcoal nibs into parchment paper, up and down, right and left. The sound of pencil nibs against paper was, to her mind, exactly the sound of waves.

One of Sharanya's classmates, who enjoyed watching her sit all by herself, tried to paint her solitary life with words:

There was once a young white virgin;

A strange girl who frowned in crinkled paper and walked on stilts of wood;

In a pitch dark attic, she was made to hide;

She uttered silence and ate dust for dinner,

She ate alone, twilight after twilight;

On the first day of her destiny, a fellow opened the door on her;

A mad fellow he was, unconvinced he roamed the world;

He took her by the hand, out and away into the real world;
Onto terraces of brick and boulder, onto gardens of insects and dew;
He hurled knives at her and she bled blue, green and red;
On her emptiness, he planted full grown trees and left a golden sun to cool;
The colours thinned her skin, burned and blemished her skin;
She was powerless by choice, any and every lover's folly;
Above a mess of torn tin cans, he rose and stared,
At how mature she suddenly became, at how her naiveties died but stayed;
Had he travelled to another time in her unmoving company?
Or was this a new reality he had created on his own earth?
Unknowingly, had he discovered through her, the nostalgia of now?
The lovechild of their union had a life of its own;
It recited in verse,
Amor Vincit Omnia, Amor Vincit Omnia, Amor Vincit Omnia,
It repeated in verse,
Amor Vincit Omnia, Amor Vincit Omnia, Amor Vincit Omnia

Sharanya knew that her art might land up in a dining room, hers or somebody else's, inviting minutes of curiosity now and then. It could be hung in a lobby, enunciating aesthetic, where passers-by could choose not to care. The energy, the muscle, the madness that gives birth to art is rarely present in the appreciation of it.

She studied in libraries that resembled cathedrals that had been carved and chiselled into gargoyles, reliefs and inscriptions; the insides would smell a little like raw and sulphurous stone, being worked on with a drill. Soaking fingers in wet paint, crushing tin tubes to ooze out the last drops of sea-green oils, leaving three sharp strokes of almond-white to create shadows on jet black, she believed that art was the highest simple pleasure of all.

In *circa* 2014, the Internet, like art, had become society's manic response to reality.

Sharanya watched documentaries on artists, on how they lived with inner strife. She read about war and what it makes of men. She read poetry that was unhinged on purpose. In art, colour wasn't to be orphaned from the family of the frame. Her mind was like colour, searching for a frame it could belong to.

Sharanya never watched the news. She couldn't handle reality at that pace. "To be is to be on the Internet," she told herself and believed the web was invented for people like her, people who lived in a parallel world. In the garden of her cyber Eden, she romanced him for weeks, or maybe months. He was Paul Bauer. Like everyone else, he didn't express in animated emotes, links to lazy humour, and borrowed music videos. He even avoided the use of exclamation marks. And when he left ellipses, the omissions in them weren't omissions of confusion, but omissions of caution. True to her trade, Sharanya appreciated the supremacy of clean, pure expression. In a world that was learning to communicate in 140 characters, he was a man of long-winded prose and knew just what to do with them. In his own kind of language, he moved between galaxies, talking of birth in animal farms, death in World War trenches and describing everything that lay between them as pure Shakespearean dilemma.

A grandchild of war-torn Germany, Paul once explained the euphoric high of guts and glory as the crest and a vacuum of inherited loss as its consequent trough. He left her thinking about how real the fear of being left out was, that the dread of disease wasn't as distant as it seemed.

There was no picture to humanise his online self, there were no customary graduation shots, no cutesy photographs of first pets, nothing at all. She knew, through their many romantic conversations, that he owned a pair of sharp shoulders and a dimpled square face; geometric paradise. 'I look like Germany,' a line Paul dropped every time she expressed curiosity in the way he looked.

On his first visit to France, they decided to meet.

Sharanya stood outside the restaurant, drawing heavy breaths, listening closely to the snap-crackle-pop of her nerves. She was in the induced delirium that romance is all about. She gathered her stray thoughts, hid them under a civilised smile and stepped inside the restaurant. The orange brightness of the Edwardian chandeliers bounced off her tiny pearls and made her fidgety about her appearance.

He hadn't arrived. There was time for another quick round of primping: 1. Swallow spit 2. Level the hems of the skirt 3. Smack on that neck, a perfume heady enough that it hits his memory 4. The neckline shouldn't drop anchor easily, so adjust and keep adjusting because that's a sexy gesture.

She did all that and sat neatly by a window. The *maître d'* stowed her red trench in a locker far away, too far actually, she was a little worried if it was safe. But, she couldn't care less.

Soon, a middle-aged sommelier appeared. He had long droopy ears, a wet nose like that of a rabbit, and white whiskers for a moustache. He began an unnecessary discussion on climate control in European vineyards. Well, wine always needed an intelligent context, otherwise it wasn't good wine. At this point, she felt cynical at any concern unrelated to her date. Besides, his resemblance to a farm animal was distracting. She didn't want to laugh carelessly. Inside her head, she repeatedly asked him to shut up, but she tee-hee-heed delicately because the man in question could walk in any moment.

Idle chatter with someone, even if he looked like a rabbit, meant an opportunity to brush up on her newfound French phrases. That feeling of ending words with a delicate sigh; long live the French. A quarter of an hour into the opaque exercise of sitting and waiting, entered the man. She saw Paul emerge from behind a mahogany Steinway, holding one anthurium. It was just one heart-shaped leaf with a long horn-like spadix rising out of its nucleus.

It was as though somebody warm and loving had clutched her from under her shoulders and embraced her inside Van Gogh's *Starry Night Over The Rhone* (1888), where the russet gold of gleaming lights emanating from the homes nearby dissolved into a river of a few ripples. Also within the frame was an imitation of the same scene unfolding in the sky, where bright yellow stars descended on the violet blue of evening; immortality on a 30-square canvas. The painting also featured a couple; bliss was a shared enterprise.

In the time he took to walk toward her, Rome was built and burnt many times over. As promised, he did look like Germany. His sharp features were mechanically drawn on a square face, as if with the use of a compass, a protractor and a scale. On his beige-tweed coat were elbow patches suede and brown. Dangling from his pants was a pocket-watch. And God bless him, he knew how to flip it open in style. He opened and shut it, just once. His chocolate-brown tresses, like dry palm leaves, fell on the surface of his creamy forehead. His eyes were satiny. She could see the glow of the restaurant multiply in them. His lips she didn't want to define, some things were to be left to the mercy of touch.

Paul bent over, planted a kiss on the back of her hand, kept the flower before her and introduced himself in a voice huskier than Batman's.

He seated himself, folded his blazer neatly on the armrest, and spoke out smoothly, 'Sharanya, may I say, you look like an Indian princess.'

'Oh. Thank you,' she replied, a shiver of excitement in her voice.

'You have more light in you than the street lights of Paris put together,' he said.

There was eye-contact at this stage. Her cheeks were pink, as pink as his clean-shaven ones. The scent of his musk made its way inside her stomach. Nothing, not a single thing, could prove she wasn't in one of Jacob Grimm's fairy tales. She could cry.

They sat across each other and so began an exchange of mutual adulation, in the mute. He liked the fact that she never thought in templates; her mind was free. He liked how she cared for detail. He liked how her long fingers arranged themselves around a ring. How her sharp nose defined the rest of her inexact face. He liked that she listened intently when he spoke. Isn't it funny when strangers aren't completely strange in each other's presence? These two had a long history of familiarity. But when they met, an accurate sense of the other's reaction didn't seem easy. As they broke bread, he advertised himself a little, 'I bake my own loaves and I know just the temperature at which they turn fluffy,' said Paul. They clinked glasses to a chorus of "santé". As Sharanya sipped on her drink, he said, 'If all sugar is consumed by the yeast, then the wine turns out dry. If fermentation is stopped, either by raising or lowering the temperature or even by adding brandy before all the sugar is converted to alcohol, the wine becomes sweet. The wine we are having isn't tannic and won't leave our tongues dry. It is sugary and slick.'

"What a glorious find," she thought. A man who chases various interests with a vengeance is just pure, unadulterated fortune. She took another sip and relished his presence.

Then rolled in the salads that were wallowing in pepper fume and diced with feta. Pine nuts glided down wet lettuce slopes. She forked her greens from dark to light, and she liked how easily his wild hawk's eye picked that out. 'You're moving to less green pastures, Sharanya. Not sure if that's a sign as healthy as your salad,' he said, and winked softly. She too was a stickler for detail. She liked how he had folded his florescent yellow-silk cravat, in mathematic swiftness, into a double-Windsor knot and then secured it with a gold buckle.

Deeper into the evening, the wine had seeped into their singular sub-conscience. The tie loosened, the skirt wasn't as stiff, and small talk was being savoured alongside entrées of French prudery.

Through the subject of cooking, he was showing off one side of his encyclopaedic oddity. Randomly, between funny anecdotes from his life, he announced, 'aprons look sexy on a man. I own a polka-dotted one, a striped one, a neon one, and one with graphic anime on it. I have one for every mood, if you know what I mean,' he disclosed. She didn't know what he meant.

'Hand-blenders make a sexy industrial noise,' he said, 'that first burn of caramel appearing around winter's first marshmallow is magical,' he said, a little later at some point. Not just domestically sorted, this man could quote Kafka and Camus and not from clever cliff notes. Sharanya felt she was the finder and keeper of this treasure, and remained starry-eyed and quiet through the evening.

Her sight was beautifully blurred. Her lips grappled onto the rim of her glass, which now felt a lot squeakier between her fingers. She locked the cuffs of his palazzo pants between her toes and rolled up her soft feet along his thighs. They felt sort of strange. In pleasurable curiosity, she bent over toward him, to lend him a wet whisper:

'Why do your legs feel the way they do, or is it just me, so very high on you?' she asked.

'They're fishnet tights from Victoria's Secret, it's just you,' he replied.

In one moment, life went from being a dream come true to a nightmare on Sesame Street. Silence was now a sound, and even the clatter of cutlery from tables nearby was piercing through it painfully. She wasn't as disturbed about his statement as she was by the nonchalance with which he made it. She fell hard from a happy high, but didn't want him to know that. So, she blunted her voice till it sounded childish and asked,

'I don't understand...do you like wearing fishnet tights?' she enquired.

'I wear everything, I don't believe in these silly gender differences, least of all in clothing. I am as comfortable in an A-line dress, as I am in a bomber jacket or a silk-wool suit, and isn't that just so liberating,' replied Paul, as his eyes and hands were engrossed in the act of scooping the jello-crust out of the caramel mousse.

Everything made sense, everything.

In a flash, his remark threw her back to all those times he spoke of the years he spent in the company of his aunts and sisters, as his warring fathers and uncles stayed aloof to serve their militaristic goals and pursue careers in nuclear science. A strange insecurity made him homebound. He preferred poetry over playing ball, and took pride in acquiring finesse that was as evident on his wardrobe racks and bookshelves, as on his kitchen shelves. Sharanya was too modern to have expressed such thoughts in public but traditional still to have thought them over in her head.

She loved him for the person he was, but she couldn't let him play her part. What seemed like an exciting departure from convention made her realise how much convention mattered to her. She found herself in a theatrical conundrum, where actors were loved and despised for the same set of character traits. Had the perception of him superseded the reality of him?

She straightened up and sipped on the cold, harsh sparkling water that lay by her side. She then pulled herself out of something much larger than the chair, stumbled across to him and left a dry peck on his left cheek. A single salty tear was felt by both. He didn't realise what was happening, maybe he did. Maybe this had happened to him before, maybe this should never have happened. He sat there unmoved.

On a slow walk back home, the only thing she felt about Montmartre was its declivity. That's also the only thing she felt about life. Her black Mary Janes were no longer elevating her self-worth. They blocked blood flow, and the cobblestone of the street felt a lot rougher on her heels. The soft curls had danced a little too much in the wind. The wild strawberry juice that once spilled around her lips had dried. The romance of things lasted only till the things lasted.

Had she lost her path and tumbled into Paul Gauguin's *Agony in the Garden* (1889) where Jesus looks exhausted, as if betrayed by his soul, as if abandoned by his own? Sharanya felt abandoned too, by her own imagination. But why was she inside a painting each time? Why did she think life was a collection of frames, each holding a different scene and sensation? Maybe, the reality within those frames was meant to be ordinary and her painterly mind was needlessly making it greater and grander.

Hunched over the Pont Alexandre III, she stole a view of the Seine; she couldn't tell if her reflection in its still waters seemed slightly wiser or greatly stupider. Next to it was a bright red bench. She walked up to it and removed her heels. She felt a strange, sensual epiphany rising up from her heels.

'Paris, you're only brick and mortar...

'You stood there feeding my fancies, you stood there watching them starve, you never spoke a word, and you found your voice in mine...

'Was I talking to you or just to myself?'

The Sleepless also Dream

Rothmans' King Size Filter Tipped cigarettes. New York. Two sleepless lovers, not sleepless in love.

Midnight had arrived. Another day of reportage and paranoia was behind her. Twitching her bare toes to the passage of seconds, Ahaana Dhar crawled into the darkest edge of her terrace. Less than a mile above the sound and fury of Manhattan, she could feel the wind. It was cold and clean. It swept frizzy hair on and off her forehead and made her elbows tingle. The light was at a distance. It peeped out of people's living rooms and danced on billboards. As her eyelids drew close, the light shrunk into glittery little dots and then got locked out on the other side of her thin-pink skin. In matter and in mind, she was above this scene.

Her brain was stained with caffeine, it was torn in a race with itself and its victory meant its own loss. One of the iron railings on that terrace touched her fragile midriff and creased her black silk robe that shone hauntingly under the moon glow. Her fourth cigarette was dying between her fingers. She was fidgety in self-reflection. Her left palm was homeless in all the restlessness. It was straying between her hair crisp from a perm, and her neck the texture of molten margarine. Her eyes were red, like dried blood. She was sleepless and overworked.

That night, as she stood there thinking, she turned to an earlier chapter in her life story and found the writings of her young and damned mind.

The autumn of '99 was shedding behind her back. Her vision was myopic to the confines of her journalistic workspace, which followed one rule: "More paper, less people". The tin temples of her cat-rimmed reading glasses dug deep into her tight ponytail. Buried somewhere in them was a pair of hazelnut eyes, melting tastily into a layer of skin that had the colour and contour of caramel. She was mostly in pencil skirts, silk shirts and slim croc-leather belts dividing the two.

Ahaana moved to New York from Calcutta to study journalism in the second last year of her teenage life, the other years of which were spent in the company of a smorgasbord of books, appetising and delicious books. She left them behind in the dusty orient, where her Bengali parents, both bleeding heart communists, still lived. They even looked like communists, the kind that fell in love during a university-level protest rally over the banning of a left-wing magazine. Outside state-owned buildings, they bickered over politics while sipping on chai.

At dinner, table talk for the Dhars was usually their reaction to newspaper articles and their disapproval of government policies. They had to be either pro or anti an issue, these liberals. The extent of their disagreement with the written word came across in the ferocity with which their bare fingers murdered their meats. Their kitchen had a plastic bin somewhere in a corner. It was lined with a clear red polythene that was fainting away at the stink of egg shells and fish bones. For the two maids who cleaned up after them, they left remains of lentils, pickle and dry salads on straw table mats. But because they were communists, they paid them adequately, each according to her need.

Ahaana's parents were cool commies, who shared alma maters with useful members of royalty, bureaucrats and politicians. They had an old Beatles poster, looking older than the wall it was crawling out of. Ringo Starr wasn't their favourite of the mop-topped pack. They had travelled to America in the '60s on academic fellowships to do their Master's in Cultural History.

'Is the revolution tonight?' Ahaana teasingly picked on them whenever they pulled out military-print trousers or a microgroove vinyl. Their living room had an unabridged *Iliad*, placed under an unabridged *Odyssey*, placed under a scholarly English translation of the *Bhagvad Gita*. There were three bronze installations of dancing gods arranged inside curio cupboards in this otherwise austere living room, merely furnished with a walnut-wood centre table and four chairs. Wet towels were left to dry in unusual places like door knobs. Spiders had woven their webs and dust bunnies hopped around unattended, because the minds that lived here were too engaged in greater causes to care.

The only child of this literature-loving and classical concert-going couple, Ahaana enjoyed the liberally charged vibes of her low-block apartment occupying a small portion on the first floor of a British-era mansion. Her mosquito-netted windows opened out to a humid Calcutta scene: a rattle of a slow yellow tram, a handful of rickshaw-pullers and commuters in need of a foam bath. Since childhood, Ahaana had been noticing an advertisement of mustard cooking oil on the tram. The company had gradually diversified into variants of sunflower and olive oil but the big picture they flashed was still of a mustard oil bottle. Calcutta evolved on its peripheries, it evolved slowly, and mostly, it didn't want to acknowledge its evolution. Calcutta was as much in the young redness of alta lining the foot of a new bride as it was in the ageing redness of paan stains at the feet of square pillars. Calcutta was in the new, Calcutta was in the old; Calcutta was the lovechild of both.

There was a shop below her house selling tangy digestives, red-chilli chips, and lemon squeezed over dry rice flakes. The dried sweat on the fingers of eaters was invisible but it made those fingers suspiciously salty from before. The tongue was as powerful as willpower. So, people stood there and ate, and ate, and then crushed the discoloured paper plates in and around a bin basket, which was teeming with waste but less smelly than her parent's bin.

Ahaana liked chaos but she wasn't the kind of liberal who went around validating it. For her, ideas needed to set sail in a powerful stream of execution, else they drowned. 'The solitude of armchairs, the quiet, cordoned state libraries, what good are they if students just waste their youth arguing with each other mostly to inflate their own egos with the little they know?' she expressed her disdain for those who idled away their energies. There were sweaty patches around their armpits as they sat cross-legged, clenching clay cups outside open air tea-stalls in college campuses, claiming to be "Neo-Marxist" about their ways.

'What good is knowledge if all we do with it is debate? And what good is debate if we can't stop debating and start doing?' was her mordant answer to her parents, who wanted her to pursue a PhD in Human Rights. For the world around her, ideologies were powerful, so powerful that they left people with no energy or intent to act on them. They clawed at everything difficult, mauled and mangled ordinary beliefs, till they became engagingly complicated. Poverty was open to statistical scrutiny and poetic licenses. It was everybody's favourite subject. Is that why it was never eliminated from the syllabus? What else would keep them engaged if they got rid of economic problems?

The floods turned Calcutta into the Venice of the East. Knee-deep in steel grey waters, yellow taxis stood on the sides of lanes. On drier afternoons, rickshaws with two passengers on them would be pulled far and wide by hands, two hands of the same person. To what extent can a man be physically strained to serve other men? Where was Neo-Marxism hiding itself now? Was it only a cheap mirage?

She happened to notice the rib cage of an exhausted rickshaw puller, Ahmed bhai. It was defined under a slim vest and looked like a coin scratched out on a sheet of tracing paper. She asked him why he does what he does. Looking down at his charred palms, as if a rope made of a thousand grass blades had rubbed against them, he replied, 'Jeevan ja raha hai, bas ja raha hai,' (In the meeting of ends is the ending of life).

Ahaana documented his life in her first written work *The Discontent of Existence*. It was published by a small economic and political journal when she was 17. It generated much debate in her high school. Her parents were thrilled at the hyperbole other students' parents and teachers sprayed in her praise, like streamers from a tin can splintered into the sky. Two months later, when the jubilation ended, Ahaana ran into Ahmed bhai once again. He was doing the same things, and was closer to his end. There was a certain lag she felt between theory and action, a widening lag. After that day, Ahaana found it harder to go to sleep. She wanted to find answers.

'Journalism. That's what I want to do, or need to do,' she said.

'But why would you leave academics? You are good at it,' her mother pointed out.

'Didn't somebody you follow religiously once say that philosophers have only interpreted the world, in various ways, and the point is to change it? Journalism is that change,' she said.

The big apple, she believed, was her orchard of scholastic bloom. 'A real liberal doesn't glorify the wrong and peacefully pray for the right. A real liberal gets up and fights,' said Ahaana Dhar, who was a woman of refreshing conviction.

At 28, she was already the youngest editor of *Corporate World*, one of New York's widely-read business magazines. Here, she witnessed from uncomfortably close quarters the rise and fall of men in pin-stripes. Her liberal parents called her up once in a while. They conveyed news about family, mostly sad news about impending deaths waiting in disease, some divorces and small-time betrayals. She kept conversations with them minimal, but greeted them on birthdays and festivals. She chose to extract only the elements that were romantic, like her educationist grandfather's Remington Rand 1930 typewriter (it didn't work). On her laptop, she worked through the night until the focus bulbs in her room succumbed to sunshine.

The nights allowed her to detach and disengage. In the blue of night, she found an entire rainbow of thoughts. She belonged to the night. If she found herself slipping into exhaustion, a Red Bull high was induced and the solitary war cry "Great Stories Make Great Papers" echoed in her great within.

She had angst, and it was existential. She wriggled out of it, each time with a newfound creative reckoning. A note-to-self pasted on her desk read: "Write, write, and write. Challenge what exists and believe in creation. There was no Hemingway before Hemingway. A good writer is a sane man's dream, but a better writer is a mad man's reality."

She wrote about empires and the characters that made and destroyed them. Those yuppies on Wall Street were like gold fish, figments of frenzy in an aquarium with inexact oxygen supply. She was watching them from a dry distance. One of the opening lines of one of her illustrious cover stories read: "In rolled back sleeves and snappable suspenders, these are men in singular, sacred lust with their first mistress and second wife—capital. It arouses in them conviction and engagement, it becomes their greatest insecurity and their only source of excitement. This game of bulls and bears is a trade of greed and greed is a good thing."

Wall Street was a deadly resolve. She was pitched in another uneasy encounter with it, this time throwing a literary cordon around the one sentiment she shared with her dark-suited subjects—the practice of sleeplessness, stylishly called Insomnia. And, that's when she faced him for the first time.

A glass lift whisked her up to Fuller Goldsteam's severely carpeted seventh floor. The doors opened up to the innocent sight of a young Chinese boy, who was acting grown up to carry the weight of his newfound designation—beaming on the badge tagged around his neck—Junior Finance Executive, Fuller Goldsteam. Arthur Lee was under strict orders from the company's Managing Director Clark Tim, whom Ahaana placed on Page 1 a week ago, to chaperone the young editor to a certain sleepless banker in their firm. He smiled like a hospitality trainee. 'I loved the last story you wrote,' 'I always wanted to be a writer.' She humoured him with a smile and kept walking along.

In five minutes, they reached Chamber No. 7 that was enclosed in deep maroon velvet walls and looked redder in the light of a fire-lamp. The chamber was inhabited by one large computer, a US Navy coffee mug, a fax machine and a burnished dustbin. This was a room without a window, a room that didn't want to impress or welcome anybody, a room comfortable within its four walls. It was a secure room just like its occupant, who came into clear view as the door creaked open.

Tucked under Tom Ford high-shine grey trousers were Ajeet Pratap Singh's impassable legs—that could easily have belonged to an elephant polo player—he stretched them out in a cross over the roller desk before him. There were perforations on his chocolate-brown brogues and spilling out of them in utter pride was a green argyle pattern on black socks. His face had a raw virginal charm, it was petite like a school girl's. Nature aided his plan of making people believe in an innocence he possibly did not possess. His crew cut was neatly gelled-back and he looked hygienic. He looked absorbed as he dabbed the Nintendo Game Boy nestled in his lap.

One slow glance and some journalistic deduction happened: "His legs are shaky as if he's restless but why is he restless, or is he planning something terrible this very minute. This looks like an especially urgent man. Urgent in some matters and absolutely not in others; the most selfish kind of urgent man. He's reeking of tobacco and perfume; he has the smell of an airport duty-free. Like an airport duty-free, I think he takes himself a little too seriously." She thought and thought over.

Ajeet Pratap Singh had done what anybody with half a dream to make it big does: move to New York. A Commerce graduate from Mumbai, he sold his first micro-finance start-up to a Multi-National Firm at the age of 17.

He didn't speak very much to his royal family, who lived in a pink-stone mansion in Udaipur. Ajeet was embarrassed by the fact that the structure resembled a fort. Submitted to the nothingness of black stallions, Swarovski chess sets and the sniff-swirl-sip of the vintage single malts in their bar, they were sworn to a sun dance of their past. His family had men in waxed moustaches and women in flowing sequined gowns. This was an ageing generation of daydreamers, swinging to a blitzkrieg of trumpets, flutes and drums, celebrating nothing in particular. In his opinion, they were all deluded in the diminishing cause of old wealth. Ajeet believed, like many others in the real world, that there was a tall glass of cold water waiting to be splashed upon his family's false universe. It was still on a tray, their own

George IV 1824 Sterling silver tray, slowly being brought toward them by one of their own loyal servants. Sooner or later, this would happen and then they wouldn't know what to do.

Like Ahaana, he too had uprooted himself from his origins. They were both nostalgic about nothing. New York happened when Ajeet was 24. Now 30, and his net worth was already a subject of the industry's intrigue.

When Ajeet was a little boy, his family owned a 200-acre property in Rajasthan. His father and two uncles spent a life throwing extravagant parties. Their wives would spend weeks planning the seating order and the menu at seven-course sit-down dinners. Ajeet tried really hard to understand why they needed to host lavish dinners. Every couple of years, his family would sell a portion of their land to maintain their lifestyle. They'd auctioned off the grandfather's 1957 Chevrolet Bel Air Convertible and a 1947 Bentley Mark VI and the great grandmother's ruby and diamond parure and her Cartier tongue cleaners, and her French fur coats. Ajeet noticed how successive generations of helpers working for his family were prospering, their children were going to the best colleges and starting businesses from the money they'd made off his family. At a very young age, he decided to save himself from doom. He wanted to be where wealth was made and not where it was spent. His life was about running as far as he could, as fast as he could. The month he turned 25, he worked at a (sleepless) stretch for two weeks till he was hit by facial nerve paralysis. Ajeet knew that the desperation of the need to matter would keep him going till he was gone.

The sharpest mind at Fuller Goldsteam, Ajeet also happened to be its resident insomniac and was thus ordered by the head of the American firm to douse a heated query raised by the press. On request, and in deliberate reluctance, he straightened up into a civil posture. An exchange of meaningless pleasantries later, Ahaana sat across him. She jerked her throat out of a long silence and dangled before him her one and only question:

'Wall Street is a tightrope. It keeps people alone, and on the edge. A glitch is a scar and it is for life. The "end" is not in the tangible, but in the manic desires that lead people to it. And, it is justified and glorified in something we simplify as the "means". And in this journey, the body ails, crumbles and collapses. What keeps going is the mind. Is insomnia a political compromise or a medical fashion? Do the sleepless also dream?'

The question stood suspended in thin air, it was infiltrating the space between them. It carried conflict.

She stopped talking. Her little outburst was like a little crash inside her head, the debris of which was still settling on the nerves. She was in the sort of distress that comprises the first few seconds after a temper rush, and he could sense it. He felt it in her body language, when she nodded a pencil robotically. He kept staring, till she came down from her sporadic high to a place where dialogue could be made.

Calmly, quite calmly, he spoke:

'Have you ever observed dynamite?' largely rhetorical, a question nonetheless.

'Yes. *The Road Runner Show* was all about it,' she said, puncturing the seriousness of his tone by throwing back to an old animated series.

And he picked up from there, this time increasing the sharpness and volume in his tone.

'Even in comic relief, life is but a ticking dynamite. At Wall Street, like in life, those who find comfort in routine will not succeed. Without conflict, there is no advance and conflict needs to happen every day and every night, and all the time. The reality of tomorrow could be greater than the capacity of our tolerance. To be awake is to be in control and there is nothing more compelling than the idea of total control. Sleep is a universal ruin; nothing less, nothing more. And to answer your last question, yes, the sleepless also dream.'

Never had a man, or anything with a pulse, attracted her at once. Foreigners from the same country, insomniacs without a physician's prescription, they were both sketching enviable career graphs, the kind that are cited in self-help books on success. They were barely conscious of each other's Indian identity. Ambition was the only commonality needed. He offered her one stick of Rothmans' King Size Filter Tipped, the rest of which lay rolled in a sterling silver case encrusted with his initials.

That very moment, she knew that the cancer stick wasn't the only thing she wanted from this man. For a full year from then on, she experienced him time and again. She met him in coffee shops where his Machiavelli clashed with her Kant, and in ballrooms over last dances, where corsets loosened, where bow ties dangled by the side of velvet lapels and stiletto straps were ultimately tied to wrists. But mostly, she met him in the nude, in a physical exchange of love juice.

Their apartments were two Manhattan streets away. They enjoyed a similar view of the Hudson, on the side of which they wined and dined in the company of ochre lights. They drove large beamers: the same model, the same colour. Sometimes, they rode together, they rode past mothers carrying children, and they rode past gardens planted with bright red benches. His bedroom had a shelf full of John Grishams, each one of them had a bookmark slipped half-way inside. His favourite was *The Pelican Brief* (1992). He only read fiction on flights. She was a utilitarian reader. She read everything from dark philosophy to political satire to extract sentiments that she could build on in her own writing.

Ahaana told time on her grandmother's HMT Kanchan Automatic 21 Jewels, which was just a sun-brushed dial with a small date counter. Ajeet wore a Longines Conquest Quartz Date that looked classic, with roman-numerals over a clean white dial. Their time machines took them to different places. One looked at preserving the glory of the past, another was building a future of glory. Yet, the common act of feeling compelled by something as little as a piece of metal beating on a wrist had made their present glorious.

She kept him connected with each business baron worth his blue blazer. Through her, he remained in tune with industry gossip, something he never cared for earlier, only to realise it was a personal inadequacy to consider small-talk a frivolous cause.

After three glasses of ale and some persuasion from his naked consort on a down-feather bed in the President Hotel's Primrose Suite, where he locked his inelastic body in her butter-soft arms on the last Sunday of every month, he confessed in a liquor-torn voice:

'Love is like caffeine. A perfect drug injected into the masses, through readily available mediums of ideological apparatus: books, television and music. It keeps them preoccupied in serendipitous fantasies. Unknowingly, it turns into a conundrum when they begin imposing their state of mind on everyone and everything that also exists in the spectrum they are the nucleus of. It's complicated, and not always, deliciously,' he spoke and kissed her forehead, hoping the innocence in the gesture would soften the edges of his intent.

Ajeet's worldview didn't differ from hers, but Ahaana didn't like the eloquence with which he made their equation blatant. She was the writer of the two; she wanted this to be her moment. When narcissists are in love with other narcissists, are they both guarded against attachment?

She rummaged through corporate archives, reached out to cronies far back in his past and collected data on a series of mishaps he might have been involved in. She found out that Bolivian escorts, parties on private jets and three-storeyed yachts were helping him win business in the Middle East. She slyly turned on her Dictaphone and distracted him with her breasts each time he was in the mood to speak about such affairs. She may have just been saving herself, don't they all?

He knew he was vulnerable and that she could, just as charmingly, strip him in public the morning after. Ink was her poison and it could give him a scary blue death. Did he care? He enjoyed the thrill of trusting her dangerous mind. He dissected with as much precision all that was detectable in her action, and all that was lying cancerous in her inaction. In their anatomical romance, she was a disease and he was the surgeon of death, mostly his own.

The deeper they are in a liaison, the greedier they are in a liaison; greedy for attention, greedy for ownership. And then there's marriage, society's way of euphemising man's greatest greed as its biggest need. Ahaana and Ajeet didn't want marriage. They knew from the start that they were headed nowhere and that might have been the only reason they came closer. Familiarity was exciting, it was stimulating. But routine, who could ever survive that? Within a year, they outgrew each other, just enough to not repulse each other; an exact science.

The calendar turned to the first September of a brand new century and Ahaana was still in bed. She was waking up at noon. She hadn't any story in mind. It was her father's birthday. She remembered to wish him the night before. She was covered in a big black Berkshire wool blanket. She reached out for the remote. Soon, she was alone with CNN's informed voice.

'In a tragic loss to Wall Street, Indian banker Ajeet Singh Pratap died in a car crash. He was on his way back from New Haven. The other two bankers from Fuller Goldsteam have been found half-dead in the smashed BMW and are now battling for their lives in New York's St Victoria Hospital. Our correspondent Helen Brent reports live from the accident scene… Helen, tell us what it's like…'

Still under the thick of her blanket, Ahaana wasn't sure if she was breathing. In the warmth of her bed, she froze. After ten slow gasps, she pushed aside the covers into a big lump, stood on her trembling legs and made her way to the shower. She turned around its shiny knob and stood under its cool strains that trickled through her frizzy hair, straightening it, making it look thinner.

She had suddenly forgotten how to dress up. Would it be too much to ask someone to pull those rough stockings up her dry thighs? On her way to work, she felt offended by Manhattan, and threatened by how it was scraping into the sky. Her team members tried their best not to murmur. That morning, silence had the fate of the hand that attempts to suppress the mouth of a fountain, fails to contain its uproar, gets wet and gives up. They knew about Ajeet's existence in Ahaana's life. She typed and typed furiously to the advance of seconds and ideas occurred and re-occurred at the same pace. She had lost the company of a man who thrilled and excited her, and those literary skills that warmed her nerves were always waiting to fill such a void.

Corporate World front-paged a picture of Ajeet with folded arms, posing in his sharpest suit, under the headline: "The Conman Who Got Away". Carefully, she put to use the findings of her investigations on him. The following week: 'May I speak to Gustav Kafri of Providence Inc., please?' Ahaana Dhar had moved on to a new hero, a new story. He was gone and she had a coming future.

An exact science, as it always was.

In high places, is a romantic relationship built like a house of cards where the risk of falling apart never leaves it alone? It is beautiful while it lasts. The balance is constructed, enjoyed and blown away. But are the cards, the aces, hearts, clowns and kings, even in their rise, inwardly aware of their approaching fall? Can they be dealt, shuffled and raised into a house identical to the one that collapsed? Has the fear of loss been lost?

The nostalgia ceased and she was back in 2009.

Seated on a bright red bench on her terrace, she stared at the last few minutes of darkness left in the night. Fatigued from the journey of her thoughts, she was nothing but a lump of flesh and a mass of bones holding together a mind. She crushed the debris of a Rothman King Size Filter Tipped under her bare foot. Her right palm was crushing something else. Once a white piece of paper, was now a grey tissue scrunched along her palm lines. It was the delivery receipt for the four baguette cut diamonds securely set on a platinum ring. She received it in a Tiffany Blue box, six months after his death. There was a note attached to the box, 'Like wealth is drawn to power, I am drawn to you. Be mine,' it read.

Ahaana lit another cigarette, she also lit the paper.

Those weren't the only memories of Ajeet she burned into the sky.

The Lesser Hero

Stars, Signs & Cynicism

Statutory Warning: Verify the document carefully before investing your critical facultises. All forecasts are subject to the movement of galactic bodies—sun, moon, whim and fancy.

ARIES

The sun enters the sign of Aries when it reaches the northern vernal equinox and that's what makes you a very special person. This week, some of your childhood dreams might come true on their own. If you uniquely aspired to be an astronaut, it'll happen regardless of that email seeking an unpaid internship that you just issued in batches.

TAURUS

You will meet a stranger and fall madly in love. Now, it is fairly inconsequential at this stage to find out their views on fundamentalism and global warming, or whether they enjoy Woody Allen movies. What matters however is whether they are cranky Cancerians, loathsome Leos or sinister Scorpios, because those are the kind you're likely to repel.

However, if a liberated Libran or a chivalrous Capricorn comes along, cling on.

GEMINI

Electric purple is the new black. Not for everyone, just for you. You need to be wearing electric purple, all the time. Job interview: electric purple tie; date by the river side: electric purple skater dress; dog-walking: at least an electric purple beanie. The colour is aligned with your chakra and it suggests you are a child at heart. It will kick start your charisma and increase your potential for higher consciousness. Even at the risk of coming across as a walking absurdity, do it!

CANCER

It's no happy coincidence that your sun sign is also a disease. This week, cliché one-liners will prove to be therapeutic once again. Try coming across the following: "If he doesn't understand your silence, he'll never understand your words"; "There will always be people who treat you wrong, make sure you thank them for making you strong". If this doesn't help, take a deep breath and caress the "KEEP CALM and do something" poster that enjoys a blindingly colourful presence on your desk. You'll be good.

LEO

Learn to see the merits in people-pleasing. In this day and age, attention means affection. If they're walking away without stopping by your display window in the social media market, you need to start selling what they want to buy. Pick an existential quote off the Internet and repackage it as your own. Everybody secretly wishes to agree with Sartre. If that fails too, try sympathy. Share a picture of a wimpy dog. A mawkish story about an injured dog nobody wants to adopt, should do the trick.

VIRGO

Travel, drop everything—your job, your kids, your partner, your debt—and travel. Break your bonds, sell your stocks, and just travel. To unlock the big secrets of life, it's important to go skydiving in the Australian outback, scale volcanic glaciers in Iceland and go hiking in the Italian Dolomites. You have to survive at least one of the above to find life's proverbial purpose. Always remember, while you warm that swivel chair at the office, somebody is clicking their new profile picture—next to corals along the Great Barrier Reef, in the sunshine of Capri, in Prague or Dublin. You only live once.

Gauri Mehra Reddy was fairly cynical about horoscopes and prophecies. She sat on the cusp of Leo and Cancer. 'My Leo self goes and does bold and bizarre things that my Cancer self keeps repenting over,' was one of her signature jokes; nobody laughed. She wasn't one person. She was many people. She believed that everybody was many people. But mostly, everybody had at least two people living inside their heads. In her case, the two-sidedness was rather defined. The 'three-years-to-go-before-I-turn-30' fashion designer, who held an MBA in Retail Management, had just launched her own clothing label Black & Pink. She was the labour of love of a "loud" Punjabi mother and an erudite South Indian father. She still lived with them.

Her mother, Neena Mehra, usually woke her up by inflicting harmless-lovable Punjabi taunts, while organising the happy litter of glassy stilettos that was dumped by Gauri's bedside. 'You should learn to take care of your things. Look at all the mess in your room,' she would say, as she capped mascara sticks that ran awry on her daughter's dresser, and folded oversized wayfarers and respectfully sent them back into their cases. 'Why do you need so many hats? If somebody enters this room right now, they'll think you have ten heads,' she'd comment, as she'd tighten the bows on wide straw hats. When her mother was alone in Gauri's room, she stared at the collection of silky thongs and strapless bras in the drawers. Did she silently regret that she couldn't blossom as freely as a flower in her own youth?

Her father, Raj Shekhar Reddy, wasn't such a South Indian when he married his girlfriend. But as she turned into his wife of every moment, his own identity came back to him strongly. He traded cargo shorts for starchy mundus. He hunted out the sacred thread that he had shunned at the start of his one and only love affair. He looked like a priest. Like most, he too began by emptying out his emotions to make room for his darling's. Is a new marriage like a new closet, where partners share space within polished plywood compartments and enjoy a messy kind of oneness? Years into the marriage, people realise that belongings have gotten mixed up in that closet. Then, each hanger begins to bear a name tag and margins are drawn. Realising what is yours after giving it away to someone else for a while, is that instinct or the misuse of it?

Gauri's father had adamantly appointed a South Indian cook who spoke chaste Telugu. Ramana was sent to Delhi by her father's parents, who lived in Kakinada. 'Ramana, where's the sambhar?' he made sure there was sambhar on every plate, in every meal. Some sort of ancestral aggression was at play in the way he requested helpings of ghee to lubricate his gunpowder with. His fingers triggered the paste that was called so for a reason. At the dinner table, he mixed pickle oil into rice using his bare fingers. He liked to own his food. He also burned sandalwood incense to a thin white smoke and made Carnatic ragas pierce through it on dusks and dawns. A family of Kondapalli bobblehead dolls had arrived like guests in the drawing room, and they were in no mood to leave. On one wall was a depiction of Vishnu in Anantashayan, in Kalamkari. It was intimidatingly large. Candle stands and ashtrays were stamped with Bidri craftsmanship. Over the years, Gauri's house had started to look like an Andhra Pradesh emporium.

He quizzed Gauri about capitals of countries of little relevance to her life (Burkina Faso, Ethiopia, and Antigua & Barbuda). Every so often, he brewed, what she declared, Delhi's best filter coffee. He was an environmental architect and ran a small practice from the two-storeyed house they lived in. Her old man specialised in building sustainable mud houses that offer thermally comfortable conditions, are labour intensive to construct and will ultimately break back into the soil. He called cement an additive. Gauri too wanted to do her bit for those thousands of artisans who were falling out of work in the rapidly digitising handloom sector. Common to the father and the daughter was good intent.

Gauri didn't look like her tall and dark father. She had skin the colour of wholewheat, eyes the colour of wholegrain, and hair-strands like noodles soaked in hot soy and drizzled with olive oil from time to time. She was attractive like an uncooked organic dish only till she dipped her lips in wine red sauce and smoked her lashes in kohl. Then, she rapidly ripened up.

Gauri wasn't rich enough to afford retailing off a sparkly store at a shopping mall that enjoyed the footfall of the easily bored and the easily amused. She wasn't totally downtrodden either. She went about setting up kiosks at weekly flea markets and founded an online fashion portal where buyers could engage with 3D images of her creations and even customise them. She managed her brand's page on Facebook and engaged with her customers.

'Oh Gauri! I love your clothes. You are so young and you are already a star,' said one girl. 'You are so lucky, I also love fashion and I want to do what you are doing,' said another. But the market wasn't easy to break into. Those who seemed on top of their game were actually struggling to keep pace. Facebook likes and website hits were not going to sell her clothes, or could they? Gauri was just another entrepreneur living out the promise of the Internet. This was the bittersweet irony of her life. Even as friends and family lauded her for making it big, only she knew how she kept herself divorced from the temper of her time to work on her craft. She doggedly marketed herself everywhere she went. Artist or entrepreneur, rich or poor, pretty or ordinary, she was in a love-hate relationship with her divided realities.

Her work was still resting in soft heaps in a 1,000 sq ft rundown boutique, in a crammed industrial pocket, somewhere in north Delhi. Real estate prices did one thing, they brought her down to earth. The crippling rent and labour cost made every little success seem necessary and ordinary. The logo of her brand Black & Pink, which was a cartoonist's portrayal of a black swan kissing a pink swan, was air-brushed on a single-panel glass door. Inside, fashion was being born in fingers, in threads, in needles. Salim bhai and Junaid bhai tuned the movement of hand and foot to the sewing machines. When they stopped to realign threads, they seemed like drummers who dab closer to the edge of the head to thin out the sound and then with a crescendo, the *ca-chunk-cha-ching* of their machines tied night to day. For those who couldn't feel it, this was only industrial noise. Under the impolite clarity of tube lights, shone the bling-and-bauble of faux pearls, jingly bells, gold lace strips and thousands of baby crystals. In coloured vests with inch-tapes dangling like suspenders over their chests, the men swung their grubby feet to the seesaw of foot pedals. All around was the roll-on-roll of fabrics. Calcutta cotton lay over Paithani brocade lay over Bhagalpuri silk, falling like a row of dominoes each time one of them was called upon. The shop would smell of wooden pulp, emulsified oils and greases and starches. The shop had a work-in-progress kind of smell.

Gauri's two other karigars, Akbar and Feroze, sat on stools with forearms and thumbs trapped in rusty-old scissors that *tchaked-tchaked* their way through organza silk. They shredded it into panels for collars and sleeves, and chiselled crimson mirrors into tiny squares to glue them onto pitch black sheath dresses. The hairy shavings of silk fell to the floor and rose up dustily.

Occasionally, Akbar would pencil in elephants and deer, and princes and princesses, along asymmetrical flair dresses. He would then paint them in fairy tale tones of fuchsia pink. In one simple act, he could awaken from antiquated slumber, years and years of craftsmanship. Her silhouettes were western, the kind her friends would venture wearing, but the artistry on them was Indian.

Gauri was part of a Delhi where the young were "creators of concepts". The owners of cafés, for instance, were celebrating junk. They fixed filament bulbs in used glass bottles and hung them in bunches. If one wall had a collage of old doors on it, another one had an installation of used utensils (plates, pans and spoons flattened and moulded into shapes). Cocktails were poured out of petrol cans and dips came served in beakers from chemistry labs. Tyre rings were turned into clocks and trays. In the spirit of jugaad, trash was given twists.

Gauri's colour palette was part-pink, part-black. She spoke the interesting language of an interesting time; it was both meaningful and meaningless.

'The pink stands for escapism, for the urge to retain innocence and the black means conceding to the constant loss of innocence. Some innocence lost, some gained,' she quoted to magazines that featured her work in tiny quarters of their glossy centre-spreads along with 20 other designers.

Everybody was speaking some kind of parallel language. Bakers dished out cakes with inedible-looking digital photographs in the name of frosting. One of Gauri's friends was a "food stylist". She was "making plating an art" by arranging the curl of salmon sushi next to a sexy splash of pumpkin sauce; colour coordination in meals enhanced appeal.

Aesthetics were becoming a moral necessity. Were aesthetics nothing more than frills or quirks for a generation that liked to think it was thinking differently? A lady was crafting leather bags from rotting pineapple leaves; sustainable luxury. One company was retailing 'cold-pressed' oils, extracted without the use of harmful heat and kept free of parabens. A group of engineers was

'3D-printing' jewellery to reduce metal loss. A whole lot was going on, even in Gauri's world.

But Gauri had other concerns. Each time there was a decision to be made, she was firmly fixed in two directions like a thumbscrew compass. Even in the dating department, Gauri was neither here nor there. Since she couldn't be one person, she couldn't find one person to be with. Each time she made peace with a guy's qualities, she painfully discovered his inadequacies.

If love was a circus out there, she was a trapeze artist in it. The centre of her spine bent itself like jelly, as she flew from one bar to another. She tried hard to cover the pain under practised grace, only to realise the bars set by her were rather high. With her divine sense of timing, she couldn't reach them and hence kept falling into the safety net. In her life, the valve against romantic failure was a conversation with her best friend Priya Patel.

Priya, who had never been on a date herself, was the self-styled 'Harsha Bhogle of Romance'. You don't have to play a game to be an expert. The fact that this Non-NRI-Gujarati friend from a family of writers could trivialise her trauma of lovesickness, made falling and failing in love all the more worthwhile. Is that why she didn't put up a better act every next turn?

It all started when Gauri was in her 23rd year, and had started making a living (a squirrel's living, just some nuts and acorns) by assisting a big designer. At the finale of a fashion show, she saw Virat Singh. He had flown in from Harvard Business School to watch his sister Natasha walk the ramp. He was beautiful like a horse, a Clydesdale draught horse. He had an arched neck and the heels of his buckle boots resembled hooves. This man of equestrian elegance was backstage gossip, where Gauri was fixing zips and steam-ironing blouses for the models. Along with a couple of others, she too sized him up in a glance fractionated by curtain drapes.

At the after-party, she noticed women border him like a pack of civic guards. They attentively listened to his story about a recent holiday in Bora Bora. Twice or thrice, he caressed the strands that fell over sloped shoulders like a long, silky mane. Snobbishly, he recounted tales of feeding sharks and stingrays. The women only wanted to know if he went with a girl, and if he slept with that girl. Gauri drowned two glasses of champagne that was nameless and naked in a glass, and went and tapped him on the back of his rawhide leather jacket. It was soft, like the thin sheet of fur carpeting a horse's neck. Below was a darker colour of chocolate on his flat-front trousers that held together his firm legs. She wanted that pair of legs to bend at her command, and carry her miles away from there.

'Hi, I'm Gauri. I'm a designer,' she said in an almost breakable, baby-voice. She then extended her hand delicately. It looked equally breakable. He looked and kept looking.

Gauri knew he was finishing his MBA, so she quickly acquainted him with her MBA background and her entrepreneurial plans and the concept of Black & Pink she was toying with. She was being her Leo self: outspoken and upbeat. She knew the kind of qualities he would appreciate. She was right. Unlike everyone else, only she managed to tame him. Of course, her white pleated skirt and black tie-back blouse that failed to reach it, made the ride smoother. In the bright ballroom of a big hotel, buzzing with skinny models and happy-high journalists, the two got chatting.

'Wealth is born in ideas. The idea could be born as earth-shatteringly in a warehouse of yarn, as in a boardroom of shirts,' was one of her statements that caught his fancy.

Gauri made a particular 'happy dog' face around the men she liked. She had liked two or three before Virat. She once tried to describe it, 'Priya, imagine if your Labrador Loki starts smiling at the wall and the smile just sits there on his sharp teeth. That's what I look like in the company of men I like. Thank god I don't have a tail that starts wagging when I'm excited about a guy. Imagine!' When she was eager beyond compare, she felt, she looked like a bad photograph of herself.

She put on her reading glasses and stopped drinking after her third glass. 'As a man sees it, a woman who can't handle her drinks shouldn't drink at all', Priya's golden rule rumbled in her ears. He left his drink too. He was drinking tea. They walked back to her car.

'Are you driving?' he checked.

'No, I've a driver,' she responded.

'Forget about him then,' he took her by the hand toward the gate.

He thumbed down the kill switch of a Harley Davidson. It woke up from the dead and they pranced through the breeze. Her arms were like long leather reins thrown around his movement, they were holding him together. At India Gate, he stopped the bike and they walked toward a bright red bench, and they locked lips on a street orphaned by the night. Deeper into the same night, she was found waltzing in her bedroom. She wrapped her head in the fair flutter of her net curtains, dreaming about loosening his tie on evenings that would magically follow from this one. Her Cancer-self liked to feel safe in clichés, in cinematic clichés where the woman is pampered, where the woman cooks and receives presents. She never showed this side to a man, but it didn't leave her.

'Priya, I'm so happy. He's studying at Harvard. He must be smart and sorted,' she gushed into her cell phone.

'What's his name?' enquired Priya. 'He's Virat. But listen, he goes to Harvard, which means I won't have to work hard on improving him,' she went on about how he chose to talk to her, what they talked about and how they stopped talking to do other things that didn't involve talking. She opened up his Facebook profile before her mother, who approved of his prosperously Punjabi existence. His distant cousins stayed in Canada, so did hers. They probably played ice hockey together, or spun Punjabi rap in minivans and crossed borders drowned in mist.

The next day, he met her at a café. She wasn't in a dress. He could see how she had hurriedly smothered her face with cheap make-up, which some blemishes were popping out of. He wasn't exactly impressed.

They sat down on cane couches. She waved the menu at a waiter and pointed to the coffee she wanted. He had already nodded his disinterest to the waiter thrice in the 20 minutes he spent waiting for her.

'Mr Harvard. What are your plans now?' she sounded like a concerned aunt.

'I am launching my start-up that will promote the use of recycled toilet paper,' he replied.

'Yuck. Are you kidding me? Who does that after a degree from Harvard?' she questioned.

'So, how many Indians in your class?' she asked, noisily slurping the sweet milk froth off.

Generally grossed out, he replied, 'Not many. I don't hang out with Indians actually.'

'Okay,' said she, hoping he'd take the conversation forward. He didn't.

'So, I see, you're not a coffee person?' she abruptly realised she was drinking alone. She put the drink back on the table, a little to the side, which meant they might as well take it away.

'So, what'll you do now?' he ignored her question and asked her one.

'I'll go back to interning with designers. So, you know, I can learn and then do something of my own one day,' she replied, locking her thumbs silly.

'Okay. I think I need to leave now. Have a flight to catch tomorrow,' he said and rose up, giving his wristwatch a tight shake.

'Oh, okay', she got up hastily. The tissues in her lap fell to the floor. He gave her a side hug that seemed like an unresolved handshake.

Just when she thought she was sitting in the centre of the saddle, he dunked her into a barren field and sped ahead. Like a wild horse on the loose, he never looked back. She messaged him sometimes, so he replied. Then he stopped replying.

'Priya, I don't get it. What a jerk! How does it matter what we're doing in life? How could he judge me like that?' she sobbed bitterly.

'But, you also knew he was going to Harvard and so you ended up liking him…,' she threw sense like a spanner in the waterworks.

'Look,' Gauri yelled, cutting her friend off. 'Look if you want to play defence diplomacy, he shouldn't be your ally. I am your ally. You're my friend. Take my side, will you!' she grumbled with her intellect intact. Priya offered her support, in silence.

'Who does he think he is? Who?' Gauri questioned in helpless and restless rhetoric.

The next few weeks, she took leave of her senses. She spent longer in bed, watching Bollywood mollycoddle NRI priorities. 'I don't understand *Kabhi Khushi Kabhie Gham*. The heir to a fortune falls in love with an uneducated girl who is also inappropriately loud. When I try to be spontaneous and eccentric, people leave. Look at *Dil Toh Pagal Hai*, the guy has an imaginary prototype of his ideal girl and the first girl he runs into falls in sync with it. Really, like what are the odds? Look at *Mohabbatein*, after all those speeches about discipline by a strict and unforgiving patriarch, young boys are ready to risk their careers to pursue romances with women they've barely spoken to,' she sighed, lying flat in front of her laptop. But she didn't stop watching. Is there a strange kind of pleasure in consuming stories that seem unjustifiably happier than one's own? For instance, the troubled marriage of a power couple, the death of the partner of a very good-looking and successful doctor, the divorce of a sultry-sexy 30-something banker, do people love the idea of a fixable crisis?

'You need to get out of the house. Virat must be poking Staedtlers at and sharing Swiss mints with his sexy classmates. And here you are, half the world away, drafting yourself into a dated idea of romance,' thus spoke Priya, like a Zen master who gets her wisdom from HBO.

Gauri's voice shrank with gloom, 'Yes. Yes...I know you're right,' she sighed louder.

'In any case, he would've looked like a horse in a suit. A horse selling toilet paper in a suit…do you really want to waste yourself over that?' came some more wisdom from Priya.

The following month, Virat updated his Facebook profile with an announcement about his new start-up. It was an environment-friendly-toilet-paper manufacturing company in New York. That helped Gauri recover from heartache.

Two months later, she ran into Prateek Panigrahi while watching a play on treason and loyalty, which was being staged on a midsummer night at the India International Centre in New Delhi. He was a five-star activist who wrote Op-Eds on Politics for at least three English broadsheet newspapers. Gauri recognised his chiselled jawline from the tiny mugshots that appeared alongside large write-ups. Her father followed the young man's writing. And whenever he found something extraordinary, he highlighted paragraphs and left copies on Gauri's desk. She never read them.

Gauri, who was then enrolled as a volunteer in the integrated skill development scheme of the Ministry of Textiles to uplift the artisans of Rajasthan, felt she had valid reason to reach out to him. And now was the right time.

He was sitting next to her in a red raw-silk kurta, skinny jeans and leather sandals. His hair firmly parted itself into two identical halves that could never again sit in harmony with each other. They made oil an ally and thwarted any ceasefire attempt by a comb or a band. A battlefield over the scalp, a battlefield under it, she thought. His arms were hefty, like they'd been packed into his sleeves forcibly. His feet were rather dirty. "He was one pedicure and two hair-spa sittings away from looking dishy," she pondered. That year, politics was the new Hollywood. Entertainment gossip was being relegated to its designated space, three pages into newspaper supplements. People were learning to debate on matters of national relevance. Minds like Prateek's had a fire in them that was impossible to put out. In their struggle with changing winds, these minds kept their flames alive.

'Hi, I am Gauri. What you do with your views, I try to do with fabric,' she hushed into his ear, covering her mouth with a well-washed palm and still facing the stage in front of them. He saw the left side of her face glow in theatrical light, it was white light strained through shifting sheets of yellow, red, blue, pink and green. Each colour took turns to break itself over the surface of her clean cheek. Some stage lights fell on her eyes, in wet splashes.

'Hi, I'm glad to meet you,' he tilted himself leftward, starting off a series of whispers. Once the play was over, they walked to the cafeteria in the complex and chit-chatted. Gauri knew which aspect of her personality he would appreciate. Of course, he wouldn't appreciate how she treats her lovesickness with song and dance, or that she hopes to make plenty of money and go idling on foreign beaches. In all fairness, she also wanted to sell novelty and nurture a community of artisans. But like many others, she wanted to think about hacking social problems only after securing her share of commercial success.

But, why should a public intellectual like him be interested in her? Appropriately, she presented herself as some sort of a catalyst of 'socio-economic change'. He was within firing distance of her smartness. That night, over wonton noodle soup and fried prawns in soy, she shot at him the cartridge of smartness stored in her brain.

'You know, the artisans of Sanganer are out of work because the market fails to differentiate between digitally-printed and hand-painted prints. Even in Benaras, there is a secret invasion of Chinese silk that people don't talk about. Have you ever seen the Hatibadi loom on which Sambalpuri sarees are made? Only a handful are left. People look at the ramp and the anorexia walking on it, and those wild hairdos, and how "unwearable" the clothes seem. A fashion show is a mere spectacle to arouse the world's awe and, somewhat insecurely, keep it aroused. Fashion is not a fashion show. Fashion is a means of creative survival for many, it is in their skills, in the history of their skills and in the future of their skills,' she curated a sentence.

'Most believe that fashion knows only two seasons: one where it kills itself and one where it resurrects itself. That isn't true. Fashion is in the in-between. Have you ever wondered how a trend is born? Who comes up with it first? Fashion is aspiration, it is revolt and an indicator of a society's state of mind,' she said, drawing his attention toward her mind.

A girl in a short skirt was making sense, thought the liberal thinker of his time. Maybe, he wasn't fully liberal.

Was anybody fully liberal, anyway? She was smart and generally conscious of fashion. In a country where the starch of a woman's saree and the circumference of her bindi ran directly proportional to her intellect, Gauri was an exciting exception.

He didn't have a car, or a cell phone. He'd rather be holding old books and chai and slaying cigarette butts in steel ashtrays, till they were completely lifeless. After dinner, she drove him to the same bright red bench where she had kissed Virat. She made her strange happy dog face, because she was really happy again. They kissed; in the political climate of their times, they kissed with fury.

Later that night: 'Priya, this is the guy. He's smart and, what a stroke of fate, he thinks I am smart. We can be this intellectual couple, you know, like Sartre and Beauvoir or Scully and Mulder, like Shabana Azmi and Javed Akhtar,' she said, as she twirled around on her bed.

'I have moved up from toilet paper to newspaper,' Gauri declared into the microphone, to an audience of exactly one person.

Over the next four weeks, the two watched plays ablaze with politic and attended concerts of bands whose songs took anarchy seriously. Sometimes, she even accompanied him to symposiums on the relationship between state and civil society, somewhere in the vast green campus of the Jawaharlal Nehru University. To keep herself awake, she jumped up and clicked pictures of him as he addressed small audiences that looked either angry, or hungry, or both. He liked her enthusiasm. Things moved forward, one event after another, one kiss after another. She told her father that she was dating Prateek. He immediately approved. 'Marry a man with a mind, you'll regret marriage a lot lesser,' he said.

She dropped him home each time they went out, because he didn't believe in owning a car.

She did it happily, just the first ten times.

'Priya, this is getting on my nerves. It's like this guy doesn't believe in public convenience. Maybe intellectuals are out there to just complicate things with their big, bulky words,' she complained.

Gauri and Prateek met for lunch the next day. She had bought him a basic cell phone (plastic keys and a torch light). It was meant to be a surprise gift. She pulled it out of her bag and kept it on her lap.

'So, I have some news, I am moving to Dhaka,' he announced, indifferently, as if it was meant to happen one day and boom.

She looked up from her pizza and went, 'What?' The cheese oozed down her chin. It hung like the tail of a mouse in the mouth of a wild cat, a mouth half-open in shock.

'Yes, I am moving to Dhaka for two years, to start an English newspaper,' he elaborated.

She slid the phone down into her bag and sucked the cheese in.

A lot later that night: 'Priya, I am so upset. Who in their right mind moves to Dhaka? This explains everything. He didn't have a car. Now I know why. To bloody never move ahead in life,' she moved from raving to ranting.

'Well, he did have an intellectually unpredictable side that you knew about…and…in fact that's the side that…' tried Priya's voice.

'No, that's not how it works,' Gauri was in no mood to hear it out.

'*Tch tch*. Come on Gauri. Get a grip. Now that we're not treading on egg shells over this man, I can freely tell you that the entire state of Kerala could have wrung out their cooking oil supply from his hair,' Priya's disapproval of men Gauri couldn't be with was cathartic. This joined up with Gauri's realisation that it would have been too much of an effort (intellectual and physical) to put up with him.

The next two years were strange and full of strangers. There was one hacker, who liked to think like a criminal. With his magic fingers, he could break into anybody's computer and anybody's cell phone. Gauri found that devastatingly attractive.

'He's super-villain material. We are most vulnerable inside our gadgets. We are completely naked inside our gadgets. Imagine the kind of power he has over people's lives,' she made a case for him before Priya, who didn't feel like agreeing at first. It was all good till the day his magic fingers tricked their way into Gauri's email account. He wanted to be aware of her every inanity, of the concepts and words she pretended to know but was privately and quickly googling, of the porn she might have watched last night, of the friendly banter she engaged in with other men. He sorely discovered that her password was 'ILOVEVIRATSINGH' and asked her to 'come clean'.

What does it mean when somebody says 'come clean' in a world where people live vaguely on the Internet? Is it still necessary to share with the partner, details of every interaction that one has had online? If there is no touch involved, and it is hard to measure tone and depth, and most conversation is had on impulse, out of boredom, then is there a point to turning it into a record and subjecting it to scrutiny?

'Being with this guy might have been like owning a beautifully iridescent snake and also sleeping with it naked,' said Priya, chasing this spineless reptile of a man out of her best friend's habitat.

There was yet another stranger. He was, in Gauri's own words, 'a sinister saint'. On the phone, he was kinky like a teenage boy learning to jerk off at the sight of German porn. He spoke of new sex toys in the market and urged her to try the 'G Spot Locator' that guaranteed 'third-level orgasms'. He said he wanted them to consume poppers (a club drug) so they could travel to 'someplace higher'. What's more, he said all that in Clint Eastwood's raspy voice. However, when they met, he behaved like a worried parent and was full of semi-solicited advice like, 'Go easy on the crushed ice in your mojito, sweetie', 'Gauri, it'll get cold in the theatre, carry a sweater babe'.

'Haha, this one's gone from being a fun Friday evening to a dull Monday morning,' said Priya, as she laughed her way off the bed.

Both these guys made it to Gauri's bench. The hacker hugged and kissed her and the other stuffed cotton buds into her ear holes to thwart traffic dust. She didn't miss either.

She also tried a dating site, briefly. Here, she met a doctor reducing vaccine-preventable diseases in Namibia. Soon, he started asking her to strip while on video call. There was also documentary filmmaker who wanted to strip, and soon made his pink and purple underwear visible. 'Good god. This dating site business is like spending evenings in parks, in skimpy clothes, during Dengue season,' said Priya, offering her bracing take on the concept.

Then landed Mudit Singh, who was finishing his MBA from Yale and was in New Delhi on a holiday. Facebook friends since three years, they had their share of harmless flirting on a chat window. They had impressed each other favourably. The two first met on a windy December night, a day or two before Christmas. They went on five magical dates, one featured a gourmet Italian dinner, another was wrapped around a period film and yet another ended with six pegs of Old Monk. They kissed in dark parking lots. He hooked back her neckpiece whenever it fell inwards into her cleavage. Firmly, he held her waist as they walked down the long flight of stairs outside restaurants in Khan Market. 'I love holding you and I love kissing you,' he messaged after the third date night.

In floodlit powder rooms, she dabbed on pink make-up, blow-dried her hair into soft curls and kept her napkin-like skirts five inches above her weak knees. They chatted about Sikhism, about Murakami, about the trip to Iceland he was planning on taking. They also talked about her brand in between. He kept forgetting what it was called.

'I think he loves me, Priya. Every minute spent with him has made me happy,' she gushed.

The frequency of his messages reduced some days after he returned to America. Slowly, he stopped replying. 'Why don't you reply or talk, Mudit?' she couldn't help but ask. 'I think we should look ahead, Gauri. I don't think I'm in the right frame of mind to be in a relationship right now. I'm sorry,' he typed.

'Then why did you spend all that time with me? Did you not mean all those things you said? Were they all lies?' she asked him. 'You can form whatever opinion about me, because I have nothing to do with all this. I have gotten over many girls, I'm sure you'll get over this easily. Good luck,' was the final sentence ever typed on the chat window—

their only common possession. He walked out, even on the memories he had with her.

'What does he mean by "I have gotten over many girls so you'll get over me"?' she asked Priya, again and again. 'Is everybody out there just to damage somebody? Are we all trapped in some kind of collective revenge?' she screeched into a pillow. 'Why did he say I'm pretty and entertaining? If he didn't find me pretty and entertaining, he wouldn't have indulged me at all,' saying this, she tore the colouring book he had brought her, from the Yale Book Store, into ugly pieces.

'He's a practical guy, Gauri. He came, had a good time with you, and left. Haven't you heard of holiday romances?' said Priya, casually, as if she too had been in many holiday romances.

Once or twice, Gauri's mother suggested suitors. Sometimes, the boys would be closely related to their neighbours, but not close enough to have visited them in a decade. The boy pool society supplied could have been the same one she'd been drinking out of. But drawing room conversations between older adults were the romantic equivalent of PVC drain pipes. Anything that trickled down that channel wasn't fit for direct consumption. A partner had to first pass through the filter of romantic autonomy. However, in the distant future, she was ready for a situation in which the sources would wring dry and then thirst would quench itself with whoever would be a stretch of an arm away. Gauri wanted to believe she was still far away from that future. She could still buy glass bottles of Evian sometimes and fool herself silly.

It was 2015, and in 2015, even mourning the loss of love had the luxury of vanity attached to it. Each time things turned sour, she dimmed the lights and soaked her spurned self in hot foam; salty bubbles she would feel on the tender curve of her knees. The other bubbles she popped down her throat were sweetly-sour like her concerns. She binge-watched the same old set of chick-flicks that featured an overachieving Sandra Bullock, an inadequately parented Julia Roberts, a pensive Tom Hanks, altogether messed up in adorable ways. In cottony nightshirts under Jodhpuri comforters, she took cinema very seriously. She liked to feel useless in familiar ways. When she purposely failed to distract herself, she missed the man who got away. She missed the sound of his hello, read old chat messages and deleted them, a new one each time. Sometimes, she felt weak and retrieved old messages. She stroked her cheeks with her own nails to relive the sensation of his beard gliding across her skin. In retrospect, she didn't enjoy it too much when it actually happened; her skin was sensitive and his unevenly-cut facial hair turned it an itchy red.

When reality leaves a memory behind, does that memory acquire a life of its own? Are they so hungry for what they want to feel that it overrides what they felt? Does it matter what happened, if all they remember is how they think it happened? If her life was one of the chick-flicks she imagined it to be, then on the morning after a weekend of emptiness, she would have found revival in Adele's voice, wrapped cigarette pants around her walk, stepped into her highest heels and dived neck-deep into work. But, since life wasn't a chick-flick, she took much longer to heal and the process wasn't half as interesting. She played the last scenes of movies and checked the guy's Facebook profile every two hours; she stalked and judged every girl he added as a "friend". Sometimes, they were prettier and smarter than she was, so she tried hard to find fault. Every event he signed up for was scrutinised, even the pictures he was tagged in were checked; nothing was trivial. To get his attention on social media, she shared updates that she knew he would notice. From artificial intelligence to Elon Musk to Amal Alamuddin to the English Premier League—these were honey-traps. Offline, her best sketches were born out of her in this vague but patterned kind of romantic hypertension.

The next year, she set up her brand Black & Pink. Her skin was still young, but from all the heartbreak, she had matured in the mind. If the face learned to reconcile with age, and the mind learned to mourn and let go, then what explained the recurrence of errors? Was existence really synonymous with experience?

She was spending a sweaty summer at her boutique with her tailors and artisans, who were sweating more heartily. In their case, sweat was far less metaphoric. Every few hours, Akbar and Junaid would step out into the balcony that faced a backstreet full of junk. Their bare feet were hotter than the food they ate. Black emissions from generator engines were pointed in the direction of this tiny outdoor space, where boiled clothes were wired up like ramen noodles and purple-and-pink dyes were being mixed into them.

Gauri felt their pain. She spent most of her time in the boutique too, hanging tags and cellophaning clothes that were sale-ready. At least, her workers didn't have to go out there in the market and pretend they did none of these things, she thought.

On one such day, a big guy in a sky-blue shirt and high-waist denims came searching for something at her door. He squealed it open. 'Excuse me,' he said. Gauri, who was perched on a counter, sticking labels, limped toward the door and saw a man with a tan. The sort of tan one would end up with after spending a month on a hammock in sunny Goa, the shack-and-beer sort of tan. It was a stylish tan, unlike the tan her workers had on them. He had a green onion of a nose and the ears were uncut ginger. 'I am Vishal Gupta, I own this building,' he stated, casually. 'Oh yes, nice to meet you,' she said. 'I just set up my personal office on the ground floor. Just came to say hello,' he explained. She was relieved that his intrusion had nothing to do with asking her to leave.

'Oh, how nice. Well, welcome to your own building,' she smiled naively. The Guptas owned half the buildings in that neighbourhood. They were rich, like a typical North Indian business family from a '90s Bollywood movie, which started its business from one room in the '70s and suddenly found itself with plenty of possessions; boundlessly, beautifully wealthy.

And after thinking all that up, he looked cuter than he was. Suddenly, his face looked endearing and it resembled Dhoni's, from a blurry distance. 'Coffee?' he checked. 'Sure,' she had no reason to hesitate.

Cold coffee from a Chinese food bus is all they could manage in this industrial colony, where catalytic converters (that reduce a car's toxic emission) were lying in the open, and gas cutters and torch cutters were being used on scrap metal by hands that bore black marks.

'My parents tell me you're doing quite well,' he said, piercing two plastic bottles with straws, and then handing one to her.

'Oh yes, God's been kind. The label is gradually finding takers' she said, looking more interested in the coffee.

They walked up to his office and sat on a couch in his waiting room. They spoke of business, rent, and his recent return from some university in the UK. That night, when she told Priya about her chance meeting with this heir to various businesses, something ticked inside her friend's head.

'Gauri, you're single. If he's cute, why don't you consider dating him,' she elbowed her, with a push of words.

'Really? You think so? He's not that cute actually. What's his selling point?' questioned Gauri.

'Selling point? He can buy and sell your label and many more,' she gave her a checkmate argument, and convinced her to give it a shot.

The next day, Gauri showed up in a floral tea-dress that was paired with an ivory and pink hair wreath. There was a pair of hot-pink Lennon's on her nose. She entered his office, where they sat on either side of his large L-shaped desk. She noticed how the desk wasn't the only large thing in his world. There was a huge double-door fridge in the office, possibly stuffed with coke and soda. There was also a mammoth round watch on his wrist, and it probably concealed a tan-free contrast. She had noticed his car was one of the most lavish looking Toyotas in town. It was fitted with a wine-chiller, small-screens that streamed movies in surround sound, and a thousand small cushions. Things were large. An impious thought later, she noticed some silver idols on his desk. Vishal saw her gaze going there. 'My family is very religious, actually,' he quickly explained. He spoke of his cousin's recent destination wedding in Thailand. He spoke of the Cartier 'His & Hers' watch set that he had bought for the couple, with his 'own money'. Vishal's family, which owned hardware stores across the city, obviously monitored the way he spent his money and his time. He was worth millions (of rupees) and they wanted to be privy to his passions and his priorities, she guessed. He had three sisters of his own, much married and much older. They took turns to call him, as did his mother and his aunt and some uncle who only discussed business. Gauri found that strange. The only person who called to check on her was Priya. His family had a long nose, which kept poking itself into his life, she inferred. Priya had a nose too, but she was only nuzzling her friend Gauri's life adorably. Can people ever see beyond the end of their noses? Was it possible that what some found in friendship, others wanted to find within their family?

Soon, Gauri and Vishal started meeting more often. Whenever they went out for a meal, he insisted he should pay, and in cash. She guessed it was because his family might be reviewing his spending habits. Since their family's treasury was one, even the discretion to spend from that treasury was a collective one. Gauri lived with her parents, but she held the weighing scale of credit and debit, which hopelessly weighed in favour of the latter.

Vishal's heartbeat was almost audible. He had no dark side to hide, and he wanted marriage. Gauri was prettier, smarter, used better words and was far more independent than he was allowed to be. Just two months after their first meeting, he asked her to marry him and become a part of his large family. Vishal was a cushy prospect. Gauri didn't make her happy dog face with him. Does the excitement of being with new people die out once they've been with one too many new people? At what point does the newness in new people become old?

While sitting cross-legged in her boutique, feeling on her fingertips the embroidered sequence that rose millimetres above the fabric, she sipped on cold coffee and envisaged what life after marriage would look like. Would she be giggling away with the women in his household, soft boiling potatoes in a large kitchen, or sewing the topmost button of his shirt before he headed out for a meeting with his father and uncles? Would she be holidaying in Switzerland with their three kids and would she have to keep reproducing till she finally popped a son?

Her brand and her love for fashion, would either last? Maybe, they would. Who knows the value of a business more than a business family, after all? She would be rent-free for life, for one. They would help her source raw materials, expand her team and pump capital into her brand. It would make the process easier. Maybe, one day, they'd even help her expand internationally. The friends she hung out with only saw the fun and fame side, and never the flip side, to her work. But Vishal and the rest of the Guptas would understand the complexities involved in running such a show. She could be her logistically-worried self in front of him, without having to come across as problem-free and proper.

'Priya, I think this guy is good for me,' she admitted, unwillingly. 'Then say yes,' said Priya, hoping Gauri wouldn't change her mind. Gauri's parents agreed.

Half a month later, he slipped a ring down her finger at a quiet farm with half-a-hundred pushy people taking turns to wish them with money and flowers. There was a DJ firing music, as if out of cannons. There was a dance floor that changed colour. At least three of Vishal's dancing aunts looked like they'd been possessed by monkeys and one uncle was jogging in place. They were a jolly lot. As any other newly-declared couple displayed on stage would do, they too divided the awkward attention between themselves. The evening ended, Gauri was engaged to be married, and the confusions of youth had come to a close. Well, almost.

Remember how people recorded contrasting genres on two sides of the same cassette, and the music, the mood and magic of that mad high they felt for those moments lasted only till the tape-reel ran out? Sometimes, they restlessly longed to re-listen and re-feel the same lines, the same beats. Sometimes, they coldly flipped from side A to side B. Inside the solitude of spongy ear-plugs that locked the wide world out, they developed their own emotions, precious and personal. Was being with different partners similar to that old habit? Even after they switched from one partner to another, was it possible to forget the sensation that pulsated from the heart to the knees and back? Those soft brown reels that crashed into junkyards might have left a lesson or two spinning.

When the song on one side ended, Gauri usually flipped the cassette in search of something else. This time, the something else was Shaurya Sarkar. He was self-made, free-thinking, effortlessly good-looking, a believer in progress, and a Senior Associate at an international law firm. He stood smiling in a well-fitted navy blue suit on his LinkedIn profile. Did Vishal even have a LinkedIn profile? Shaurya paid massive rent. He lived in a voguish South Delhi apartment that had French windows, wooden flooring, and a fireplace. He had ordered one of her jumpsuits (Jamdani weave on hand-woven linen; one of her classics) for his colleague, and that's what brought him to her. Gauri, the chance conversationalist that she was, made a plan to hand it over to him over drinks and dinner in Connaught Place.

She showed up in a supple grey sweater, a little gold chain was kept a little under its turtle neck. The gold chain was a gift from Vishal's mother. She pulled one sleeve over her mounted solitaire and got to know him. At the table, were Coca Colas spiked with rum, there was the wax and wane of a restless olive in vermouth, and the death of wobbly caramel under a silver knife. They spoke of hard work, of travel, of living from the end of one pay cheque to the beginning of the next one. They talked about rent, money and stability, as they puffed out rings of hookah smoke. 'That's mathematical despair, life is beyond the smoke,' he stated, and they smiled. The evening had a democratic passion about it. She was free from the noisy attention of a large family, and the talk of marriage and babies, and bedroom curtains and surname changing. She was free.

'Priya. I don't know if I want to marry Vishal anymore. He's a lovely guy, he loves me and all that. But Shaurya is his own person,' Gauri convinced herself.

'I knew it. I just knew it,' exclaimed Priya.

Over the next two months, she tried to graduate out of this dilemma and failed. She spent her days at Vishal's office, which was just below her own, and kept engaging with him on marriage plans. She met Shaurya almost every evening.

In his company, she wore Chanel No.5, which Vishal had gifted her. Whenever Shaurya suggested how unreasonably individualistic he gets, she caught its scent and thought about what she was doing. She hid all this from Priya. She went on long drives with the two and hummed along to the same songs on the radio. The thick air-conditioning in Vishal's complicated car didn't welcome the breeze. In Shaurya's smaller, snazzier car, she rolled the windows down and shared a smoke. Vishal would stop the car to attend a phone call or three from his family. Shaurya stopped for nobody, not even for her.

Back at her boutique, the workers raised their eyes from their machines to observe how she changed tones to talk to these two boys on the phone. They couldn't understand her words, but it wasn't hard to guess what the hell was going on. Her parents wouldn't like the idea of her marrying a Muslim, but these Muslim men were the only abiding feature in her life. The relationship she shared with them was more honest and mature, than any of her other relationships.

Vishal always called back after if she hung up on him by mistake. He held her hand in front of sexy women, and he didn't want to debate and argue. He had no mystery left in him, or maybe he never had any mystery to begin with. Shaurya knew good lines, he watched her kind of cinema, and he spoke of travel. Vishal was land-locked and Shaurya was in love with foreign lands. One had nothing to lose, the other had nothing to gain.

Vishal could buy the wine that Shaurya could appreciate. The charm of Shaurya's youth wouldn't last forever and there's a good chance that he'd have multiple affairs. Vishal was tolerant. She could picture him standing by her side as she threw up, swelled up, or developed lumps in place of what were once curves. Would Shaurya sharpen his teeth and walk away at the sight of her ageing body? Gauri did the math.

She took them both to her bright red bench. And on the courage of her calculations, she kissed them both on her bright red bench. Vishal meant imaginary refuge from practical problems. On one side was her Punjabi mother's insecurity of not marrying into a business family. Gauri's unsure self, soft and part-Cancerian, pushed her toward him. On the other edge stood her father, telling her to chase knowledge and have faith in the unknown. He had married a woman unlettered in higher wisdom, one who didn't grow old with him. Without saying anything, he provoked the chutzpah of her Leo side. He didn't know about Shaurya, but that's what he would have told her.

One side was pink, the other side was black. 'Like a shuttlecock, you are flying from the force of one racquet to land atop another one. So you better watch it,' Priya warned her, and begged her to make a decision, when she found out what was going on. 'Make a decision. Make a decision. The decision is yours to make. Make a decision,' she rang the bell of sense, till it was heard.

Gauri Mehra Reddy, on a Friday evening, in that quiet park near India Gate, invited them both to the bright red bench and told them what was going on.

After the first few weird minutes, she looked at Vishal with eyes that resembled those of an errant child in the hope that he would understand and hold her hand, as Shaurya would curse her and walk away from their lives forever. Instead, Vishal stood up and looked the other way. He extended his palm and asked her to remove the ring. Still looking away, hysterically, he requested her to never call him again and then walked up to his big car with the ring. When she turned back and looked at Shaurya, he was sitting on the red bench, one leg over the other, lighting a cigarette and grinning like a thief.

'You're a nice girl, Gauri. Find yourself before you find someone for yourself,' he said, pulling the cigarette swiftly away from his mouth. He might have been disgusted, but he appeared unaffected, like a mere witness to someone else's life.

He tapped her on the shoulder, said a brotherly good luck and left her alone on the bright red bench.

She sat there alone, hid her face with her anxious-cold palms and began to sob. How many men had she sat on that bright red bench with?

They have voids, and like empty tanks, these need to be filled from time to time. Then, they drive around in neat lanes, on open freeways, through valleys and nooks, depleting themselves, only to come back and experience the euphoria of a freshly-filled void.

Gauri went back to her label, to her parents, to Priya, to the ordinary press of every day. She still opened the horoscope cynically, every morning, with the inkling that her Cancerian self was a void half-empty and her Leo self a void half-filled. While she was busy finding out what her bent of mind really was, the fact that there was half a void in each of her two selves remained largely unexamined. When she searched for qualities in a partner, was she searching for defects that defeated hers?

Soon after, 'Priya, guess what? So, I met this amazing guy, and…'

The Talkative Colleague

She could be in the countryside of Spain under an orange sun, soaking in sour smells of vineyards. On a wicker chair, over a wooden deck, she is swirling sangria, purple with plums and prunes. Those distances of cobbled-stone, she covers on foot. She watches a town square where people haggle over art, over fruit. There is a young boy on it, a red handkerchief around his neck. He blows into his harmonica for money. There is also an old man, a weaker man, clanking castanets in a pastel shirt. They wish to bring neighbourhoods to a halt, but end up making the air eternal; a beautiful failure on their part.

Are these the delights of Marrakech, where shadows of minarets stand raised like the legs of tennis racquets, aiming to hit the crescent moon tossing above and between them? Here, she meanders into bazaars, brushes shoulders with buyers who bend over to pluck out dried dates that rise up in mounts. She is startled by a laden donkey that has abandoned its animal instincts to join up with civil society. Africa meets Arabia in tented shops. Here, she buys magic supplies she will never learn to use.

Or is this Tokyo on a Monday morning, where she is amidst an ageing workforce ebbing and flowing in and out of the city's metro lines. She walks into crammed markets, where stuffed Doraemons share rack space with glitter-lined facemasks. She spills a few thousand yen on them. Those sharp red pagodas, could they puncture her skin if she parachute-lands on them? She lights incense cones, and at once, becomes one with an alien faith. The slow slide of a blonde woodscreen leads her into a tea-house where fat, suited men sit cross-legged on tatami reed mats. They sip on mint tea and chopstick the whitest of white soba noodles out of karakusa-patterned bowls. Here come the tiny-footed geishas, the watercolour prints on their glossy silk kimonos look as edible as the white paint smeared on their faces. What she doesn't see are those patriarchs in moustaches (two tapered tendrils growing downward from a clean-shaven lip) the ones who rhapsodise tea-riddles on the street. Do they only exist in books? At night, she discovers Ginza, where giant screens stream Japanese scripts in the universally loved language of neon. In tall glass buildings, she finds karaoke parlours to sing along to. And for sake's sake, is she drunk on rice?

Maybe these are the Maldives, where islands are named after hotels, where waters are greener than yellow and bluer than green. She runs around in bare nothings of spandex, little knots on either side of an abdomen sullied in white sand. She dips herself in clear waters. In seconds, she is calmed and cured. She sinks, feels weightless and numb. Hiding under a bed of clear water wasn't a clever move. Here comes the sun. It cuts through the waters and begins melting on her ears, her forehead, her chin, and her pits.

Its brightness blinds her and makes red boils on her. She is burning and burning more. 'Somebody call the fire brigade,' she shouts. Here it comes now, its electric bell ringing in panic, ringing and ringing away.

Ringing and ringing like an alarm clock. Was it her alarm clock?

It was almost noon. The air-conditioning had struck off its eight-hour deadline and retired into inaction. The maid halted the blades of the fan. Doing that was a part of her job but there was a trace of inverse superiority in the way she executed it. Archana Kapur was still under her blanket, legs warmer than the chicken legs she roasted the night before. She was possibly sweating butter. 'The heck do you sleep under a pile of faux fur in this humid-as-hell Mumbai,' her flatmate Khyati Kapoor, "aka: the poor Kapoor" pointed out. The girl had already returned from a breakfast meeting in the other side of town. She opened a can of Diet Coke and hovered over Archana's half-dead body like a health inspector condemning lazy life choices, throwing offhanded remarks on the lack of fresh air et cetera. For Archana, Khyati was a fly. She wanted to squat her flat on a wall and reduce her annoyance to a black blotch.

'Can you please shut up and do your own thing,' Archana retaliated. Still blanketed, she turned her back on the wider world and shut eyes that were groggy with morning waste. She wanted to return to that lost paradise, to reimagine and relive it once more. Archana tried and tried hard, as if sucking the sucrose out of coarse cane stalk at the risk of rotting her gums in germ. Are dreams like sugarcane, whose sweetness is a diminishing return? Sooner or later, are dreamers left with a mouth full of golden straw, inside a mind full of golden straw?

One reason why Archana Kapur couldn't wake up early was her inability to detach from the unreal and return to the real. That's also what made it harder for her to fall asleep. She had given up on her dreams of becoming a novelist, because her middle-class parents insisted on the necessity of an MBA. She could have put up a fight. She didn't, she was lazy. So, she dreamt along, demonising society, victimising herself, wherever she roamed.

'You still haven't done your homework? What were you doing since morning?' her mother would say, whenever she caught her daughter staring blankly at a wall.

'I am thinking. I will do it. I will,' Archana would say, not knowing what else to say.

Is daydreaming a slippery affair, in which one forgets when to stop enjoying the weightless slide and when to hold on to the closest handrail? Archana kept sliding along a floor that was soapy before a mop; toes and fingers soggy and clothes covered in foam. Life seemed to be elsewhere, somewhere far away from there. When she was growing up, with the toothpaste spewed between her teeth, she kept looking at the mirror until her younger brother commanded that she vacate the bathroom at once. This dreamer had pin-straight hair that she left unattended on her round face. Her eyes belonged to a mountain goat, cheerful as tearful. Her hourglass curves emptied out inside straight-cut jeans and one-size-fits-all T-shirts.

She had completed her MBA in Marketing & Sales and had moved to Mumbai from its windier and sleepier neighbourhood, Pune. Her physical move to Mumbai may have been recent, but like many others, she had romanced the city's vibe in matinee and gala.

Mumbai had the gleam of a currency coin. It was resting heads-side-up on a table. Heads represented wine-stocked refrigerators, lavender-scented hotel lobbies, and landscaped balconies that were in an open relationship with sea breeze. The visionaries who instituted banking corporations, law firms, advertising companies, and those whose capital powered movie sets and factories and shipping ports, had found the path that started in their hard work and ended in their fortune. This side of Mumbai lived the magical thrill of being identified and revered, even in messy side plaits and dark glasses worn over hung-over eyes. This side of Mumbai could afford to be spoilt, and it was written and talked about. Its struggle was now a story, a great story.

The other side of the coin was tails, and it bore the weight of the other side. Here, houses could be attacked by leopards. So, they camouflaged each other for survival. The men who came here in search of livelihood, were made to live with mice and live like mice. This side of Mumbai made thirst wait in a queue. Bathing didn't involve privacy, let alone ease. There was the fear of electrocution from open wiring during the rains. This side of Mumbai was more likely to drown. Living here meant competing with a million others for the attention of a single doctor, a single teacher. This side of Mumbai also struggled, to survive.

Between the two sides of the coin was a ribbed edge. It didn't matter if it was engraved or polished, nobody looked at it dramatically. These were middle-class citizens with unromantic worries like college admissions, difficult bosses, traffic and pollution. Both sides were on the same coin. At any point, one fist pump against the table could fling the coin and turn fate on its head. Mumbai was the coin; Mumbai was the fist. Mumbai was the reaction to its own action.

In a city populated with dreams, were they all dreaming the same dream? Archana's dreams weren't usually unusual. She hoped to bump into her future husband in the local train, and within a year of their first meeting, she expected his stocks to soar on the Bombay Stock Exchange. This is how she wanted their life story to play out: first, she would stop taking the train altogether so she'd no longer feel the urge to bathe as soon as she entered the office. Maybe, she wouldn't need to work anymore. All day, she would sit in her airy south Mumbai flat, beside big windows. These imaginary windows would be so high-up that they wouldn't require ugly grills (the kind that protrude seven inches to hold potted plants) to avert theft. In this beautiful imaginary place, she would write on romance and on murder. Then one day, like celebrities do, she would get pregnant only in the womb, and show no sign of fat anywhere else. She would have twins, one of each kind. In this imagined world, the husband would gift her diamond tiaras and spa vacations. Her novels would get written easily, mostly on their own. They'd receive good reviews, famous authors would scribble blurbs, she'd be on bestselling lists and at least three of her works would be turned into film scripts. Students would bother her for autographed copies, she would scrawl on them disinterestedly, because how many copies can one sign in a lifetime? Her rich and famous husband wouldn't be fevered by her mercurial fame.

Isn't the imagined far better than the real? Good fame is the most heartening of imagined circumstances. It permanently guards people against rejection and makes their cheer a matter of public interest. Famous people may be misunderstood, but they're never neglected, she would think.

It was all going to happen. She believed, like many others who came to Mumbai to believe. Mumbai seemed to be headed somewhere. No one knew where, but it was on its way. Meanwhile, Archana too was on her way to work. In the local train, a prototype of every face in the country travelled with her. "It's going to be hard to take the train at peak hours and every week day, that's like ten times a week," she counted. She stood between men, at least a hundred men, at least ten of whom were flattened against her curves. The compulsions of metropolitan existence were permitting everything, briefly. These men, crushed in their grinding commute, might be deriving minutes and minutes of excitement by touching her body. But she was guarded against any fragment of intrusion in their intent. Her mind had trained her body to believe that this was a harmless act of survival. "Is there any other option, except to board the train with these men?" she thought, as she stood protected by her perception. Some evenings, when the trains were immovably crowded, and she was trapped between better-looking boys for a change, she enjoyed losing control of her body as it surrendered before them. Nobody would ever know that she enjoyed a touch she was supposed to socially resent. She felt what a child feels on peeing in a swimming pool, on peeing into the rain. Was there a charm, a dark, discreet charm to that feeling of letting go publicly? The muted touch of a masseurs' palm pressing a grown woman's breast, or that of an attractive surgeon examining the crevice of her vagina with two lubricated fingers...how common were these pleasures, how wicked were these pleasures?

Archana, like a monkey swinging on a rickety branch, danced to the beat of the train. Examining the faces in the train, she thought, "The world is full of strangers who want the same things from life: to find a seat in a train, to reach home safe, to work hard for a family, to gain access to discounts and sales, and to be able to afford foreign trips and host great weddings."

Archana joined the job two weeks after a bomb exploded inside a compartment exactly like the one she was in. People couldn't stop taking the train, so they erased the memory of disaster and assumed nothing wrong will ever happen again, at least not immediately. Archana didn't worry about that instance of death, where one crash-bang of a feral box of grenade would bring flesh and memory to rubble. But she thought about death, a lot. The moment of death would be faster than the hours spent in its anticipation. Even if her blood-soaked intestines were stuck (like a juicy steak) on the roof of a train, she wouldn't feel the pain. Even if her hair was blasted afar from her head, and hung off a bar like a witchy wig, she wouldn't be alive to see it. What scared her was the idea of the death of her unfulfilled dreams.

Back in the real world, it was her first week as management trainee at Market Watch Inc. This was a 3,000 square foot workplace on the ninth floor of a tower in Nariman Point. She was welcomed by a receptionist whose smile was a reflex action. It expanded and retracted, like a door stopper, as people entered and exited. Cubicles fitted with sound-proof glass were emblazoned by white light and chilled to a numbing high; a cold and hard place.

"How the hell will I work here? The light is so bright, it's brighter than moonlight I think. Should have never done that MBA," she lamented.

The corporate world believed in first impressions. And, except in warm and fuzzy hindsight, first impressions were mostly last impressions. Archana was the sort of person who made a good first impression to negate the need to make another impression, good or bad. "I don't like the idea of getting into wrinkle-resistant trousers and (75 per cent polyester) shirts. I feel uncomfortable in them," she felt pushed, as she hurriedly got dressed. But she had to, because it was part of the system's general idea of how lasting impressions are made.

'What do you want to do with your life, Archana,' her classmates would ask, as they wasted evenings on campus lawns. 'I want to be somewhere I feel free. I don't think I can ever work in the corporate sector like you guys. Actually, I don't know if I can work in any sector that involves going to an office and sitting next to people all the time. I like being alone in a room,' she would reply, breaking leaves and watching the evening sky.

The free spirit she had chosen for herself in the university was being monitored in biometric records and close-circuit cameras that emitted broken red dots, as was the plan. There was a grown-up unimaginativeness about staring blindly at a screen, all day. Making matters unbearable, the contents of each screen were always visible to a number of peering eyes. Capitalism was bifurcating human emotions into spreadsheets. In the glorious cause of making a living, Archana felt, these conditioned fools were unlearning how to live. The savagery of victory and rivalry was being given the civil veneer of promotions, assessments and appraisals. The system pitched them against each other. In the name of professionalism, they tried not to pour out their personal lives before each other or participate in sexual encounters.

On the first few days, Archana was friendless and quiet. She listened to the tap dance of keyboards and to the loud chatter of corporate inmates. There was heaviness in the feeling of being the outsider amidst a group that had already blended into each other's lives. She felt that their laughter was directed at her. She stared into the screen of the laptop that was handed over to her. When they laughed harder, she straightened up and quickly removed the pop-tinted clips from her hair. They kept laughing. "Are they laughing at my clips or the new pimple on my nose?" she tried to guess. "I wish I could remove this pimple. Just who do these people think they are?" When people haven't been introduced formally, and they first experience each other in silence, do they mostly hate each other? Archana hated each one of them, for not trying to warm up to her, for not trying to understand that she might be interesting or worthy of conversation. Where were their social graces? What would it take to turn the taciturn?

She waited around awkwardly for supervisors to return from their long luncheons and give her something to work on, mostly drafting bulk mail and browsing through sales trends of rival companies. Everybody knew the salary of a management trainee. She was fully exposed. The only respect and self-worth this job could get her, would come from friends, parents and boys.

The clock struck 10. Archana was dragging herself into the fourth day of her professional existence, which felt like four years. 'Hey, is that Archana,' said a honeyed voice from a distance. She searched in three directions for the owner of this surprisingly sweet voice. 'Hey, over here,' said the voice again. She saw a perfectly plump woman sitting on a square sofa near the entrance. A loose Pathani pant was covering her two legs, one of them crossed on the seat and the other one hanging below. An aqua blue scarf was placed on her pearl white tunic, there was also a dying ponytail somewhere. Archana wished she was in something equally loose and comfortable, her trousers were pricking her thighs dry. The face of the owner of that voice was oval like a potato, and like a potato, her skin was a dusky film with yellow blood inside. She was reading Sydney Sheldon's *Tell Me Your Dreams*. She sprung up and extended her hand toward Archana. 'Hi, I'm Meera, Meera Sahni,' she said in a voice, decidedly lively.

'I am the head of your team. And, that means, I am your boss. Boo!' she made a small, witty roar and raised her palms before Archana's face to fake-scare her.

'I was on leave for three days, but now I'm back. You see, my son was being felicitated at a special ceremony in his school. He's a brilliant student, he goes to Doon School. Raghav and I had chosen the school the day the doctor announced "it's a boy". I mean, both of us could never afford attending an elite school, but we sold our ancestral lands in Dehradun for the child's sake,' she went on for another minute, describing her son Rohan's accomplishments as class topper and tennis champion. The teachers eulogised this boy with encouraging adjectives—intelligent, conscientious, attentive, discerning, among others. Archana was utterly happy. She loved the idea of a personal conversation.

'Oh wow, I am sure you are a proud mother,' said Archana, sounding a lot more interested than she was. 'We sacrificed our togetherness to put him there. You see, Raghav's family runs a real estate business in Dehradun and he lives there too. I live here to earn. I earn well enough to support Raghav. They hate Bombay. My Bombay. But I keep visiting so it's all good…' she quacked, hastily on. She still called it Bombay. Archana was immediately attracted toward such people, she found them less frivolous and felt they had deeper secrets.

'I'm sorry, I talk a lot. Please stop me whenever you feel I'm deviating from matters of work,' Meera interrupted herself. Archana didn't have the heart to tell her that she hadn't raised a single work-related concern till now.

In coldly arranged offices, renditions of personal stories brought in human warmth. At some point or another, there was the graphic minute-to-minute reliving of a recent adventure holiday with a new girlfriend. The tongue hopped in and out of little stories till the audience started suppressing yawns. Sometimes, there was a courageous retelling of a son's accident, one where he almost lost his life, or stories from a daughter's elaborate wedding with gossipy slippages. To keep pace with monotony, death was de-stigmatised and little joys were exaggerated. The new daughters-in-law were uneasy about going back to new homes with newer and stricter rules. The whiny lovers slouched and stared ecstatically at their inboxes, waiting for that one message from the one they've been pining over; a depressing song was left on loop.

At her time in Market Watch Inc., Archana watched these lives closely. Corporate jobs were hung around them like neckties. Whenever they wanted to be real and honest about their likes and dislikes, they loosened up to breathe. A flop movie, an extra-marital kiss, a breast augmentation surgery, they wanted to share more and more with those they spent their weeks with. But before anybody saw them easing up, they tightened the knot and stiffened up again. Rank and file ensured they were professionals first and people later.

'Come, young lady, let's go in and get started,' Meera snapped Archana out of her over-elaborate thoughts. Meera's desk was wider than Archana's. A purple notice board was thumb-pinned with pictures of Meera's family. Archana went through these photographs carefully. There was one with her husband from their trip to Kashmir, the date stamp said 26-10-87. Right below, the marking moved forward to 03-04-89 as if to the spin of a slot machine. Here was a tiny picture of her son, fragile and fresh from the womb. Adorably, his tiny vital stats were embossed below: 8.1 pounds, 21.1 inches. To the left, the stamp reeled back to an older date: 19-02-88. Inside a cheap-looking frame, this was a picture from her wedding. Many women (old and young) held an excessively-bejewelled Meera from each side. Archana felt this scene resembled a hunted tiger and a group of forest officers posing with its remains, to condemn its death.

Just as she was beginning to pick up pictorial clues to Meera's life, she was given a tough pat her on the back, and a tremor of shock ran in and out of her body. 'Here you go, girl,' Meera handed out a sheet of rules Archana was to follow. For the first time in four days, Archana felt comfortable discussing work, because it suddenly didn't feel like the cold and impersonal orders she'd been receiving from random supervisors.

'So, we're basically a funny organisation. In fact, I like to think of us as a "un-organisation" actually,' she laughed and jumped up to sit cross-legged on the desk. She looked just as comfortable as she was on the couch some time ago. Archana stared at her, barefacedly. There was something special about Meera's happiness. It wasn't the kind of happiness that the crestfallen searched for on a sermon's mount. It was happiness that hadn't been cultivated or earned. It was natural happiness. It was cosy like a hand-woven sweater. It was cosy like coloured socks on wooden floors. The happy Meera spoke with a sugary lilt, as if her voice had been treated for years with honey and milk.

With the rhythm of an opera conductor, she grabbed a red receiver with one arm and swirled a coffee mug with the other. She was calling the other two trainees, who were sitting at another end of the large room. Within minutes, they ran in, with notepads and pencils. 'Sorry. Ma'am, are we late?' said a tall girl, possibly the tallest girl in the world. The other one, victim of relativity, looked much shorter than she was. 'Not at all. I'm sorry about the ill-planned seating arrangement. I am your team leader. I was just telling your fellow-trainee Archana that we're a "un-organisation" and that means we've accepted that we can go wrong,' she smiled. Archana felt relieved there were others as directionless as she was. She also felt a little cheated that the two girls were suffering the generally belittling experience of being a trainee in each other's company, while Archana was all by her nervous lonesome.

'Every year, I train three morons for a job they shouldn't be in,' Archana felt this remark deeply, as if her new boss had read her mind. She straightened up and asked, 'Why do you say that?' Meera smiled and replied, 'Now, I know exactly which one is the most moronic of the three.' Archana smiled, as did the other two: Anuja and Saumya (in descending order).

Then, in an almost bulleted fashion, she went over the dos and don'ts of the job. She pulled out a white board that could easily double up as a projection screen. With a red marker, she wrote three things: How, What and Why. 'We're in the most common trade in the world. Man is always selling something or the other. And, when he has nothing left to sell, he starts selling himself,' she said. 'The How stands for How the hell, The What stands for What the fuck and The Why stands for Why on earth,' said Meera. She turned back from the board jumpily, looked at their startled faces and laughed aloud. The three girls, still dreamy from school, unsurely smiled along. 'The problem with sales is that there are one too many rules. But, success comes when you bend the hell out of them and make your own. And, you don't have forever to do that. You'll have to come up with intuitive plans, the night before a sales pitch or during a 10-minute meeting with a key client. Be always prepared,' Meera chanted the mantra of every responsible sales manager in the world. After an hour-long talk, where she kept suggesting how hard-working her husband Raghav is and how focussed her 13-year-old son Rohan is, she handed the girls a mock sales task typed out in expressionless Times New Roman.

'Don't befriend clients. Friendships demand transparency. But, only friends can deceive, so one has to fake a warm and lasting friendship,' said Meera. 'Wait a minute, deception? Are we deceiving people?' spoke Archana, like a brain-washed socialist. 'Every business is its own form of legitimate deception, otherwise money will never be made,' said Meera, like a fair and square capitalist.

Through the next half hour, they asked silly questions, one even asked where the closest washroom was. She answered each one, spiritedly. "This woman has the energy of an 889 MVA hydroelectric generator," wondered Archana, who was just about to start searching for the wires snaking about under the carpeting and leading up to her.

'So, my three musketeers. Now, for the most crucial segment of our day,' Meera further tightened her tone. 'Yo! Gurt!' she cheered unexpectedly and invited them to a treat of frozen yogurt.

Following Meera's lead, the three of them stormed into their building cafeteria, looking homeless and hungry. Then began a quick gamble of crunchy toppings; some colourful gems broke more and more under plastic spoons, and mixed up with some chocolate snails, some broken biscuit, and fruit in every shape—fresh, dried, cut, solid. The girls took their own sweet time to romance all these flourishes and walked back with cups, out of which creamy waves rose up in white and pink. By then, Meera had scooped halfway into her tiny treat. 'I never have to choose. I always go for caramel because that's what Rohan likes and he's never able to finish it,' she said. 'I miss my baby so much. I spent the last three days with him. You know, these little breaks are so refreshing for me. I work hard for him,' her voice mellowed.

'Was it the frozen dish or the hardship of being away from her child? She's a long way from home,' thought Archana, as she kept staring at her warmly.

'I'd love to meet your son,' said Saumya. 'Oh yes. But he can't come to Bombay. I don't know if he'll ever come to Bombay. Besides, we have a big family in Dehradun. It makes sense for me to fly down, every now and then. Just one ticket,' said Meera, as she licked her spoon dry. Meera was brilliant at her work, Archana hated that the system was cheating her and failing her. She deserved to be with her son, with her husband. Why did anybody have to sacrifice? Archana loved blaming the system so she could keep dreaming of a place outside of it. 'I guess, life is elsewhere,' Archana's feelings fell out of her mouth. 'No way!' said Meera, taken aback by the young lady's remark.

'Life is right here, Archana. It's in front of you, every minute, every second. I am away from my family. But, we are one in soul and spirit. I know that sooner or later, I will be back with them and that gives me the energy to wake up and win over each day,' said Meera.

On an optimistic high, the first two months of training ended. Every morning, when people walked in through the gates, Meera yelled out their names. She had strange nicknames for many of them. The receptionist Dolly was renamed 'candy-floss' because her voice stuck like sticky sugar to the telephone receiver and then melted into its pores. The company's oldest employee, who was its senior accountant, was christened 'Sir Sahab' as an ode to his years and years of honest service. These people, whom life had quietened and trained to accept routine, smiled at the sound of her voice. Meera's angelic energy was contagious.

From the difficult first hour of Monday to the lightest last minute of Friday, Meera furthered the sanity and strength of these girls. 'Raghav always says a brand is as good as the way it's branded,' her husband's wisdom was often offered to them. The girls agreed on how cute he was (courtesy: the grainy picture of him on her desk). Meera never answered any personal calls at work, so nobody called her. In Meera's world, single-minded commitment was paramount.

There were all kinds of colleagues in Archana's workplace. There was "the funny colleague" who came up with puns, 'I'm reading a book about gravity, it's impossible to put down'; 'Need an ark? I Noah a guy.' Besides planning to ram something thoroughly spiky into the stomach of such a person, once in a while, Archana had deep respect for people with humour in them. Then, there was "the hypochondriac colleague" who made a drippy nose sound like the start of a pandemic. This one always had half-consumed, foil-wrapped pills and dark bottles with final sips of bitter syrup stashed away on the work station. The sound of sniffles would attract "the wannabe-physician colleague" who would then advise: 'Just two teaspoons of honey in boiling water and crush some ginger and turmeric into the mix.' The sniffles came and went, so did the advice. Then there was "the superstitious colleague" who had placed a small laughing Buddha on a possibly sacred spot somewhere in the office; not necessarily the most competent worker. At least once, he or she had argued with the management or offended co-workers to occupy an East-facing seat. In some offices, there was "the distantly-related-to-everybody-important colleague" who could draw a kinship chart linking herself or himself to the

RBI governor, to a legendary test cricketer, to the winner of a reality show. Meera was "the talkative colleague." Could she be called chirpy? She wasn't pointlessly happy at silly things. 'She was more the uplifting kind, like an old army general who had risen above death and loss. With episodes from her experience, she could wake up her tired army's spirit. Like those generals of armies, her proud smile was a reminder of the good times, of victory, of glory. Her face was post-war peaceful.' Archana wrote all this in her notebook, on the way to work in the train. After many days, she had written something.

Archana found herself enjoying this new reality, she was complaining less and doing more. She daydreamed in the train, in Meera's voice. In the crowded mornings, she sensed a hint of citrusy musk, of peels of lemon and orange preserved with glycerine and chloride, she felt it escaping the collar vents of shirts. First, she visualised how the scent was advertised: there were sexy women shaking their posteriors to an energetic number under cascading streams, celebrating the first white of froth along the lime-green soap cake that was being tossed, in break-dance rhythm, from the length of one arm to another. Then, something got into her and she tried to picture the real fate of those soap cakes, mashed wet into cheap plastic dishes, next to buckets also made of cheap plastic. Next, she visualised those burning copper taps that released broken strains of hot water, causing a steam that fused soapy scent with the smell of shit and toothpaste and shaving cream. In extreme amazement, from that one scent, Archana pulled out a difference between the real and the imagined. She etched these quaint thoughts in a notepad, instead of losing them to train rides that felt the same every day. The writer inside her was finding itself.

"Does each face in the train have a story behind it?" she questioned herself.

Archana jotted down every single emotion that fell into her imagination: "Take for example that uncle over there in a steam-pressed office shirt, the metallic clip of a fountain pen neatly placed in his front pocket, a line of chalky talcum filling up a skin-bend along the neck; old habits of old people. I'm sure neither his decisions nor his time belongs to him. His responsibilities are real, and it might take him years and years to fulfil them."

"That lady in a chiffon saree who has been ruing her son's inability to find a job since twenty minutes. Is she putting forward a brave front, while he is away in Goa tripping over a powdery substance? I think some heroes are heroines, waiting for their heroes to wake up."

On the train, there were household maids in packs of three and four. They railed southward to accompany rich kids to swing parks and to push their prams in shopping malls. "Did the maids have children of their own, who are back home eating mud, chewing on rubber slippers, sipping on their own sour nose leaks?"

There were also students on the train. Their backpacks possibly had steel tiffin boxes because they jingled at every start and stop. There were two black cords connecting their hot ear holes to a device in their pockets. "Were they switching radio channels every second in search of that one song that could fit the mood? And, at what point did they fail and settle for something unpleasant? Radio channels seemed undecided, they made and remade collective mood after every couple of minutes; a noisy ad right after a sweet birdsong. Why?"

At the close of the second month, the inexperienced team earned the chance to secure a small but important sales contract. Meera, the army general within her, summoned her force. She led from the front, but this war wasn't hers to fight. 'The last lesson in management, and in life, is that of discretion,' said Meera, sounding at least 20 years older than she was. 'You have before you, an opportunity to put to use the theory and conjectures the last few months have been about. Go win this war, it is yours,' said Meera. She was one of those who could make an order sound like a request, a humble but powerful request.

The girls didn't wait a second to get down to work. Meera typed and typed till her nail paint chipped. She felt like taking a blade and grazing it off, but it didn't hold her interest for that long. On late nights, Meera would order dinner for the girls. In between great life lessons, there was always a twinge of personal detail. By now, they all knew her son Rohan liked his greens, and it was his father Raghav who was unhealthier of the two. Raghav's drinking binges were increasing, and so was his cholesterol. 'He's a grown man. He can't depend on me to mother him all the time,' Meera said, as she tore powdery chapatis.

During the final week before the presentation, the girls were killing themselves softly. Two days before D-day, Meera casually asked Archana to deliver the presentation in front of the other two girls. Archana could see the noble intent in her passive-aggressive tone. 'I will do it,' said Archana, who, till three months ago, had wished to sit pretty in the woodwork.

The night before the presentation of the sales pitch, Meera received a phone call. She approached them, a frown wrinkling up her entire forehead like that of a Pug. 'Rohan has had an accident, I need to leave for Dehradun immediately,' she said. And, without giving them the time to come toward her in affection, she ran back to her desk and began packing her stuff. While they were still deciding what to say, she sprinted out the door. Like the first 60 seconds of silence after a loud noise, everything seemed empty. Archana first felt a little cheated. She was left with a big task and without anyone to guide her through it. Then, a flush of shame warmed her over. This wasn't about her. She went ahead and delivered a great presentation. She wished Meera watched her do it.

The young team, Meera's team, got its first big contract. Archana called up her parents and narrated the entire story, excitedly. They were elated. They had heard the name Meera on multiple occasions. Meera was away from her own child, but beautifully nurturing theirs. 'We are proud of you, Archana. Send us the presentation, so your mother and I can see how hard you worked,' said Archana's father, who was a retired civil engineer. Archana plugged in the hard-drive into her computer to email the file. That's when she realised she had been using Meera's hard-drive, which carried most of her work-related documents. There was a file called "Personal". Sometimes, when people open up their lives before others, do they fail to consider that the others might want to know a little more than they share? She clicked it open. It had nothing but a record of electricity and water bills. It also had her address. Surprisingly, it was two streets away from Archana's. Funny, Meera never mentioned they were neighbours in this mammoth metropolis. In fact, Meera never mentioned if she stayed with somebody. Archana decided to drop off the device at her place, greedily wishing she'd find Meera in town, so she could tell her all about the presentation.

On her way home, she carried the device with her. Soon, she reached A-408 on the fourth floor of Alaknanda Apartments. Archana felt strange entering a building she crossed every day on her way to work. The main door wasn't shut properly; frail light was escaping it in one vertical strain. Before she could ring the bell, an old lady in a cotton saree appeared and made things awkward. She had an aged, seasoned and somewhat troubled version of Meera's face.

'Ma'am, actually I work with Meera. I came here to return her hard disk drive, Ma'am. I live close by, Ma'am,' she overcompensated, only to prove she was an innocent bystander and was outside the door with a purpose far nobler than prying.

'Come in,' said the lady. Archana followed her into a drawing room that seemed trapped in another decade, in the '70s, or the '80s maybe. There were bead curtains with sea shells in them, crocheted sofa covers, and crocheted table mats. Even the big round carpet looked more crocheted than it was. There were three dusty old transistors, and in poor presumption of acoustic, they were placed next to each other. A pair of military binoculars had wrapped a thin string round and round its throat and was committing suicide by hanging off a hook on a wall. There was a sheaf of photographs in a wooden basket on the dining table, as if to be pulled out for a lucky draw prize. These were placed next to, heaven knows why, a purely plastic apple. Some more photographs were wedged between leather-bound books.

Just as Archana was examining the room, the lady returned with a glass of Limca. 'Here, have something to drink. It's hot outside,' she said. This is not how Archana had imagined Meera's home to be. She pictured her as a domestic Goddess (Martha Stewart grade), toasting marshmallows and reading biographies nestled into a neat suede loveseat with floofy slippers on a patterned floorboard below; everything spick, span and squeaky clean.

'Ma'am, are you her mother? She has never mentioned you,' asked Archana, feeling the tongue-tied uneasiness of a guest. 'Yes, I am. I stay with Meera now,' she spoke in an older version of Meera's voice. She came and sat on a cane-rattan-cheap rocking chair. The edge of twin rockers knock-knocked into the wall behind her and forced a faint fall of grey sand, at each knock.

'Do you visit Dehradun with Meera, often?' enquired Archana. 'No, we have nobody there now,' the old-world gentility in her tone disappeared, abruptly. 'Raghav and Rohan?' said Archana, wondering if she had said something wrong.

'My dear, Raghav and Rohan went missing after the bomb blasts in Dehradun on Raghav's 13th birthday. And, that happened three years ago,' she said matter-of-factly. All of a sudden, the knock-knock of the rocking chair seemed like the only sound left in the world. Archana, stunned and confounded, wasn't even sure who she was and where she was.

'But Meera said she's…' The lady interrupted, 'Meera hallucinates they are still alive. It's what gives her the strength to live her life normally. If she overtly accepts they are gone, she will die.' Archana didn't have words to keep this conversation going. But, she wanted answers, 'So, nobody knows she's living a lie?' she enquired. 'I know, now you know, some other people know, her friends know, and maybe even she knows,' said the lady, whose casual tone was rather questionable at this point. She picked up the plastic apple and started wiping it unintentionally.

'So, we just let her believe this whole thing is real. Why don't we save her?' said Archana, sounding territorial about her colleague. 'You think we didn't try. This was the only way she could find the strength to face life. She pays the rent, takes care of my medical expenses. She is a son to Raghav's devastated parents, the son they lost…' the lady suddenly stopped and started staring into thin air. Raghav's parents were old. The death of their son and their grandson dissolved into their medicines, their silence and their static lives. But Meera had to pick herself up and go out there and live. Meera had to face those faces that had nothing but sympathy and pity for her, and those faces reminded her of the faces of her dead husband and her dead son.

'Every three months, she goes to Dehradun to look for them, and fantasises that everything is normal, the way it used to be,' she spoke and retreated into silence, the same silence from a couple of minutes ago.

'What does she do over there? Does she hurt herself?' checked Archana.

'No. She goes and walks around in the market where the blasts took place. She tries to locate the place where they might have been killed. I know she doesn't cry,' replied the old lady.

'Have you tried speaking to a counsellor, a psychiatrist?' suggested Archana.

'You think we didn't,' retorted the lady, a little insulted.

Archana's eyeballs were leaking and before they brimmed over, she left the device on the table and ran out the door. The body was running down the stairwell, but the mind was slowly reeling forward and backward. Meera's voice was echoing inside her head and Meera's face was forming and fading into colourful pixels, inside her mind. She spotted a bright red bench in the playground below her building, where a group of boys were playing a rough game of cricket. Almost blacking out, she went and crashed on the bench. She didn't know why she was feeling cheated and let down. All this had nothing to do with her.

The greater escapist of the two, who was it? Was it Meera? Drawing strength from something that had left her behind? Or was it Archana, draining her mind in dreaming what wasn't? Whose existence was finer? Archana had an open green field before her, all she had to do was start running around on it like a bulldog, and the world would rejoice with her. Meera was locked inside a cold, dark attic, with just one wilted candle, commonly defined as denial. Yet, she lit it bright, and she was painting, and she was reading, and she was creating and thriving in its soft glow. She had learned to be happy with what she had. Yet, this world wouldn't approve of this definition of happiness. The world would call it madness. But, which was this so-called world? A world where men hide their amazement so they don't end up coming across as juvenile? A world where people fake being content, even complete, to be accepted as normal functioning members of the circles they call themselves a part of? A world where people lie to their bosses and their partners to earn their daily peace? A world where people deny what's happening and believe in what can happen? A world where people killed by people are asked to rest in peace by other people? A world where the meaning of life is more and more centred on what the majority accepts as morality? Meera Sahni didn't want to live to please a world that lies to itself and believes it never lies.

Circa 2015. One long decade had passed. Archana was still in Mumbai, still living in the suburbs. Her flatmate had found love in a Silicon Valley techie and crossed seas to live a life of opportunities with him. She had a pool, twin daughters and a Dalmatian named Rex. Archana too was married, to the same guy she was in love with in college. He was now the CEO of his own online travel company. He could still make it big on Bombay Stock Exchange. She had a daughter named Meera and a son named Rohan. Contrary to her aspiration of ageing like a movie star, she was plump and there were age lines on her cheeks, and she was perfectly happy the way she was.

Those strange and passionate three months she spent at Market Watch Inc. as a marketing trainee sat on her resume, which she never needed to update thenceforth. Archana Kapur was now the author of three novels (all bestsellers) that she mostly wrote on the power of an ordinary person's ability to imagine. She was a regular at book signings and literature festivals. She had thousands of attentive followers on Twitter and Facebook. Young girls and boys tapped her shoulders and brought along dog-eared copies for autographing. Her handwriting wasn't messy as she thought it would be. Reality might be humbler than the dreamy anticipation of it. She never went back to that office, to Meera's made-up stories, to Meera's listeners, who either ignored or were ignorant of what was really her reality.

Archana's mind was inspired by that unreal reality she had once faced, the reality she couldn't tell anybody about, the reality her conscience was completely spellbound by. Meera was probably still living a lie, a lie far truer and purer than most things people accept as the truth.

Archana remembered, like yesterday, that New Years' eve, when she ran back from that bright red bench with a strange, scary strength in her nerves. It was Meera's strength that Archana felt within her. She climbed two steps at a time to her apartment on the fourth floor, entered her room, locked out a half-drunk party, and wired up an old computer. She then began beating on its stiff keys, the first passage of her first novel *The Talkative Colleague:*

Solitude is in those writers, those bankers, those students who choose to live alone in large foreign lands. Solitude is in pouring red wine into a single goblet throughout a weekend that one spends binge-watching a gripping murder series on a couch. Solitude is in making a plate of rich and creamy pasta for oneself. Solitude is in poetry, and war. But mostly, solitude is in knowing that the nearest neighbour lives alone too.

Loneliness can happen in a crowd, it can happen on a fluffy bed with one's wedded partner and it can happen in the subway before going home to that partner. Solitude is a choice. The rest is a very real, a very rustic kind of loneliness.

My talkative colleague turned loneliness into solitude on the strength of her perception. It is the same perception that kept her alive. As I write her story minutes before the start of a new year, I realise everlastingly that the difference between the last evening of December and the first morning of January is precisely that perception. Few people understand the tremendous strength that lies in perception. Fewer are able to put it to a mad and wild use. Go, blur the real and the unreal and find your truth, however and wherever it lies.

Candle in the Gulf

All the world's a runway. And, all men and women merely fliers. In search of dream and dollar, they make their exits and their entrances.

Like young cadets forming pyramids in a physical training regimen, hundreds and hundreds of glass panels clambered atop each another in angular curves, in high arches, in round domes and in towering façade. They were made to stand upright in attention as the audience to the drama of coming and going. But, the glass of airports was a looking glass. It looked at the carloads of passengers who poured in on its gates, it looked at them entering in small, quiet queues and immediately scattering their anxiety and excitement like confetti across one big, marbled concourse.

Somewhere, a grown man was dabbing a cheap ballpoint nib again and again. Like a school boy doing his homework, he hunched over a tiny immigration form. Meanwhile, one suitcase felt confused. Was it receiving respect or being humiliated by being mummified in bubble wrap in front of everybody? Meanwhile, the conveyer belt disappeared inward, into the airport one couldn't see. What happened to these bags once out of sight? Were they secretly hacked into? Was a group of delinquents waiting to fiddle their locks open, to gawk at leopard-print silk thongs? To gape at a stash of porn with rubber bands tied over it to hide the rousing artwork? Were the half-read books smelled? Did bookmarks then fall out and move ahead a few pages? Were the socks spat into? Oblivion, it seems, is its own kind of spiritual awakening.

Back at the gates, the passengers arrived to depart. They piled the load of their journey onto the plastic handle of a nylon suitcase. The handle was furious, as if made to stretch its pelvis in childbirth, it wanted to scream for its life. Soon, a task force of four wheels was launched on the ground to ease the strange friction that had developed between man and his own baggage. Passengers carried their baggage around. Flying norms compelled them to divide and choose. They kept one bag close to their heart, and it never left their sight. They sent one or two away to lighten the load. The passenger did have discretion over which baggage to hold on to, and which baggage to let go off (temporarily).

Adding to the load of baggage present on the scene, on just another airport day, was the baggage of Seeta Ranjan and Sriram Ravishankar. This was tied to the carrier of a Toyota Etios, painted and then dented. The two, who were moving to the Gulf on a year-long placement, weren't a couple. The girl was the lady of Arjun Ranjan's life and the boy had committed his life to the loving company of the Aishwarya Rai-eyed Aditi Ravishankar. All in their late 20s, they were friends and colleagues at the Bangalore-based tech-solution company ThinkBeyond.

Cramped into one car, they were approaching the city's international airport, each in their own way. Seeta was rolling her orange iPod, in white wires. She then placed it in her purse, next to a copy of Jonathan Franzen's *Farther Away*. Sriram had an Abe Lincoln-like goatee and wore a black T-shirt with a faded Al Pacino on it. He looked like an erstwhile member of a hard-metal band possibly called 'The Reflectionists' and it probably played at a beer pub every Friday night until its members fell apart, jobless and clueless. Like everyone else, he too had a set of million-dollar start-up ideas.

Sriram felt under his fingers the number engravings on his new forex card. He flipped it around to learn the code, then flipped it back and slid it inside his cheap-looking croc-leather wallet that also carried a colour-printed picture of him with his wife from their honeymoon in Malaysia.

His wife Aditi was feeling closer to one of her basic feelings: sadness, definitely. She kept her beautifully broad forehead on his shoulder and held his little finger like a child. She was comfortable in her skin. It was the skin from a Vaseline advertisement, after the Vaseline had been applied. It was soft and glossy. She was a poor dresser. An ill-fitted T-shirt, baggy jeans, uncombed hair circling her ears and muddy floaters, made her look like a college girl (broke and uncaring). If she dressed well, would she still have sincere woman friends, without a trace of envy in them? Would men still make civil conversation with her, without cherishing the intent of sucking on her neck? Maybe, deep down, Aditi knew that a slow, graceful blink of her blue eyes could put everything and everyone else to stupid shame. She was happy just knowing that. Sriram held her hand, which was lovably rubbed with white water lily-moisturiser, and kissed it aloud. They smiled naïvely.

Inches away, the slightly overweight Arjun, who was balding from the crown, was going through his wife Seeta's travel documents. He ticked them off the checklist on his phone one by one. Then, he dispensed last-minute advice on foreign exchange rules, on excess baggage allowances and customs clearances. Seeta, who was the brightest of the four, was busy stretching her thin lips, dotting and filling them up with colour. 'Seeta, you need to be careful about your handbag when you use the washroom. I think you should take it with you. It has your passport and money,' he pointed out. Still smacking her lips into an even tone, she raised her eyebrows angrily, hoping he would shut up. He didn't. 'Also, when you use the lavatory in the…,' as he hastened to explain, she interrupted. 'Arjun, please! Just please relax! This isn't the first time I'm boarding a flight,' she screamed, clicking her lipstick close in the same harsh tone. His almost-parental concerns were grounding the fancy there is in flight. He was one of those who felt that the aviation industry was going to deny them their due. He was usually expecting to be held back by security for another gruesome round of frisking or worried that the airline would pack his luggage off to Egypt or Moscow, and then do nothing to bring it back. If everything were to flow smoothly, he'd expect at least a crash into the first blue sea the damn plane flies over. He couldn't make every fear public, so he centred his paranoia on the most common of all fears: that of missing the flight. His plan of action was such: tear through the traffic, reach the airport only to realise you have left either the passport or the ticket back at home, tear through the traffic, raid your own home like a thief, tear through the traffic and still have enough time to spend at the boarding gate. To make Arjun happy, they agreed to reach the airport at 8.30 a.m. for a flight scheduled to take off at noon.

The driver steered them along a ramp, which had a foliage of palms on its either side. Landscape architects were doing their bit to ensure that people in concrete jungles were able to botanically identify at least three trees. Arjun quickly got off and caught hold of two trolleys. The rest of them, tired from the ride, slowly pulled themselves out and stretched and looked around. They took turns to take dry sips of mineral water from the same bottle, till its blue cap dwindled and disappeared on its own will. Arjun opened his wife's bag thrice to check if the square-folded printout of the e-ticket was still bookmarked inside her passport. She stopped his hands, and in aggression mixed with affection, she begged him to relax. They huddled with their respective partners warmly, in their private goodbyes.

Arjun was still worried about something or the other and Seeta seemed slightly relieved. The other two snuggled. Briefly, they forgot their concerns and posed for a group selfie for Facebook. They were all tagged: #DubaiCalling #Thubai #Gelf; 100 likes, 30 comments. The fliers waved out to the partners they were leaving behind. Within minutes, the existence of those partners beamed into the back-lit screens of their partner's phones and laptops. Distance, isn't it known to turn people into numbers, into icons, into pictures, into things?

Meanwhile, against Arjun's better judgement, the fliers had a smooth check-in and had two hours to kill at this airport of limited amusement. After plates of juicy chicken burgers, with onion and peas falling out of hurried blends of mustard, mayo and ketchup, they ordered tall cups of Vanilla latte. Clutching them, they walked and walked in search of two empty seats. In places of rapid public use, why did everybody want to court a corner seat that was as distant from the others as possible? And, at the behest of this desire for whatever little isolation, they walked longer, peered harder and finally found an empty place to spend the time that would seem longer than it was. The two threw open their laptops, immediately distancing themselves from each other. Soon, they noticed a crowd in front of a screen that flashed the sign: Emirates Flight 567: BLR to DXB. Some girls, in red pill-box hats and white handkerchiefs rolled on the sides of their necks, stood before it. As if a dragon had rolled out its tongue, the chute leading to the airplane was waiting to suck people in and whisk them away.

'Oh god. I wish there was Wi-Fi on this plane,' Seeta grunted irritably as she turned off her phone. 'Huh, you said something,' Sriram, in his usual lost self, was humming Coldplay's *Hymn for the Weekend* and staring at another plane reversing into the runway. 'I said, if all flights came with Wi-Fi, it would be such a step forward in communication, wouldn't it?' she questioned, rhetorically. 'Well. It's just four hours and there's plenty on-board entertainment. Honestly, it doesn't matter to me,' he replied.

His coolness was bugging her. 'How could he be so casual about leaving behind his pretty partner, alone on one side of a double bed? How easily could he give up on the comfort his sideburns enjoyed under his beloved barber's blade? Wouldn't he miss those long walks to his fridge, and in each of those walks, reminding himself to clean up that stain of orange curry that chose to harden across his off-white kitchen tiles? And what would happen to those Chinese leftovers in that fridge? Won't he miss the rattle of his ceiling fan that was the background score to his dreams for so many years? Or his favourite bar stool in his favourite pub or just his favourite fruity-estery ales foamingly falling from the tap?' she brooded over his decision to fly away.

She looked at Sriram's emotionless face staring at the scene around, around and below. The plane, like a weightlifter, exerted every ounce of its usable energy to lift itself above the ground. When people are torn away from the urgency of their little joys and grandest concerns, do they remain the same people? How much of their health and peace was lost in the making of the houses they were now flying over and away from? Within those walls, they received the news of a brother's cancer report, of a son's admission to Oxford, of a daughter's miscarriage in the eighth month. In those homes, they hid high-cholesterol reports, repaired wall clocks, and soaked taper candles into creamy pineapple cakes on birthday midnights. Where they once spread out floral bed sheets and spring-cleaned shoe cabinets, those houses looked tiny from the sky; tiny like toys made of cardboard and silver foil. When viewed objectively, from a height, did the meaning of those lives within them also shrink? What they feel they are leaving behind, is that ever really left behind? In the age of sail, men travelled to find. In the age of wind, did they travel to forget?

'I can't wait to land, flights give me an identity crisis,' she made a strange confession and began tapping her fingers on the armrest. 'Huh? Why would you say that?' he asked, and turned himself toward her, attentively. 'Why should the journey between giving up a life that I had and embracing a life that I know nothing about be spent miles above ground in a space where the drawing of a curtain will make me realise I didn't work hard enough, and the wrap of a tiny skirt around a firm butt makes me feel fat,' she blurted, fingers still moving up and down the armrest.

'I don't like this feeling. I feel like I'm leaving something behind and I need the people I love around me to comfort me but since I am going away from them, that's not possible. Maybe, Arjun should have accompanied us and stayed over for a week,' she cribbed.

For the first time since Sriram had known her, this go-getter came across as weak of will. 'Hey, are you all right?' he asked unsurely, and calmed her down by rubbing her shoulders twice, uncaringly actually. 'Relax. I know you're strong. We're not leaving anything behind,' he added. 'Of course we are, Sriram. You know, it didn't seem like such a big decision till yesterday. Do you think we're taking our marriages too casually by just taking off like this? Won't you miss Aditi?' she raised a set of concerns.

Sriram took some time to think about what he was going to say. 'Seeta, let me see, how should I explain this... Hmm...You've a steel metal chain, right? You've noticed the vacuum between two loops. That vacuum is necessary, it's deliberate, it keeps the loops together and the chain stronger,' he said, tapping her shoulder again. 'Don't worry, we'll be fine,' he reassured her. Seeta was pleasantly surprised. Sriram was leaking wisdom and had managed to distract her. She didn't expect either from him. She switched on her phone and took a selfie; #Flying #SoExcited #Jitters; 87 likes, 10 comments. A sepia tint and a Steve Jobs quote on that selfie seemed befitting, because it was indeed a new and exciting professional move. She sucked in her worries and smiled.

After two small movies on either side of fidgety naps that left legs and elbows in a quandary, they lowered into the Gulf.

In 1991, Dubai had 1 skyscraper and now it has 400, the Gulf declared on a billboard that ran unencumbered along the length of a wall, below which immigration queues kept building and breaking. After a tiresome wait, Sriram and Seeta were summoned to two counters, where men uniformed in cool white thobes sat inspecting passports. Dubai saw two kinds of arrivals. First, of those who came to earn, to save and return home with much more than they had left with. Second, of those who came to earn debt by spending more than they had ever earned. Everybody earned something in Dubai.

Seeta quickly logged on to the airport's Wi-Fi and messaged Arjun, 'The Falcon Has Landed'. Quickly came his replies: 'Thank god', 'How was the flight?', 'Is it too hot?', 'Did you catch up on your sleep?' She was really happy about how much he cared, and that he hadn't forgotten her in these four hours. Soon, she felt strong again.

Meanwhile, Sriram messaged their Pakistani broker, Aadil, to check if the twin apartments were ready to move into. He messaged back promptly, 'Sir, Syrian tenants have vacated now only. But houses ready.' And, so began their cab ride on Dubai's smooth, elevated roads that flew into every horizon of a dressed-up desert. Erected on either side of the road were billboards for American perfumes, Swiss watches, and European sweaters and boots. The Arabic tag lines on these implied that luxury consumption is a global ideal. At regular intervals showed up air-conditioned metro stations and air-conditioned bus stops. The cab too was air-conditioned. In Dubai, life was hiding itself behind air-conditioned glass and watching the heat, defiantly. The heat was cleverer, it could cool itself a little and manage to strain in through the silver film of reflective windows. The desert tried its best to escape the sun, which still waxed and waned on its own command.

Dubai was peopled with buildings. The two engineers alighted at the front porch of their apartment tower that had a million windows dotting its 100 floors. It was a tower in a sea of towers that had washed over all barrenness. The two young Indians were in the neighbourhood of Jumeirah Lake Towers (JLT).

'Wow, this looks stunning,' said Seeta as she threw her head back to size up the structure in one, upward glare. The top edge of the building had melted into the sky that was as yellow as white, almost like the first poor attempt at a sunny side-up omelette. She looked at Sriram, who now looked blue from her retinal strain, and exclaimed, 'The building looks better and bigger than its picture in the ad.' Together, they checked into their respective studio apartments—904 & 905. Their Pakistani broker had kept his promise. The old tenants had vacated, although mere hours before the new ones checked in. 'Slaalekoom. Nice flight?' asked Aadil, who stood wearing formals and holding ten sheets of the issueless rent agreement. 'Walaykum Salaam, Aadil. Where do we sign?' asked Seeta.

Within 10 minutes, the homes had new owners and their doors were closed from inside. Sriram got into his apartment, furnished with only one springy mattress, two folded sheets and two pillows. He threw his tired body on the mattress and looked up at his fan-less ceiling, and felt he wasn't at home anymore. He took out his phone and saw 11 missed calls from Aditi. He quickly called her. She carped, accusing him of having forgotten her. He spent a few minutes calming her down.

Meanwhile, Seeta was trying to open the one window in her stuffy apartment for a breath of fresh air. She quickly realised it could only open an inch-and-a-half into the wind. She felt the breeze on her fingers. It was warm. She thought of her balcony back home in Bangalore, she thought of herself in a soft night shirt standing barefoot on its wet granite, next to her oily green plants that too were awash and happy. She then admired how beautifully big and shiny the view from her new window was. The building next to hers had a limpid pool on the first floor. She saw couples lounging around, as their toddlers splashed around in pink-and-blue swim tubes. Suddenly, she missed Arjun. She thought of all those times he suggested they should have a baby. The wallpaper on his phone was a picture of his little niece, and he spent Sunday mornings watching cartoons with the neighbour's cranky kid. Like a child tying on a leash to a stuffed puppy and dragging it around till the parents melted and bought him an actual one, Arjun's subtle hints were adorable and made her feel crippled by her choices. 'We don't have savings, Arjun,' she got herself to tell him.

A knock on the door pulled her out of these thoughts. It was Sriram, checking if she wanted to join him for dinner at the salad bar in their building. She did. The two had to report to their new office the next day. They ate at the ground floor of their building complex and went to a departmental store next to it to stock up on shampoo, toothpaste, biscuits, eggs, cans of cola and some utensils. 'This is why moving into unfurnished homes is a bad idea. We don't even have refrigerators. Let's take half a dozen eggs and a small loaf of bread, we'll place them before the AC vent,' he spoke, facing a colourful collection of cereal boxes. Meanwhile, Seeta was having an NRI achaar-papad moment. In pensive poise, she stared at the shiny array of packets carrying oily spices, dry chillies, and circular crackers that were ready for a roast. She remembered stopping over at the convenience store near her Bangalore house, where the manager knew her by name. Her picky husband checked expiry dates and took out his glasses to read out the list of ingredients in fine print, specifically checking for coconut oil, which she was allergic to. Back then, she sped past sections and picked out whatever was needed. That day, miles away, even the empty shopping cart felt heavier. When Sriram's palm fell on top of its handle by mistake, it felt a lot lighter.

'Sriram, have you already forgotten your likes and dislikes?' she didn't know what she was saying, neither did he. She looked lost. 'I mean… I am no good at buying groceries. I don't know how this thing works. I mean, let's pick out whatever we like and can have tomorrow. You're right about the dairy products though,' she covered up for her previous question, slowly regaining her senses. 'I think you are tired from the flight, Seeta. Come, let's get you some rest,' he rubbed her shoulder, sensing something was wrong with her.

A week passed. The two foreigners blended like sweetened lime juice in this cosmopolitan cocktail of a workspace. There was one Cypriot, gambolling about in it like a black olive. One Jordanian, sweeter than canned cranberry juice. And a British boss, who shook (and not stirred) them from time to time. In Dubai, Thursday was Friday and Friday was Saturday and by that logic, Sunday was a working day. On a relatively easy Thursday evening, Seeta was sitting at her desk, tired of feeling homesick. Something got into her and she spread out her new business cards, displaying them like tarot cards, in front of her Macbook. She didn't put herself in the picture, for she was dark-circled from the lack of sleep on a cheap mattress. She added a noir effect and a Sam Altman quote as a caption; #NewDesk #NewOffice #NewLife; 56 likes, 5 comments.

'Do you want to watch *The Great Gatsby*? It's playing in Marina Mall, just across the road from our building,' said Sriram, when he saw Seeta play around with her business cards. 'Yes, let's do that. I really feel like going out. I love Lana Del Rey's *Young and Beautiful* from the movie's soundtrack,' she started to chirp. After the movie, they walked around the mall. She asked him to pronounce the names of some brands that retailed there: Balmain, Juicy Couture, Vacheron Constantin and (the hardest) BCBGMAXAZRIA. He got each one wrong, and she laughed and laughed at his ignorance. He made silly faces and laughed along.

Both Seeta and Sriram were good at what they did, and better than their partners at what they did. Sriram saw Dubai as a year-long transit before he could migrate to the

Silicon Valley. Seeta's computing skills held considerable sway in her office in Bangalore. She was fluent in the languages that machines responded to: HTML, JavaScript and CSS. She was an expert in designing a Graphical User Interface (GUI) that provided non-tech users with point-and-click menu options that made it possible for them to operate websites. Seeta was a translator between man and machine, she knew the language both would understand. However, these days, the codes in the repository of her own mind were becoming harder to decipher. She remained entangled in them.

Not only was she missing the admiration of her 30 co-workers, she was also missing the way Arjun pampered her with a shoulder massage and how he placed a steaming glass of tangy rasam on a straw coaster in front of her, after each hard day. Things were ordered. And, order wasn't easy to re-establish. To put things in place, to get people to believe in one's rareness and notice one's "at-the-end-of-the-day" goodness, wasn't exactly easy. When life presents newer and greater chances, old orders are smashed to establish newer ones. But, after people abolish the old order and till they establish a new order, do they feel both hopeful and hopeless? There seems to exist, during this phase, a strange kind of duality that refuses to balance itself out, like a coin that won't stop rolling along a floor.

'You said you're not good at buying groceries, want to try furniture?' said Sriram. She smiled and said yes.

Expats in a city of expats, they plucked two Ikea brochures and encircled wall shelves, hooks & hangers, storage beds with headboards, lamps and rugs. Together, they dressed up their homes. Sriram coat-tailed her and bought whatever she was buying. They followed up the shopping spree with tequila at an Irish bar in downtown Dubai. They walked a mile to locate the bar in a concrete complex, across the road from Burj Khalifa. That was the tallest building in the world. For some reason, it resembled the steel rod antenna of an old radio, the kind that stretches up in broken lengths and then stubbornly corrodes and refuses to recede. Only, it wasn't corroded. It was sparkling. It looked celestial, as if it was making satellite transmissions to another universe.

This city had its alcohol behind bars. Seated on the visitor's side of its most popular Irish bar Fibber Magee's, he spoke, 'Did you know that tequila made from 100% blue agave doesn't require the lick-and-suck of salt and lime?'

Suddenly, Seeta was lost again. She remembered her time in Bangalore, when Sriram used to play barman at those shindigs he hosted on his terrace. Their happy friends uncorked chilled pints of beer, and poured white wine into cheap plastic glasses. She also remembered a hassled Arjun on that terrace, waiting to go back home and keeping count of her drinks. 'What was Arjun even doing in the midst of beer froth and the good times,' she asked herself.

Back at the Irish bar, a three-drinks-down Seeta looked at Sriram and thought of Arjun, more and more, and of how he would never let her take three shots in the first place.

She couldn't even call up and tell him she was homesick, he would be worried. Her worries were largely wasted on him. She drank, she drank, and she drank to this freeness, to this newness, to this openness that he had uncorked from within her.

Minutes close to midnight, they dawdled into their building arm-in-arm, whistling a Flo Rida number, fumbling for door knobs. Then, something hit them. There was no electricity in their apartments. Instantly, they sobered down, as though they were pretending to be drunk to endorse their foolishness all this while. On inspecting further, they realised there wasn't any water either.

'Oh my god,' she gasped. 'What will we do now?' she gasped harder.

'Calm down. I'll check with Aadil,' he said, as he paced up and down the corridor.

Soon, Aadil found out that the previous tenants hadn't cleared their Dubai Electricity and Water Authority (DEWA) dues for the last three months. And, this could only be undone on Sunday morning, because the office was shut for the weekend.

'What? Just what on earth are you saying?!' she questioned, almost blaming him for the situation. When the agitator is unknown and away, the agitation is deflected on those who did nothing to trigger it. He sat down on the edge of Seeta's mattress and held his face, in helpless exhaustion. They left the door ajar, so the light and air-conditioning from the corridors could keep bucketing in. She rummaged through the drawers and found one tall candle and a matchbox. She lit it on the kitchen slab that was still cold from the residual air-conditioning. She sat next to it, just staring at its infantile flame. He looked up and saw her smiling at the candle. It was the kind of smile that shows up before the last tear has been wiped off, the involuntary smile that stands for a simple, but life-altering realisation. The unexpectedness of bliss in that troubled moment made it all the more adorable. He shut the door close, so the candle would discern that its own blonde radiance was as intelligent as the filament of a light bulb.

Dubai was like that candle. A thousand palms from around the world were caressing its glow. A couple of palms were pouring in oil, slowly, from a height, to keep the flame alive. They were silhouetted in the candle's long shadow, and they couldn't be seen. Whenever the fire would dim to a cool blue, other palms would labour hard to pile on new layers of scented and glittered wax. The old wax would freeze in shavings around the candle's spherical pillar. Nobody thought about this used wax, not even those palms that were here only to draw pleasant warmth. The rest of the world believed that the oil this candle drank would dry out one day, and the hands it ate out of would soon gather hideous burns, and that stringy wick beating at the centre of its heart would die a black death. Like the candle, Dubai compelled viewers to see only the present, and called itself the "centre of now". There is the certainty of uncertainty to a candle's flame and it does stretch over to all that lies within the flash of that flame. For the first time, the two felt engulfed by the Gulf.

'Have we lit the first candle in the gulf?' she asked. He walked up to her, enclosed the flame in his palm and said, 'Yes'. The alcohol in their nerves felt a lot less anonymous. He gave her warm signals and she received them. He kissed her, once, twice, and thrice. He lifted her and put her on the mattress. She wasn't as light as Aditi, he thought of Aditi and decided to pull himself back after leaving a kiss on her forehead. In the amber of the moment, he saw her lips widening in want of a kiss. She looked tired and he wanted to comfort her. She was smarter than Aditi, who at this point could only attract his attention by childishly whining into a video-call window. There was no fun in saving Aditi, she was a weak person. He could save her with the little finger of his left hand. And, with the rest of that hand and his other hand, he now wanted to hold Seeta. Was this desperation? Aren't people ultimately desperate for touch, desperate for giggling under a bed sheet with someone, casing their arms around someone else's, and needing someone's lips on their own? When they are far away from their partners, does the healing effect of touch stop working? And then, like wax, does good sense also go down in dribs and drabs?

The morning found them slumbered, awkwardly in a lazy, loose grip. She was alarmed by the beep of her phone. It was Arjun. She was still in last night's clothes, a shift dress that had crawled above her knee, over which lay Sriram's leg. She pushed it aside, sprang out of that setting and ran barefoot into the corridor with her phone. Those minutes before waking up completely; before repossessing their natural energy, before they realise they are mourning something these days, or that it's their wedding day, or the first morning in their new job; those minutes before gadgets are switched on and the first coffee is brewed...are those minutes spineless? Three long, monotonic beeps of her mobile were enough for Seeta to recall what she had done.

'Where are you?' he asked. 'Nothing, nowhere,' she said, hyperventilating, her voice felt trapped as though in asthmatic cough. 'Where else would I be? Where are you?' she cross-questioned to take the focus of discussion far, far away from where she was.

Seeta was sweating, from the lack of electricity. Arjun asked her about her appetite, and about her weekend plans. He told her that he managed to fix a pipe on his own. For once, she was thrilled at his peripheral concerns. She went back in. Sriram had left and entered his own apartment. His door was open and she could hear him talk. Seeta was anxious that he might have been talking to Aditi. An hour later, she knocked on his door. It was awkward. What they didn't have was the luxury of avoiding this awkwardness. Promiscuous guilt wasn't their only common problem. They had electricity, water, the lack of food and so much heat to worry about.

'Don't worry, I've spoken to Aadil. He said the payment has been made and an engineer will come and switch on our power supply by tonight,' Sriram conveyed the information in the tone of a delivery boy in a cap, who had no emotional connect with the buyer or the seller, or even the job he was in. 'So he wasn't speaking to Aditi,' guessed Seeta.

In the evening, their apartments were back on their feet. The next day, their furniture showed up in pieces. It wasn't broken. It acquired character as they assembled it. The week after, the Wi-Fi was geared to top speed. Life was comfortably basic. A month passed, Dubai seemed friendlier and easier. Sriram and Seeta tried to talk about work. In each other's presence, they behaved more and more like their earlier selves, their selves before that night. Deep down, Sriram still felt the warmth of that candle, he remembered that kiss, and he missed the kiss even as he looked at Aditi's face on video chat, every night. On the other side of the wall was Seeta's apartment, where Sriram was once lying on top of her, where he was once the desire of her fatigue.

If they had brought this up, they would have dismissed it as an 'abrupt exchange of saliva' and moved on. Maybe it was a little more than that, so they chose not to talk about it. Soon, they became friends again. They worked intently through their days, went back home and video chatted with their partners. On weekends, they strolled aimlessly in Dubai's colossal malls, losing track of how much they had walked. Seeta, medium-in-her-sweaters, medium-in-her-pizzas, saw mall-walking as an amusing variant of fat burning.

'These people have so much to sell,' he joked.

'There's always so much more to buy,' she replied, hopping from one overwhelmingly well-stocked store to the other.

After that kiss, for no particular reason, Seeta was careful about her wardrobe choices. She tried on dresses as Sriram waited outside curtained trial rooms. Sometimes, with a price tag dangling between her half-zipped back, she stepped out to ask his opinion and rivet his attention. Initially, he enjoyed being in a position of authority over her vanity. He then developed an eye for her vanity. Because of her textbook charm, Aditi never felt the need to dress up. Sriram felt he had been missing out on partaking in the effort a woman makes to look elegant.

Be it a naked glass of malt or a fruity cocktail with a paper umbrella decorating its rim, no matter how much they loved one, they didn't give up on the other. Every weekend, they discovered Dubai.

She Instagrammed pictures of the food she ate, the clothes she bought, and the sunsets she soaked in. She was alone in each of her pictures, his presence was cropped out.

Sriram's wife looked at his pictures and dreamt about living the good life with him. Seeta's husband inspected how sunny it was in the frame, and why she wasn't sleeping instead of burning about in the heat; his concerns were mechanical. Occasionally, they clicked a picture together, smiling socially like distant cousins who only met at family gatherings. Through photographs, life was being made to judge life.

Together, they walked past kiosks selling copper coffee pots, their snouts curved like that of elephants and grime trapped in their dense engravings. There were pretty Persian carpets hanging from ropes. The two tested perfume from the delicate hands of French girls, Filipino girls, Indian girls, all of whom broke racial barriers and smiled the same soft smile, and clinking tiny crystal bottles on shop shelves. In Dubai, gold wasn't in a rush. Shackled in hundreds of chains and wound like millipede inside bracelets, it sat there with the surety that it will be claimed. Seeta always wore gold earrings with pearl droppings. These were gifted by her mother on her graduation. But she would never stock up on gold out of financial insecurity, she sensed a menace in the metal.

'Gold makes people selfish, wars are fought over gold. Families lock up their wealth in gold. The same money can be spent on travelling to new countries. And, if a situation arises where they have to sell the gold, it is considered a massive misfortune. Let's not look at gold,' she would say casually powerful things and drag him away from the souks. There were some women who dumped ancestral gold and ran away with men who wouldn't measure their worth against this metal, and there were others who came enveloped in this metal, and all their life they felt guarded by this metal. Had this metal not been there, wouldn't they have led bolder and more prolific lives?

He would notice sheikhs in cottony white thobes and feel jealous of the comfort they must have been in. She would notice bands of women in hijabs. So many heads were guarded against the sun, the dust, and amped-up air-conditioning. Unlike many others, the two were not interested in deciphering the political symbolism in these outfits, but they appreciated their practical merit. The friendship between Seeta and Sriram was growing, new memories were being strapped on to it. Each time they were on the road together, they jokingly guessed where their next cabbie would be from: Hindi music: Islamabad; English Music: Kerala. In blameless ways, they distanced their partners from their simple pleasures.

One evening, a hardware mechanic who worked in their building, followed Seeta to the café in the complex. He introduced himself as Sunil Pillai from Marottichal, a village in Kerala. He politely asked if he could sit next to her. She shut her laptop and gave him a wordless go-ahead. He kept his head on the table and began to howl. The crying made his spine rise up and down in waves.

'What happened?'

'Why are you crying?'

'Tell me,' she questioned more and more to get him to talk, and quickly, because other people were now watching.

'Madam,' he said, wiping his face. He pulled out his voice, it was tear-sodden.

'I am living in Naif Street, in a small room with six others. There is no window in room. I am sharing rent,' he took a break to breathe in. At this point, Seeta was gauging what he possibly wanted from her. Was it money or a ticket to go back home, or if he had committed some vague crime and wanted to seek shelter in her tiny studio apartment? Coldly, she listened. 'They are cooking meat every day. There is smoke in my room. I cannot cook my own food in that smell. They are not taking bath. I send my daughter to medical school, I send my wife AED 1,000 every month,' he elaborated. 'I came to Dubai for my daughter. I pay her medical college fees. I cannot leave. One time…I try to kill myself,' he confessed.

She looked at his helplessness and found herself in the middle of a mysterious squall. Beneath the expansionist desire of glistening steel and polished glass, the earth was basically, brutally cracked. After promising that she'll look for another place for him to stay, she fled.

She ran into her apartment and began crying, 'Oh god, the world is so unfair'.

The noise startled Sriram and pulled him out of his house, bare-chested. He found her door open and got in. 'Hey, what happened?' he asked. Seeta narrated the story, between three puffs and four pants, and then hugged him. 'It's okay. Life isn't as rosy as it looks,' he consoled her with clichés. She was still fluttery from the incident, so he held her tight to restore her strength. She had never been held by a man so firm and fit.

He kissed her, and this time in full possession of his senses. He noticed behind the washed utensils upturned on her kitchen shelf, another candle and another matchbox. This time, he lit it. On a fluffy couch, he put himself over her. They had coped with difficulties and earned this comfort together. It was theirs. Soon, she flipped him under and copied his moves. 'Aditi never displays such courage,' he thought. 'Arjun would be so uncomfortable if I tried to ride him,' were her thoughts. He had a head full of hair. She sniffed and touched it. It was a sprightly break from Arjun's bald crown that had patches of sticky dandruff stuck on it. Sriram had a tattoo on his upper arm, and it resembled the Bentley logo. She had glimpsed it in the past. His short sleeved T-shirts exposed it stylishly. It looked different on his nudity. It looked imposing. Arjun had a black birthmark around the same place, a black scratch on that Bentley.

They made love, every other day, for the next couple of weeks. Whenever their spouses voiced the need for a quick video chat, caution was taken to hide any evidence that could be fatally visible through those blurred chat windows. But, this stemmed from a lack of confidence, the kind that makes criminals leave behind a trail of silly clues. Those semen stains between two uneven pillows, four slippers on the same side of the bed, shaving cream in both bathrooms and four stained cups of coffee on the kitchen slab, could still be easily hidden in this age of digital closeness.

For some unexpected reason, they didn't think of this as cheating. He still wanted to spend the rest of his life with Aditi. Of course, the rest of his life would only resume once he got back with her physically. Till then, he was on a pleasurable detour. Sleeping with Sriram was making Arjun's methodical ways tolerable. The more crudely she slept with Sriram, the more deeply she wanted to have a child with her husband. Their minds claimed to be divorced from their own bodies. They looked at this as a vacation from their respective marriages, a harmless delight. Had the term "affair" fallen out of fashion? This didn't seem like a beautiful blunder they were committing. The lies they told seemed to be serving a genuine purpose.

This strange relationship might have well been an extension of their job contracts that made them move a continent away from their homes, and check into hotel buildings and spend "workations" in beach towns with colleagues. The jobs had summoned their minds to Dubai. But, the bodies that had tagged along, could they keep whiling away their time at the reception desk? They had to do something.

Seeta and Sriram were alone in this togetherness. When people travel far from the comfort of what is known, they learn to hold new fingers, to laugh at the unfunny jokes of strangers in the lure of befriending them.

They know full well that during the time they spend walking back from the subway to their apartments, many miles away, their fathers could be collapsing in heart attacks in dark slumber, unaware of life leaving their nerves. When their partners might be tucked under blankets with leaky red noses in the silence of Cole Porter's voice spinning out of a warped vinyl, they themselves could be caught between the wiggle-waggle of suitably-oiled bellies to revoltingly loud music, in a nightclub. And, when partners are conveying their dismay in lengthy text messages, they might end up receiving them with little or no emotional cognizance, while watching John Oliver do his thing. Even an exchange of erotic messages can be felt differently by two people. Maybe one partner isn't even turned on.

Had those fabled rivers lost to antiquity, deposited them, like silt, onto the vast sands of the gulf? Was the romance between them like the candle they lit somewhere in the beige depths of the gulf, so momentary that it was almost functional in its delight?

Nine months later, their spouses paid them a weekend-long visit. Seeta and Sriram did their bit to ensure the tourists remained wholly unmindful of their little arrangement and didn't discover a detail or two that might alter the course of their happily-ever-afters. The couples posed romantically with Dubai's yacht-shaped hotel twinkling in the backdrop. Aditi bought pairs of salt-and-pepper shakers, each painted like a Sheikh and Sheikha. She also picked out paperweights stuffed with sand and a large camel stuffy. For Arjun, the thrill lay in comparing the prices of electronic devices to the ones available in shopping malls back in India. 'Maybe, it's cheaper to buy this stuff online,' he remarked, and then got drawn toward red-yellow stickers that screamed discounts.

This visit, which was spent mostly outdoors, was far less awkward than they had expected it to be. All they had to do was act as if everything was normal, and then everything would become normal.

On the last morning of their trip, something bizarre happened. While Arjun was still asleep, his phone vibrated on the side table. The constant buzz, like that of a bee, shook Seeta out of her sleep.

'Hello, who's this?' she spoke in a manly morning voice.

'This is Dilip from Sun Travels, Sir,' the man on the other side refused to acknowledge that the voice was that of a woman.

'Yeah okay, Dilip. Tell me, how can I help you?' she played along hesitantly; she wanted to go back to sleep.

'Sir, the honeymoon suite you have booked for your wife Aditi for the 17th won't be available if you delay the payment. It is holiday season and we are getting a lot of requests,' he informed. The phone slipped from her fingers and fell between two pillows. She quickly cut the call, deleted the number from the call log, fell on her back, and feigned sleep. Behind shut eyes lay a settling storm. She hadn't cheated on him, if he had cheated on her too. Seeta didn't mention any of this to the three of them, not even to Sriram. She kept pretending everything was normal, with a lot more effort this time. Once the partners left, she mustered the courage to talk to Sriram. At first, he was angry at Arjun and Aditi, and then at himself for being in no position to be angry. Over cigarette, coffee and work, he reconciled naturally.

A year after they left for Dubai, they returned. Sriram and his wife were all set to leave for the US in a week's time. He had landed his dream job in Palo Alto and Aditi had conceived their first child. Seeta and her husband were planning to set up their own business, and hopefully start their own family, in Hyderabad. On a bright red bench outside their old office, they all sipped on coffee, in silence. When they were done, they took another group selfie; #NewLife #NewBeginnings #NewStories; 150 likes, 23 comments. 'I am so proud of you. You inspire my children. God bless you,' commented Sriram's aunt. 'Two perfect couples,' commented Seeta's mother.

Does the living of life happen in the backstage of life, where props are messy, the lighting is improper and performers look mostly hurried and unprepared? To the world, what shines under spotlights comes across as real. Are they putting up an opera in the hope that the world would watch and cherish it? And if they want to make the world believe in their perfection, do they also want their partners to think they are perfect so they can expect perfection in return? Bar to bar, string to string, these four young minds tried and tried harder to strike a chord between their conscience and that of the other.

"There was failure on my part and failure on your part. In a way indescribable and in a way known only to us, if we are both wrong, then we are both right."

That One Photograph

If everything out there has been made known by those men of science and industry who break the world down to fact and math, and the rest of what remains unexplained falls on a philosopher's plate and whatever is still left surrenders itself before a poet's nib, then what is it that the others are dying to find out? They still wander with wonder to see anything they haven't seen before. And, if the excitement of seeing anew isn't something that gets them going, why are they told they might as well be blind?

Ravi was a restless little boy. His parents ran a small shop in the temple town of Haridwar, where sin and ash were drained in the brown flood of the Ganga. His shop looked like a hut made of scrap wood, with saw shavings that drifted out of it and blackened up around the edges. Nails had lowered into these graves of wood and died a death of corrosion. His parents didn't care about the wood and how gracelessly it was ageing. Crushingly stacked in its tiny centre were accessories of faith. There were packets over packets of cotton wicks, and more packets of camphor that was machine-cut into tiny square slabs, and five, or six, or seven plastic bottles of sesame oil. These were a source of fire, fire one could trust and control. Mostly, the shop sold idols made of painted clay. This was the market of myth. A slim street made of big broken stones ran between shops. Drained water seeped through the cracks, and mucky-footed stray dogs sipped on it. Some shops sold harem pants with patterns of Sanskrit verses and ponytails of key chains with 3D images of gods were hung around. Another shop spun discs, one more jarring than the other, mostly Bollywood numbers remixed with devotional messages. Between songs, temple bells could be heard; a therapy of sound from noise. At the temple shops, pilgrims were customers and they liked to bargain.

One day, when Ravi's family hadn't sold anything since morning, a lady insisted on buying three clay figurines for half the price. She flashed her money before his father's eyes. The man stood there, exhausted from the heat, wiping the sweat off his forehead. His father's every impulse was absorbed by the sight of that banknote folded between her fingers. Ravi could never forget this incident. It used to take his mother all day to make three idols, which his father would paint later. If pilgrims were in search for peace, how could they oversee somebody else's peace? Ravi had grown up in and around this shop. He had learned to man it as a child.

His family of eight lived in a big room, or a little house, right behind the shop. His grandfather was a bearded soothsayer, accompanied by a parakeet as frail as himself. His beard was dirty, it mostly had cloves and rice flakes trapped in it. He spent his days on a cement seat under a peepul tree, making his bird beak out forecast cards from a box. As a child, Ravi would sit behind him and watch him go about his business. He saw him repeat the same stories to different people, day after day. Why was he fooling them, and why did they not look fooled? The old man's broad, wrinkled forehead had a large swathe of sandalwood paste that broke itself along his age lines. The old man had a wife, who behaved like a widow. She abandoned herself on temple stairs, in corners of marble courtyards that burned but couldn't cease the march of bare feet. She fed herself at community meals that were funded by those pilgrims who believed charity was a route to salvation. Ravi had seen his grandmother tuck the inner edge of her saree into the waistband of her petticoat, to scuffle with other women for an extra puri or another slam-dunk of boiled rice. Charity was a moral and social obligation and it sustained the economies of faith. His parents worked as a team, painting clay idols and clothing them in coloured skirts, as if these were dolls for adults to play with.

Sometimes, the clay idols cracked clandestinely, under their clothes, and there was no way to tell the damaged idol apart. The presence of a broken idol is inauspicious, for then it is not even an artefact or a paperweight. If not discarded with respect, it is basically taboo. The broken idols knew they were broken, so they stood quietly among the crowd, enjoying reverence that wasn't theirs. One broken idol didn't know if another in the lot was broken as well. Like many others, was Ravi also an unfounded broken idol, concealing his inner confusions, pretending to be in conformity with beliefs he didn't appreciate? Ravi was alienated, constantly.

The boy attended a small government school that was shaped like a temple. It had domes. Here, he found it hard to read books. His teachers, who sent the students out to fetch fried snacks and tea on rainy days, didn't seem too convinced about the point of education either. Like the carcass of a cat, his head lay on a desk. He stared out of his classroom windows at a wall that couldn't move, at a street that didn't want to move. Nothing outside was exciting enough for him to get up and leave. A belly full of helplessness, hunger and worms made loud noises. Like everybody else in a pilgrim town, he too was seeking release, from an existence so static that it felt like sin. The eldest of four siblings, Ravi slept his nights on a thin cotton sheet in a corner of his single-room house, where the breeze of the ceiling fan failed to reach him. He lay on his back, with his hands folded behind his sweaty head, and watched the light from the temples. He barely slept. On occasion, monkeys hanging upside down peeped inside at his sleeping family. What were they searching for in this house of meek and mired comfort? They jumped upon the roof, and jumped more and more. Sometimes, when it wasn't totally dark, he could see his parents forcing themselves on top of each other, trying to procreate or recreate, or both. He would turn the other side, in complete disgust. He would cover his ears under the fold of his elbows, hoping his parents would see how badly affected he was by all this. At some point, he stopped caring and slept right through the action. He was paralysed. He could feel it all and not act on anything he felt. Once he grew up and realised he had physical needs of his own, he forgave them.

He felt attracted to the girls in his school. He wanted to touch their hair, their hands, just touch them to see how they felt. Could he have found his answers in a woman's companionship, he wondered? Ravi wanted to drain out the battery of boredom and fear that life had placed inside him. In his town, the rising sun was first seen through clear strains of water by priests, who stood a few feet deep into the river. The sun was as much a creator and a preserver, as it was a destroyer. Would it, in some ways, be kinder to those who saw it first? The mornings woke up to the sound of bells big and small, turning evermore lyrical inside a chorus of chants by freshly-cleansed throats. In Haridwar, eternity was an everyday effort. The wheel of birth, death and rebirth was churning night and day, day and night, in song and light, to restore something that wasn't even fully destroyed. Was order being feared or was it being desired? Some believed in higher powers, others believed in their own. None however had the power to deal with a change they couldn't understand or handle. So, they wished that the waves should be only scarcely animated like in a desktop wallpaper; the mountains shouldn't crumble into a debris of man, cattle and car; any volcanic eruption should happen thousands of years from now; the beasts should follow the rules of the wild, and yes, there are rules in the wild; sunny mornings should follow from dark nights; and the marriage of skin to skin should be able to renew life. Ravi's mornings were stationary and his nights motionless. In a land that was closer to the higher forces than it was to those who were trying to survive on it, he made sense of day and night.

Around his 16th birthday, he found a discarded cycle in a heap of junk and repaired it. It was the best gift he could have given himself. He peddled around town. Mostly, he peddled along the ghats. Here, priests and the pious folk sat huddled under giant umbrellas around small sacrificial fires, trying to establish contact with celestial bodies. Empowered by the wheels of his vehicle, he rode as far as the strength of his muscles took him. Ravi noticed riders vroom into town. They wore washed-out jeans, held packets of cigarettes and had sacred red threads tied around their wrists. They could well be riding into the wind, kissing the floor at hairpin bends, and standing brazenly erect at the edge of perilous cliffs. They had freedom. Then, what brought them here? He noticed white-skinned men, who were freshly bald and white-skinned women with hair partially wet from a holy dip. They wore ochre and blue kurtas, with 'Om' and 'Swastika' imprints and black sunglasses, and cameras that defied gravity dangling from their necks. They came in, acquainted with terms from the Vedas, the Upanishads, and the Gita. They sat on warm chipped floors, in a silence almost spiritual. They clapped along during the evening arati, and didn't fuss over the purity of bottled mineral water. Miles away from where he was, were those lands of flyovers and skyscrapers, where atheists bandy about, mocking idols as a backward habit. Were those good men—with the possibility of construction and expansion lying within their palms—liberated from the fear of God? Then, whatever were they hoping to find over here? The other group that caught Ravi's interest consisted of research scholars and journalists. It was as though they willingly placed themselves on a rotisserie in oven-like temperatures, and slowed their lives to observe and listen to sadhus, pundits, devotees, shopkeepers and even beggars. Ethnographers of faith they were, searching not information but knowledge. What sort of vitality brought these people to small pilgrim towns? They seemed different from the regular horde of day trippers that came packed in buses, dried vomit stuck on every third window. The families always featured apathetic children, who didn't want to be here.

Once every twilight, he balanced his bike on its kickstand and climbed up crumbly, muddy steps to join a group of ascetics. A saffron wrap short of nakedness, they crouched and clutched chillum pipes, turning breath into smoke without a worry in the world. Sometimes, he borrowed their smokes, and felt relieved. Lying on his back, he whistled the smoke out and saw the stars that looked like the sprinkle of salt grains over a poor man's plate. Yet, the night sky was rich. The smoke that men made, in ritual and release, was as adrift as the clouds in that sky. In narcotic numbness, he kept gazing at the stars. His gaze, like any gaze, was a wordless wait for motive to flow into action. Then, one day, it happened.

On a cloudy August afternoon, some priests were squabbling. The point of contention was a five-hour long yagna that was to be conducted for the health and welfare of a wealthy merchant family from Allahabad. The sum involved was a staggering 25,000 rupees. Some shrieking happened, a hand or two were raised, and passers-by began walking toward what was turning into a mob. Ravi stood a metre-and-a-half away from the rowdy crowd that worked in the department of peace. Through the gaps in their feet, he noticed a person sitting all alone by the ghats. He walked toward that person. It was a girl. With her eyes half-shut and her legs half-dipped into the water, she sat there playing with a basket full of marigold petals. Orange like the sinking sun, therapeutic like turmeric and bright like fire, the marigold looked like art in her company. In the cup of her palms, she flung them up and a few of them fell back in and even fewer stuck to her small cheeks and her slender neck, both of which were wet with the love of the Ganga. She sat in a sleeveless white salwar kameez. He flapped his shoulders and flew forward. He went and sat next to her, hoping to discover something in her eyes. She didn't disappoint him. She had the golden brown eyes of a calm wolf, with a sparkle of mischief in them. The world outside was cold and harsh and she was sitting here, peacefully. She didn't notice him or talk to him. She kept playing. Her relaxed jaws moved to the tune of an old song, "Na tum humein jaano, na hum tumhey jaane, magar lagta hai kuch aisa, mera humdum mil gaya," (You may not know me, I may not know you, but in your company, I feel I have found the soulmate I was searching for all over). Ravi hummed along. She heard his voice and felt his presence. It didn't have an effect on her. She kept singing, so did he. Ravi and this stranger were far away from everything that was wrong around them. He made conversation with her. She told him she was staying at an ashram with her brother, sister-in-law and their teenage daughter.

He offered to walk her back. Her legs were jammed in one place, he helped her get up and they treaded softly through the crowd. She closed her eyes and gently breathed in the scent of jasmine from garlands. She bent to take in the freshness of the gulkand, the cardamom and the lime paste that was being brushed over betel leaves. She told him that leaves have a scent of their own, and it is just as deep as the scent of flowers. As they walked, she held her slippers in her right hand and felt the dust and heat of the ground on her feet. Doing that, she said, brought her closer to where she belonged. He tried not to stare at those two brown diamonds she had in place of eyes. On their journey to the ashram, she rubbed her forehead on a temple wall. She then kneeled down next to a cow on a muddy lane. She took out a polythene bag full of grass and fed the cow. Ravi stood at a distance, arms crossed, just watching the scene. How many times had he seen a mismanaged herd of cows inconveniently reduce the width of streets? It was difficult to tell if the creatures had life in them, up until the wag of their dung-laden tails. It was economically rational to worship a cow. The Brahmins said they wanted to preserve cows, but they didn't act too much on their decision. The lower castes were in charge of disposing off their carcasses, sometimes they cooked them to derive protein, a vital source of energy for the back-breaking work they did to earn the right to exist. A mention in the scriptures earned this animal several treats. While the world was busy chalking out its fate, this girl was caressing its soft white forehead. Whenever she did that, the cow shut its eyes and let out a long weep. It was a response so human it failed the power of language. Ravi stood there, absorbed. Right behind him, a boy was trying to take a picture of a monkey. With quivering hands, Ravi grabbed his camera. The physical act of taking a photograph of her brought to an end, a journey of years and years. Inertia ended and Ravi was hugely aware, and alive, in the moment.

Together, they reached the ashram. Her brother opened the door with a barrage of questions and her sister-in-law pulled her inward. They shut the door on his face and screamed ugly taunts. Ravi eavesdropped and found out that her name was Sailaja, and that her brother and his wife were waiting for her to turn 18 so they could find her a husband and 'get rid of her'. They were probably as rich as he was, and that was reassuring. Ravi turned his back on these lives and began walking away. He was nobody to interfere. Something got into him. He pole-vaulted over a barbed-wire wall and went and stood under her balcony on the other side. And there she was, wearing that same calm smile on her face, trying to wrap a thick strand of hair around two tiny fingers, lost in her own thoughts. Was this person above it all? He stood there till her sister-in-law pulled her inside again. Ravi walked back home, thinking of Sailaja.

The next morning, he went back to the ashram that was run by young volunteers. The two girls at the reception counter informed him that the family had left for Delhi earlier that morning. In his sweetest voice, he requested for their address. One of the receptionists scribbled it on a ruled register page. That evening, he told his parents he wanted to work as a photowala in Delhi, where he would be paid to take pictures at weddings. When he clicked that one photograph of Sailaja feeding the cow, as he pressed that button with his fat thumb, all his questions turned into one answer: all of life is buried in moments and these moments now need to be lived. His parents couldn't understand the concept, because it wasn't as ordinary as their lives. Before they could form their own opinion about his decision, he sat on the floor and strapped on his father's leather sandals. In one oil-stained canvas bag, he kept two shirts, a pair of pants, a six-month-old toothbrush and the broken clay idol that his mother had asked him to discard a long time ago. He boarded the interstate bus that was Delhi-bound. At quarter past midnight, with that one bag and 500 rupees in modest denominations, Ravi left Haridwar behind.

The next morning, the bus dropped him off at a crowded terminal. He took the Delhi metro to his uncle's house. This ride was air-conditioned and comfortable. He had only experienced air-conditioning once, when he had accompanied his father to deliver a big box of clay idols at a government guesthouse.

Ravi looked at the many faces of Delhi. Some were chit-chatting, some were knocking back their heads in short naps, and others were reading notebooks and encircling them. They weren't like those sightseers and worshippers he was used to seeing in Haridwar. These people didn't look like they were in search of anything in particular. Thirsty from the night before, he saw a young girl pouring water down her throat, and the water looked cold and clean. His white and flaky tongue came out to stare at it. He closed his eyes and remembered Sailaja. How would she have lived this very moment? Where was she living this very moment? Something in him cooled down. An hour later, he deboarded at the Uttam Nagar station. His uncle was standing outside in a sweaty vest and brown pants, there was chalky distemper splattered in one pattern over his malnutritioned legs. He was a contract painter, and his house stood atop a single-counter meat shop in the least developed pocket of the urban village. Never had Ravi seen shiny cleavers mincing bloody breasts and legs. The sight made him realise how far away he was from his home town.

His uncle's house was furnished with junk metal. There was a dismantled iron cooler in one corner. There were several skeletons of electric motors and a two-seater bench that looked like it had been uprooted from a municipal park. The uncle lived in the company of a pivoting stand fan. Its breeze came and went as if catching its breath in between a conversation, but the voice of its blades spoke to him all the time. There were pots and pans that played into the hands of rapid rats. Ravi noticed that a two-pit toilet had been constructed on the small terrace attached to the house. After having received compensation from the government, his uncle was using it as a storeroom.

Within the confines of his uncle's home, Ravi found his comforts. He placed his broken idol on the windowsill and felt at home. The next morning, on his uncle's insistence, he asked his way around to Rawat Wedding Photo Studio. The sun had turned its back on the building. Disoriented and still sort of thirsty, Ravi showed up at this small studio shop that was cluttered with half-a-dozen round lens caps, tripod stands, crystalline lenses and wires that ran from the mouth of chargers to the ear-holes of plugs. There were photographs on display: couples holding roses, families posing in front of snowy backdrops, children wearing sunglasses, and girls standing straight to tell the world they're ready for marriage. The place looked like the drawing room of many families. Seeing an underfed Ravi who hadn't any experience with a camera, the owner Mr Manoj Rawat got worried. But he had his own problems. Two of his photographers had called in sick during the wedding season. He sat down the young man and asked him if he'd be able to do this. Ravi answered, 'Pathar ki duniya hai, kaanch mein kaid karni hai, kar lenge, Sir, jab nazaria hai, toh nazar bhi aa jayegi' (My task is to capture a world of stone in the glass lens of a camera. Sir, if I have a vision, I will also find the sight.) Mr Rawat was floored. The businessman that he was, he promised to pay Ravi only if he did a good job. Ravi, with the uniquely amazing thirst for moments that Sailaja had left him with, was ready to do a good job. How would Sailaja have made sense of this wedding? What would she have observed and celebrated?

Ravi captured the uneasiness of the groom's mother as she adjusted the pendant on the bride's 22-carat orange-gold headpiece. She stepped back to let another woman come first in the life of the man born to her. He captured her bittersweet joy. He photographed the bride's distressed uncles as they counted the banknotes they would have to hand over to the groom's father once the noisy nuptials came to a halt. They sat away from the party, drowning their differences in half-filled whisky glasses. That night, they were all fathers of the bride. He saw them inside his tiny viewfinder, the heated edges of which lay on his right eye. He noticed the disinterest of the guests in the ceremony, he saw them loiter about. He focused on one excited and excessively dressed cousin and juxtaposed her against a dull crowd. He noticed how the placards had fallen by the side of serving containers—both, the vegetarians and the non-vegetarians first checked if the food was vegetarian. He photographed the food delicately, with all its intricate garnishing. He twirled the plastic lens to zoom into girls raising their arms to take pictures of themselves, to justify all the effort that went into getting dressed up at a salon. He shot the ladies who were touching each other's jewellery to inspect weight and shine. He caught young bachelors teasing spinsters from the other side, in playfully sexual ways; weddings legitimised innuendo. Ravi shut one eye and hid the other one behind that black piece of plastic. His hands cupped its ribbed lens. Sometimes, his fingers got trapped in the grip strap and stroked tripod mount holes. At someone else's wedding, he was becoming one with a machine that was already pregnant with possibility. An 18x135mm orgasm was coming and going, and going and coming.

With his camera, he froze the flames of the ceremony and the fall of rice and coins during the bride's parting ritual. He hooked his sight on tears to capture the emotions of those who were giving a daughter away. Ravi noticed a range of emotions in a wedding. There was fear, excitement, worry, loss and panic lurking around jubilation. Ravi didn't know he was using a worn-out, overused, probably second-hand Nikon D80. It was enough for him to know that all that was amorphous out there could be dwindled to the point of 10.20 megapixels. Imagine a telescope that traps the galactic expanse of twinkles and the chance glitter of a comet inside a small black tunnel. Once the sights are trapped, the camera changes form from a telescope to a microscope in which every detail of that distant scene is enlarged by a 7.50x zoom. Now imagine a leaf kept under a microscope. There are gooey veins and yellowish bacteria glued to cell walls, but on the outside it looks like a leaf no different than another. Each moment is as high as it is low, as majestic as it is delicate, and all that the cameraman wants to ever do is feel the moment in every vital impulse that occupies its stretched limits.

The candid freshness of Ravi's photographs was appreciated. He earned himself a total of 9,000 rupees and Rawat Photo Studio its next six contracts. A year and a month later, Ravi was earning 15,000 in rupees and double of that in goodwill, each month. Mr Rawat gifted him the old Nikon D80 he had started his photography on. It was then that he went back to his canvas bag and pulled out the paper that carried Sailaja's address. On the last Sunday of August, he wore a new shirt, touched his broken idol and decided to show up at Sailaja's house. Outside the door, he stood listening in on her sister-in-law, who called her a burden and a headache and other uncharitable things. Nothing had changed. Ravi walked in and proposed that he'd relieve them of this pain. With a complete stranger's idea, they agreed.

A month later, Ravi brought home his Sailaja, whose liquid-centred eyes were lively like that of a fish. Sailaja left her aquarium behind and found her place in a freshwater lake. Ravi believed she could swim, elegantly, in any depth. That is how she lived in the moment. They will never know where the ocean ends, they will never sail to its edges. What glides along their scales, through their gills, and on their fins, is the freshness of the water they are in. The oxygen that they breathe and the fact that they breathe, every second, how do they forget so easily something as incredible as that? Sailaja knew how to breathe in the big sea, and breathe in the midst of each wave. And thanks to Sailaja, Ravi too had found a philosophy to live by. His uncle vacated the house and moved back to a village on the border of Uttar Pradesh and Bihar. Among all the junk he had left behind were small cans of paint testers. Ravi and Sailaja made this home theirs. They painted the door blue, the windows green and the discarded bench a beautiful bright red. They revived the bench with their combined effort. They smiled as they soaked their fingers in red paint and left shabby imprints on it. His salary was small, so were their pleasures.

Ravi worked on contracts for photo studios and had spare time during the day. Come sun, come rain, come storm, he walked around town with his camera and rented lenses, capturing everyday scenes in this big city. Sailaja sensed that his heart was scared, and defenceless in the lingering sense of "now what". She let him sulk, and mask in the moment with her.

One day, he walked far away, wandering aimlessly towards the end of the city and noticed a large landfill. Here, he saw children, who slept like cats and dogs, inside empty cement pipes. They scouted for big and small recyclable items inside mountains partly made up of maroon sanitary napkins, busted thermometers exposing mercury and half-pulled tins that gashed their tender skin. He snapped and snapped as they made hats by sticking junk metal on jute and giggled wickedly. They did little jigs and when they saw Ravi chasing them for a week, they hunted a pen and paper and gave him their autographs. He captured their haunting smiles, as they gleefully dived into piles of filth. If they found a tube of pain ointment in the garbage, slices of white bread were brought and smeared with it. They ate this strange mixture to find a high in the lowest of lows. A vision came to him in the form of a photograph, a grainy photograph of a little girl with pigtails, sitting quietly in between Sailaja and him. Then the picture grew grainier and was torn up by his doubt. Could he take yet another life from darkness to light? He returned to the brightness of day, feeling burdened by something weightless.

Time felt cold on his elbows and nose as he photographed:

The dolls of little girls who had been raped in Haryana;

Empty hospital beds of victims of crime in Chhattisgarh;

Shovels and sickels of farmers who had turned suicidal and surrendered to their will, in Punjab.

People had gone and the things that mattered to them stayed, quite selfishly, alive.

The emotional ironies that life unfurled before Ravi, deepened his intrigue. Ravi had to chase one misery after another. He began selling his photographs to media houses. He didn't get any credit, just some money for every dozen images that he submitted. There wasn't a scintilla of doubt that media houses were addicted to anxiety. He came back home slightly ashamed, slightly assured. The source of his relief was someone else's misery? The thought crept into his mind and sat there.

Sailaja heard the reality behind the images, the names of the people who suffered violence, how they smelled, and if they had rough voices. She imagined in her head what his lens captured. She had been told stories of how some of them only looked abject in pictures, and were otherwise refusing to help themselves. Others smiled as soon as they were done striking a pitiable pose for him. She didn't even frown. The evenness in her attitude started to bother Ravi.

Ravi was upset. Here he was, walking into the debris of buildings after earthquakes. To what pleasure did he take pictures of clocks that were still ticking in the rubble? He felt like a drama-maker. Like he had found a release in doing something socially destructive. The woman who once patted a cow like it was her own child and lent it so much love that it cried in silent reception of it, and made him click that one photograph of that scene and put him on this unusual path to self-realisation, was leaving him alone and midway.

Ravi stored all kinds of strife in the glass jar of his lens and tried not to let it trickle into his eyes, but sometimes he felt like failing. He could watch her calmness and copy her calmness, but he couldn't touch it or kiss it. She looked like a wax statue of herself. She wasn't only blissfully away from the rest of the world, she was also away from him.

On the bright red bench that they revived, Ravi slowly returned to the weaknesses of childhood. That visitor called anxiety decided to stay on, illegally.

One afternoon, Sailaja stuffed a pillow under the armrest of the bench and comfortably tucked herself in for an afternoon siesta. Ravi, prepared to tie a coarse cloth round his neck. He shook faintly like the wind chime on the window. She closed her eyes, trailed the sound of little tinkles and hummed a familiar song, "Na tum humein jaano, na hum tumhey jaane..."

Ravi stopped. Sailaja's blind eyes couldn't even see the drastic turn her life was about to take, then how could she have stopped him? He remembered why he loved her. Her being was his answer, and his strength. And it was right where it had been since the moment he took that one photograph. He hurtled back to her, and hugged her.

There is always a deep cut right down the centre of two eyes, the scene crashes into it and breaks into two. When opposites attract, why do they behave like eyes, trying to urgently complete one picture after another?

Couple of Words

The tarmac was grey. His court coat was black. Her doctor's coat was white. They were together on the tarmac grey; they were two shades of the tarmac grey. Advocate Vijay Pandey was driving his wife Dr Kalpana Misra to the hospital, which was on the way to his place of work.

It was a Monday morning after a long weekend and Delhi's traffic was well-rested. A broken red light had caused a bottleneck on one of the radial roads leading to the Dhaula Kuan flyover. Vijay was saving his white Maruti Suzuki Swift Dzire from drowning in the sea of white, black, silver hatchbacks, sedans, rickshaws, buses, trucks, cycles and some walkers. On four long lanes, cars moved one by one like beads on abacus rods. Those commuters who swished past the traffic in the super-fast Airport Metro were in a position to see how the roads resembled this geometric exercise. The long jams looked both adorable and ugly from a height. Some pedestrians parried cars by hitting their bonnets to halt them and then crossed over to the other side; foolishly fearless. There were others who waited for the lights to switch in their favour. They were losing body fluids and gaining tanned patches, a costly barter, cheaper than death. The petrol, greasy and warm, seeped into coal-tarred roads and made rainbow rings that resembled the shimmery necks of Indian pigeons.

Inside Kalpana and Vijay's car, the air-conditioning was doing all the talking. Outside, the road pilfered a broken strain of water that dropped from a municipal tank truck. The windows and sunroofs sliced up sunlight into small triangles, the chrome panels on door handles and the bonnet grills trapped swelter and threw back shine. Stained by exhaust-fumes was the skin of little boys and girls who sold things. They offered Chinese helicopters, latex balloons and pink rose buds, all three possibly had the same shelf-life. They also sold books they couldn't read, and calculators and multi-pin car charges they didn't know how to use. This road had a little village on wheels. If everything else in the world dashed into apocalypse and just this one road survived, the people here would find partners, procreate, and build a thriving community in no time.

Back in the white car, Vijay and Kalpana were much into their daily activities to notice the scenes the windows were live-steaming. The biggest cars behaved like hard-to-impress mistresses. They were proper and they made others feel inadequate. The smallest cars, like college girlfriends, made bumpy rides carefree. There were three bright red cement benches under a shed at the bus stop. Kalpana had been noticing the benches. Nobody was sitting on them. It was too hot and the buses only stopped for less than a minute, many metres away.

Those who are stationed on the road are hardly lucky on the road. Bumper to bumper, a staged protest of honk-and-beep happens; the pressure to accelerate is unstoppable. A brake is only a break. The shift of gears in a small box, changes the path of life. On the road, the wheel of thought turns inward again and again. It remains unresolved in friction, but steers ahead because of a sense of duty.

And this was what this young couple's life was also like. The two had fallen in love over daily phone conversations while he was completing his LLB in Pune and she was in medical college in Bangalore. Once they started living together, they felt suffocated by the persistence of each other's presence. To put it mildly, they were bored. To kill the boredom, they gave birth to a daughter. She was now seven and had completely cog-blocked the one and only vent in their claustrophobic relationship: personal space. Kalpana had become irritable over the years, and Vijay, who once impressed her with his comic timing, didn't want to risk offending her with his borrowed jokes. His silver-tongue had lost its spit shine.

Initially, she didn't want him to give up on her. Soon enough, she accepted that she wanted to be peaceful, with or without him. She didn't want arguments to emotionally exhaust her, especially as work became harder. Kalpana wasn't comfortable with the marks motherhood had left on her skin that once had the tonal quality of velvet. He shared that discontent.

She sat in the car elegantly in a rayon chiffon saree, with a black leather bag nestled in her lap. Her deep-cut blouse left most of her back vacant. She made back-handed attempts to attract him every morning, mostly by taking longer than usual to delicately drape the folds of her saree as he gelled up his hair with both hands in front of the same mirror. He looked at the slant of her back, just looked at it and then looked away. Sometimes, he felt invited. But he didn't want morning grumpiness on his hands. He saved his humour for the workplace. His colleagues cracked up at his often chauvinistic one-liners. She was composed around her colleagues. Outside this relationship, they were quite the same people.

Why are they exceedingly tender-minded in the company of those they are closest to, by virtue of blood and law? Would it be easier if they just made their intentions known to them? Or, is it just more romantic to pocket expectations and want their partners to scavenge-hunt them out?

Released from the crush of traffic, Vijay sped in the direction of the hospital and then circled the roundabout toward the High Court. He had to attend an important hearing. Vijay wasn't fighting this case but his friend Swapnil was the accused. Ten months ago, his new wife committed suicide. Her parents, in complete denial of the possibility that their child might have been depressed, put the blame on Swapnil and his family. They slapped Sections 304 (B) for dowry death, 498 (A) for demanding dowry and section 34 of the Indian Penal Code for acts done by several persons for furtherance of common intention. Vijay had attended the wedding and knew that Swapnil doted on the girl, who was a 23-year-old Economics teacher in a school. Though the match was arranged, the two sneaked out of their homes at night and went on long drives, and made weekend trips to Dharamshala. They were just about getting to know each other. Swapnil's family accepted whatever the girl's parents offered during the wedding—a Honda City (Diesel), a lavish farmhouse reception party and a trousseau full of gold, diamonds and gems. After her parents filed the case, Swapnil lost his corporate job and his credibility. His father had a heart attack and his mother went into depression, she couldn't bear to listen to the accusations the women's rights activists hurled at her son.

Kalpana's workplace was sterile. The floor tiles were phenol-clean. The bitter smell of disinfectants had some desperation in it. It rebelled against the salty smell of blood and skinless limbs that exposed gooey flesh, strains of blue-and-yellow on wild red. There was white froth in fresh suicide attempts and faces that were burnt maroon. Emergencies came and went.

That morning, as Kalpana was holding a little boy's upper arm taut to pin a syringe full of chemicals into it, a nurse walked up to her carrying samples of blood and urine in a tray of transparent tubes. She informed her that the patient in Room No. 17 was serious. Kalpana didn't react to the news till the job at hand was done. The little boy didn't react to the pain either. He was a good boy. Calmly, she released her fingers from her rubber gloves. Alongside swooping stretchers and concerned nurses, she walked towards Room No. 17. This room had been the home of R Ramakrishna for the last six weeks. The 54-year-old was in the senior management of an American global cruise company. He was used to spending six months at sea every year, and had been doing that since three decades.

Affectionately called 'nautical star' by his friends and family, Rama described this single-patient room with green shower curtains as his 'last port of call'. Kalpana was the junior oncologist on the team of doctors treating this patient of lung cancer. To the surprise of the medical staff, the terminally-ill Rama acted quite normally. He didn't worry or cry or say morose things about the nearness of death. 'On the cruise deck, we're all living one life. Wouldn't life be nicer if every place had the openness of a cruise deck,' he said to a senior doctor. He pointed to pictures of Italy, Mexico and Australia on his iPhone. In those waters, he said, he had sailed the most. He didn't trust these pictures to be worth a thousand words on their own, so he provided the thousand words. He had stories to tell. Stories of empty martini glasses rolling on wooden decks, stories of delicately-gloved hands falling into suited arms on a sweet corner of a long bar, stories of the champagne people shared next to the synth and string of the cruise band. On the cosier side of the portholes that dotted the hulls of his large ships, lasting friendships were made. Rama was a friend to the waves and he could still hear them clashing against his ears. He wanted to believe he was drowning in them, only to belong everlastingly to them. Kalpana, a doctor by profession, found it hard to accept that a patient was stronger and more objective about his death than the doctors treating him.

He had recently sent out emails to his bosses, asking them to relieve him of all his corporate responsibilities. Rama didn't have good savings, his family travelled a fair amount. He sold his family home in Pune to support his son, who was completing his MBA in the States. His wife came to the hospital every second morning and his daughter stayed over on Wednesdays and Fridays. A couple of times, Kalpana saw the daughter talking to her friends in the corridor—she would make movie plans and discuss online shopping sales. Twice, she even had e-commerce sites deliver products at the hospital's reception. "Is this person mad? Why isn't she upset about the fact her father is going to die? Why can't she at least be upset enough to look upset?" wondered Kalpana. For a sick man, Rama signed a ton of documents. He withdrew his membership from his social clubs to retrieve the safety deposits, and paid his final EMIs. While in his full senses, he also met up with insurance agents and lawyers, who walked in with briefcases full of formalities once or twice. Kalpana was a doctor and she knew what it meant to be detached from the process of dying. As she was trained to think, patients were mere rotting bodies in a world where everything is bound to come to a rot one day. Why was she taken aback at Rama's readiness to rot? Rama often suggested cruise trips that Kalpana and her family should take.

'Alaska, you must see Alaska. Snow on still waters and oh yes, the great glaciers,' he shakily pulled out his phone and showed Kalpana pictures. This was shortly after the doctors had told him that he won't survive longer than a week.

Kalpana was unnerved at the unaffectedness of this family. Even his wife didn't drop tears. She played Sudoku on her iPad and remained largely quiet. They must have wept, wailed and reconciled at home before he was brought to the hospital, Kalpana guessed and hoped. Four days ago, his son turned up with the latest issue of *The Economist* and a tall box of Irish whisky chocolates. His father had jokingly termed these his 'last Duty-free gifts'. By then, Rama's fruity voice had turned sour. His wife pointed out that he sounded more and more like his own grandmother. But his hair, which the radiation had eaten up, looked like his grandfather's. 'Why didn't he inherit their long lives instead?' Kalpana thought. The skin around his eyes was ageing in dog years. Had those dark blotches around his eyes fallen from the skies while he was asleep? He was breathing in chain strokes. His breath had solid deposits in it, grey and salty.

In Vijay's world, where judges entered courtrooms like Mughal emperors and went on summer vacations like British viceroys, nobody was in a hurry to save anybody. The clerks and stenographers worked in shifts, as did the judges. Yet, they all came back with belief in the system.

Justice was signed, sealed and delivered. Since the victim wasn't on anti-depressants and hadn't exhibited any suspicious behaviour in the past that was documented or witnessed, it became all the more difficult for Swapnil's lawyer to prove it was in fact a suicide that too within weeks of the wedding. Swapnil and his family were taken into custody. Vijay felt infuriated, he felt cheated and helpless and angry at himself for not being able to do anything.

'Ammaaa...,' the glucose pouch tied to his arm trembled from Rama's long and painful wrestle with air. The catheter tube that still had warm urine in it, unscrewed itself slightly and stuck out. The telemetry monitor that played the rhythm of his runaway heartbeat resembled the last few names that appear on the screen before the movie ends into a blank, mute screen. Rama was dead. His family covered his face and shortly after, the discussion shifted to last rites and hospital paperwork. Kalpana wanted to fall over his body and cry, because nobody else was doing that. Why were the rest of them in such a hurry to let go of him?

Both Kalpana and Vijay lived through the exact same emotion, that of helplessness. In medicine, like in law, some is left to method and some is left to mercy. Sometimes, mercy is balanced on bronze scales, sometimes it is restored by a pair of steel forceps. The methods differ each and every time. Between method and mercy are untold stories of how easily lives are broken and repaired by other lives. Kalpana cried into a bathroom sink and Vijay poured his heart out before his fellow lawyers.

The evening of that morning, they were back in that Maruti Suzuki Swift Dzire and on the other side of the same road, going back to where they came from.

'How was your day?' asked the husband.

'Good. How was yours?' the wife replied.

'Not too bad,' he said, drawing the curtain on the happenings of the day.

'Have you noticed, the evenings are much warmer these days? It'll be a terrible summer,' she pointed, increasing the fan speed of the AC.

'Yes, let's get the AC in the small bedroom serviced on Sunday,' he suggested.

'What do you want for breakfast tomorrow?' she questioned.

'Nothing too oily and spicy. This new cook doesn't know what she's doing,' he answered.

She pursed her lips and turned toward her window for an answer. Soon, she forgot her questions and stared at the same scenes on the road as she did every morning and every evening. The three bright red benches on that bus-stop were only one such scene. They whizzed past them before she could realise how much that one particular scene could have revived her. If only she had chosen to sit on those bright red benches with her husband, if only she had chosen to spill her heart out and wipe his mind clean.

The Radio Mirchi clock struck 6.47. Vijay was trying to pull the car over a flyover without touching any of the thousand bumpers or bonnets around them. In Delhi, driving was almost like a newspaper dance game; more and more cars shrank huge roads to tiny lanes and challenged big cars to scoot out scratch free. Stationed behind a bus, they saw two eunuchs walk up toward Vijay's window. They knocked a couple of times, announcing blessings between tight claps. They knocked again and again promising to bless more in return for something they didn't directly ask for. Vijay turned up the volume of the radio and Kalpana looked into her phone. The eunuchs kept knocking on their window, until the couple was grossed out. Soon, the bus cleared out and they drove away from that unpleasant situation.

How difficult is it to accept the difference of the other? And, instead of adapting to this difference, is it easier to turn a blind eye to the other? What they do to the other, they do to their own. When they call it circumstance, are they already trapped in it?

Still a Bright Red Bench

They cry in the rain, they sing and dance in the rain,
As they watch the rain, why do they miss the rain?
They wish to whistle and chirp along the open spring. They wish and do nothing more.
When summer sets fire to their sky, they wish they had done more with the open spring.
When trees change colour and fall to the floor, leaf by leaf,
They arrest them in poetry and paint;
They fill meaning in autumn, to find meaning in autumn.
Then when winter shovels them indoors, they dream on about the freedoms of summer.
And that is how they live out their years, in nature's neighbourhood,
At once delighted and dismayed at its certainty.

I am a bright red bench. Unlike them, I have accepted the turn of seasons. It is not something I consider inescapable; it is something I don't want to escape. I may be a bright red bench, but I know that the experience of seasons is as universal as it is personal.

Each life is stolen out of seasons that exist. Just like the high-tide is made of the same water that it rises out of. Briefly, it acquires a colour, a temperature, a texture, even a scent of its own. Sooner or later, it falls back in a splash, stirring up a salty froth that instantly dissolves into a vast oceanic vortex as if it never was.

Once people have lived and gone, their characters, their faces, their voices and their problems merge with the crowds that surround them. Their stories, whether fascinating in details or frivolous on the surface, are lost in the history of the time they lived and loved in.

I am still a bright red bench. I will stand and stare at the living of life through seasons. And I will marvel at the mutability of it.

Acknowledgements

My wooden desk has been mightier than a chopping board, quietly bearing the hits of my bony elbows. My lamp (plastic and Ikea) developed a crack or three, but its saffron glow didn't go sour. My black mug has acted like a pivot door to the passage of brews. There was also a nearly unusable quill pen, a pearl necklace I'd bitten into, and a Remington Rand 1930 (eBay UK) that I couldn't find ink ribbons for. Big book over small book over big book sat in a rack that started to smell like time. Then, one amazingly vague quote and one Instagram filter (Nashville) later, things didn't seem as unmoving as they were. Outside my window was no sunny beach and no mountain at a hazy distance, in fact, there wasn't even breeze. But, there was a dusty red bench in a tiny park. And, the presence of that red bench in every moment through my empty nights, made it seem brighter than it was. I lent it a voice and a sight.

I penned *Upon a Bright Red Bench* through those nights whose days were spent at a noisy newspaper office. The book has grown up with me. We started out when my uncle, who is no more, read out Zauq, Ghalib and Faiz whenever I had trouble falling asleep. I still find it hard to go to sleep, and then it is poetry that speaks to me. At Carmel Convent School, New Delhi, our great teachers taught us how to think with our hearts and feel with our minds. Until I made mistakes of my own, it was harder to understand what that meant. I am ideologically indebted to my professors at Sri Venkateswara College, Delhi University, where I earned my Bachelor's degree in Sociology. The subject made it easier to accept that in life, like in literature, what will take us forward is conflict and not consensus. At the Delhi School of Economics, India's finest social scientists enabled us to understand the point of theories that could seem absurd to the naked eye; there is a point to everything that exists. I thank my editors in the media, who sent me far and wide to hunt out stories and made me fight till I found my own voice. I am still fighting. The Yale Writers' Conference made this book happen. It was conceived in Richard Jackson's Poetry for Prose class, for which I had to write a piece in the voice of a handrail. A community of America's finest poets, essayists and novelists at YWC made me believe in my writing.

I thank my brother Aditya for filling up my life with his cathartic sense of humour. I thank Sijo, who asked me to stop thinking about writing fiction and start writing fiction! I thank Nabila for making my life ridiculously interesting and Rajat for showing me the strength in simplicity. I thank all those who made memories with me and talked to me about loss, about rejection, and about that wild kind of madness they casually walk around with.

I am grateful to Ipshita Mitra from Om Books International who helped me take these stories told by a bright red bench back to where they came from.

From Haruki Murakami's attractive mind to Woody Allen's sepia-tinted cinema to Gay Talese's literary journalism to Frank Sinatra's Cadbury blues, the book is several feelings now stored in one place.

We are the sum of our parts and those parts are as ordinary as we believe them to be.

Life isn't elsewhere.